To Mila

Always B.

My favorite English Professor,

Evert Jigner

Mildred Relawy

1 2

THE SECRETS OF
CRAIG STREET

THE SECRETS OF CRAIG STREET

Evert Tigner

VANTAGE PRESS
New York

Published by Vantage Press, Inc.
516 West 34th Street, New York, New York 10001

Manufactured in the United States of America
ISBN: 0-533-12571-5

Library of Congress Catalog Card No.: 97-91115

0 9 8 7 6 5 4 3 2 1

To the memory of my parents,
Frank and Lessie Tigner

Contents

Part Four

Part Five

Introduction

Writing *The Secrets of Craig Street* has been a pleasure for me. I have always enjoyed writing, but I never considered having my work published before. The story and characters are totally fictional even though I used a real place for the setting.

The characters and the events of the work originated with me during long motor trips from California to Texas, where I have homes. I enjoy describing characters, and I could hardly wait to arrive at my destination so that I could begin a new chapter.

The houses in the story play an important role. I have always had an affinity for interesting houses. When I visit a town or place for the first time, I am anxious to determine which house would be for me.

There are many interesting old houses on Craig Street where I live part-time. I have used different houses with modifications for my story.

I wish to thank a few individuals who have been helpful and encouraging during the writing of the story. I wish to especially thank Dr. John C. Morris and Mrs. Catherine Morris, who read the entire manuscript and made valuable suggestions and corrections on many events in the story.

In addition, I wish to thank Maureen Daly, whom I consider my mentor in becoming an author. Other individuals who have been most helpful to me are Allene Arthur, Ian Gibson, and Harvey Sarner.

In closing, I wish to thank the residents of Hillsboro who answered my questions so patiently, especially Horace Cliett and Paul Crews.

THE SECRETS OF
CRAIG STREET

PART ONE

I

R. W. and Rebecca Campbell

Robert Campbell and his beautiful bride, Rebecca Randolph, said good-bye to her family in Virginia a few days after the elaborate wedding at the bride's home, Fernwood Plantation. It had been a most beautiful wedding. Robert was a handsome groom and Rebecca was a lovely southern bride. She loved Robert and she took her wedding vows seriously. She was happy "to honor and cherish him in sickness and in health and to love him the remaining days of her life."

Robert had convinced Rebecca to marry him and then go West to start a new life together. They would make their way to St. Louis, where they could board a steamship and sail the Mississippi River until they could connect with the Cypress River. Then they would take a stern-wheeler to Jefferson, Texas, the state's largest city and inland port, which was under consideration to be selected as the new capital of Texas.

Jefferson was a thriving community with new people arriving weekly. The inland port brought many new residents from the southern states and the East Coast of the United States who were interested in a new beginning after the Civil War from 1861 to 1865.

After several days journey, Robert Campbell and his wife, Rebecca, arrived in Jefferson. Robert had enough money saved to rent a small house for them. Rebecca had brought many of her wedding gifts and the small cottage was soon comfortable and cozy. Rebecca thought the green trees and shrubs of East Texas were beautiful, but she did not enjoy the hordes of large mosquitoes that came with the humid, hot weather. But she wanted to please her new husband and complained as little as possible.

Robert wasted no time in finding a new job in Jefferson. Many new houses and businesses were being built, and most buyers wanted an insurance policy on their property. Robert began working for the best insurance agent in Jefferson, and he immediately sold many new insurance policies. Robert had a most pleasant personality, and he knew how to keep a potential customer interested. He seldom lost a sale or a customer. Robert's successful selling of insurance continued for many months.

One evening Robert came home from the insurance office for his evening meal and told Rebecca that he had quit his job. Rebecca was shocked and upset. She said to Robert, "But, darling, you are doing so well, and we are living so much better than many of the new people who have come here." She continued, "Why would you jeopardize our secure way of life?" And then she burst into tears.

Robert finally pleaded with Rebecca to become calm, explaining that he had already made plans to open his own office to sell insurance and real estate to the newcomers. Rebecca calmed down and began to listen to her husband's new ideas and reasons for opening his own office. She eventually admitted that life was never dull with Robert as he often had many surprises for her.

Robert did very well in his new business. He used several approaches that his competitors had never considered, including cultivating the captains of the boats which anchored at the city's port. He told Rebecca always to be prepared for an extra guest for dinner; Robert often invited a ship's captain home for dinner. These captains were happy to leave the boats for a few hours to enjoy dinner in a private home. Rebecca prepared and served a fine dinner every night and could add more food if necessary. Robert kept an adequate amount of good whisky in the kitchen cabinet and some captains enjoyed a good libation before eating dinner. After a pleasant dinner was served, Rebecca served dessert and coffee in the parlor. Robert would then seize the opportunity to give the captain a supply of brochures telling about Jefferson and its fine possibilities. The captain would agree to distribute the Campbell Insurance and Real Estate brochures to his passengers who appeared to have the finances that would enable them to purchase property from Robert Campbell. Robert received many good sales from the boat captains' recommendations.

Robert sent pamphlets about Texas and his business to his relatives and friends who lived throughout the southern and eastern states. These contacts generated considerable new business for him. Robert always had a sharp mind for business matters, and he constantly thought of ways to improve and enhance his business. He was very dependable, kept his promises to clients, and took pride in his honesty.

Business continued to grow and be successful for several more years, until, suddenly, the river transportation declined in the 1870's, and the growth and development of Jefferson slowly came to an end. Robert was from a Scottish background, and, fortunately, he had saved enough money to meet a setback in business.

Robert Campbell continued to work harder at his insurance business but the income was not increasing. Robert studied for many hours his situation. He realized that other parts of Texas were growing and developing so he made a decision to leave Jefferson and move to central Texas, where new settlers had been arriving for several years to seek economic opportunities.

Robert closed his business, and they tearfully said good-bye to their friends, neighbors, and clients. They took the nearest train and headed West for two hundred miles. Their destination was Hill County, Texas which had a small town called Hillsboro located between Austin and Dallas. The Texas hill country was different from the lush, green shrubs and trees of east Texas. It was more severe, and the wind blew almost daily. The terrain was more hilly, and the trees were shorter than the tall east Texas trees. It would take them some time to discover the beauty of the hill country of Texas.

This was a new beginning for Robert and Rebecca Campbell who had originally come from North Carolina and Virginia. The big question was, "could Robert Campbell succeed in the insurance and real estate business in the small town of Hillsboro?" It was never said aloud but Robert and Rebecca knew the answer to that question.

Robert opened a small office on Elm Street in Hillsboro. He greeted everyone he met cordially and invited them to visit his office any time. It was his general nature to be friendly and people reacted favorably to his friendliness. His business began to grow and he had to hire a secretary to help him with the new increase in work. Robert Campbell was pleased and felt secure that his business was beginning to grow. In addition to town residents, Robert contacted the cotton farmers of Hill County and offered them a special insurance for their houses and barns. Cotton was the king crop of Hill County and there were many prosperous cotton farmers who had never considered the need for insurance for their property before. He emphasized the frequent hail storms in Texas which could ruin roofs. He also hoped it would never happen but advised that occasional Texas tornadoes could destroy all a client's property if it was unfortunate enough to be in the path of destruction.

Robert and Rebecca Campbell loved the small town of Hillsboro and the nearby hill country of Texas. The Texas hill country consisted of many rolling hills with creeks and winding rivers. The wind blew occasionally but you became accustomed to it. Weather changes were constant and newcomers were told if they did not like the present weather, to wait a few hours for something different.

Hillsboro had been selected as the county seat for Hill County in 1853, a few years after the new county had been formed. The town was planned around a square with the County Court House to be built in the center of the square. When the large Court House was finally completed in 1889, many different opinions were expressed by architectural critics. *Harper's* magazine described the new Court House as having the appearance of an outstanding cathedral, but an article in the *Saturday Evening Post* labeled the new Court House as a monstrosity. Most residents of Hillsboro and Hill County were very proud of their large and impressive Court House, which was the largest and tallest building in Hill County Texas when it was completed.

Robert began to acquire considerable property as his insurance business prospered. He bought houses in Hillsboro and stores from his constant cash flow. Robert also bought choice farm and ranch land in Hill County. He always believed that the real wealth of this country was in the ownership of land. He knew that many people have left the place of their birth so they could acquire and own land. Robert also knew that everyone who came to Texas did not succeed as he and Rebecca had done. But Robert rationalized that others did not dream, plan, or work as he and Rebecca had done in order to accomplish their success. Robert Campbell believed in having dreams, but also in some plans to accomplish those dreams.

He worked long hours each day and he awakened each morning shortly before 5:00 A.M. He started a fire in the fireplace and the cook stove so that the house would be warm when Rebecca arose at 5:30. Rebecca always prepared him a warm cooked breakfast each morning.

The day continued to be long for Robert. His insurance office was opened from 8:00 to 5:00 each day except Sundays. He believed that his office must be opened consistently in case a new customer should be in the need of insurance or real estate.

Rebecca admired the successful approach of her husband toward life. She used to tell friends the secret of his success was due to three things: dreaming, organizing, and working. She said, "My husband dreams, and he knows how to organize. He is not afraid of hard work." She always added, "A good combination for anyone who wishes to become successful."

II

Robert William Campbell, Jr.

Judge Robert William Campbell, Jr. had lived most of his life in the large white house on Craig Street called Hillsboro House. His parents, Robert W. Campbell Sr. and his mother, Rebecca Ann Campbell, had built the enormous, two-story house at the beginning of the century. Some of the most beautiful homes were located on Craig Street in this small Texas town. There were many large, two-story, white and brick houses with classical columns on Craig Street, and large, green elm trees contributed to the beauty of the street.

The parents of Judge Campbell had arrived in Hillsboro after their move from Jefferson, Texas. The Civil War from 1861 to 1865 had ravished their home states of North Carolina and Virginia. They decided that Texas might offer more opportunities for them when they were first married.

The people of Hillsboro called Judge Campbell's father R. W. R. W. Campbell had created a successful insurance and real estate business in Hillsboro. Some of the old timers said that R. W. could sell you the socks he was wearing. Other people declared, "Don't go into R. W.'s office unless you want to purchase a house with a new insurance policy on it." There was a lot of truth in those statements. R. W. Campbell had made a large fortune by the time of his death yet he had been good for the town of Hillsboro. He helped organize many civic organizations, and was among the first to contribute to charitable events or any worthy cause even though he was considered to be very frugal in his business and private life.

Rebecca Ann Randolph Campbell, the mother of Judge Campbell, was born in Virginia. Her family had been plantation owners and she had lived graciously while growing up in Virginia. She was accustomed to the life which large southern plantation owners enjoyed. The Randolphs were important in Virginia, and they had many social and political connections. It was often rumored that Rebecca's family were distant relatives of Thomas Jefferson. Rebecca never denied this rumor.

Hillsboro was an adjustment for Rebecca. She was not readily impressed with the small Texas town and its plain living. She did not like the black sticky soil of Texas when it rained. She frowned upon the name of Becky which the townspeople insisted on calling her. She missed the many servants that her family retained. She and R. W. could only afford one servant part-time who was named Ettabelle Jackson.

Ettabelle was called Aunt Ettie or just plain Ettie by the Campbell family. Aunt Ettie was the best black cook in Hillsboro. No one could fry chicken and make cream gravy better than Aunt Ettie. R. W. said, "Her fried chicken is the greatest, but you must try her mashed potatoes, fried okra, black-eyed peas, and corn bread in a cast-iron pan." Aunt Ettie helped with the Campbell's house-cleaning and cooking on alternate days. Ettie was a widow; she lived in a small wood-frame house in the southern part of town.

Becky Campbell finally accepted the ways of a small town in Texas and she began to organize many women's clubs. She was pleased with the success of her husband whose ability for making money was doubted by her parents in Virginia. Becky was happy. She loved her husband and believed in his ability. She enjoyed teasing him when he proudly talked about his Scottish heritage— R. W. Campbell's grandparents had emigrated from Scotland to North Carolina.

On a very cold and damp night in February of 1894, Becky Campbell began to have childbirth pains. R. W. suggested calling Dr. Blackburn at once but Aunt Ettie thought it was too soon. A few hours later, Ettie said, "Mr. R. W., it is time for the doctor because you is going to be a proud father." Within a short time, an eight-pound son was born to Becky. She and her husband agreed on a name for the new son—Robert William Campbell, Jr. The new baby was healthy and it grew very quickly.

Their present house seemed smaller than ever with the new baby, and Ettie was staying most of the time. Becky would be glad when they could move to a larger house but she would let R. W. decide because he was in the real estate business.

Becky was disappointed one evening when R. W. came home very late from his office. The dinner was cold; R. W. could sense her disappointment. When R. W. explained the reason for his delay, his wife was almost in tears with joy. Her husband, that day, purchased the largest and best situated building lot on Craig Street for their future home. Becky was even more elated when her husband told her they could begin building immediately.

The large house began to take shape quickly. When the big house was completed a few months later, it had two stories with a large central hall in the neo-Greco style. Four Grecian columns graced the front entrance on Craig Street and there was a large portico on the side street with a circular driveway for the carriages. The house was impressive, indicating the affluence of the new owners.

The spacious entry hall was magnificent where a Victorian Gothic, octagonal wood table with a large pedestal and claw feet gave a touch of elegance. A beautiful bouquet of red roses was on the table. A large Empire mirror with a gold, gilt frame was on the wall. The wood floor had a lovely oriental carpet. An elegant staircase led to the second floor of the house.

On the right of the entry hall was an immense drawing room with a large white marble fireplace in the center. It was furnished in the Victorian style by Henry Belter. The large settee and the two matching chairs were in dark wood with light green satin upholstery. A marble-topped Victorian coffee table stood in front of the settee. Two other large and elaborate Victorian marble-topped console tables helped to complete the furnishing of the room together with a tall curio cabinet. The walls of the drawing room were covered with an intricate Victorian wallpaper with borders at the ceiling and the large windows were covered with dark green velvet drapes.

The left side of the entry hall had a spacious dining room with an elaborate crystal chandelier. A large mahogany dining table with twelve chairs in Chippendale style and a large matching buffet furnished the dining room. The best china and silver were kept in a tall china cabinet. They had been sent from Virginia by the Randolphs as a housewarming gift.

Elaborate dinner parties were given by the Campbells where

important Texas legislators and politicians dined at the Hillsboro House, including the governor of Texas. The governor asked to meet Aunt Ettie who had prepared the meal, and told her that he had never eaten southern homemade pecan pie comparable to hers, thanked her for the splendid dinner, and told her if she was ever looking for a job to let him know.

Life continued to be pleasant at Hillsboro House. The young master, Robert William Campbell, grew and matured quickly. He was an excellent student at Hillsboro Elementary School. He read books constantly. Emily Blackburn and Robert Campbell were in the same class and they lived on the same block of Craig Street. They often did their homework together.

When Robert was old enough, his father suggested that Robert work in his insurance and real estate office to learn the business and to earn an allowance. Young Robert enjoyed the work. He could speak well and answer questions effectively. If he believed he was right on a business matter, he insisted on stating his point of view. One day R. W. said to his son, "I think you would make a good Texas lawyer."

The young people, Robert Campbell and Emily Blackburn, did many things together. They attended the same school events, parties in the community, and their parents were members of the Episcopal Church on Craig Street.

When Robert and Emily enrolled in high school, they arranged to have most of their classes together. They walked home from school each afternoon. Emily hardly noticed when Robert carried most of her books and held her hand as they made their way home. One afternoon Robert squeezed Emily's hand firmer than usual. She glanced at Robert and observed how handsome he was becoming. Her heart beat faster than ever as Robert walked closer by her side. He was going to be tall and she preferred tall men to short men. She was glad her father, Dr. Blackburn, was over six feet tall.

Robert was beginning to develop a strong physical interest in Emily. He began to notice aspects of Emily he had never studied before. Her beautiful white complexion and dark hair appealed to him. Her body was soft and gentle to touch.

Robert asked Emily before they reached her home if she

would accompany him to the basketball game on the following Friday evening. They would sip Coca-Colas during the game, and maybe have an ice-cream soda somewhere in the town afterwards. Emily said that she would enjoy joining him and she would have to get permission from her parents. The parents agreed and the young people went to the Friday night basketball game, where they met their fellow classmates. The Hillsboro team defeated the Corsicana team. Emily glanced at her wristwatch. It was a few minutes until nine o'clock, and she had to be home by 9:45. This gave almost another hour with her date.

Robert took Emily to the ice-cream parlor on the town square, where they sat at a corner table. They enjoyed the evening talking and holding hands. When it was time to leave, Robert escorted Emily to her home on Craig Street. Careful that her parents and neighbors might not observe, Robert took Emily in his arms and held her tightly to his body while giving her the most intimate kiss she had ever received from anyone. Emily passionately said good night to Robert before entering her parent's home. She tried to brush her hair with her hands and make her dress look neater before she entered her home.

Emily and Robert were more than friends for the remainder of their high school days in Hillsboro. They saw one another almost every day and they shared many private thoughts with each other. They were sad when it was time to graduate from high school because each one would enter a different college in a different city. They promised to never lose touch and would always write letters to each other.

After graduation from high school, Robert Campbell entered the University of Texas Law School in Austin. Emily decided to become a school teacher. Her parents sent her to Tulane University in New Orleans to study for a degree in education. Emily and Robert corresponded often, and they cherished the times they would meet in Hillsboro during Christmas and summer vacations.

Emily Blackburn graduated from college after three years of study as an honor student. She took more classes than most students did each semester and she participated in several college organizations and honor societies. Most students took four or more years to receive a college degree.

Emily majored in English and American literature. Her ultimate goal was to teach literature at the college level, but because of the age and health of her parents, she decided to remain in Hillsboro and apply for a position teaching senior English at Hillsboro High School. The local school board was pleased when Emily applied for the position, and Emily was quickly selected for the new post.

Emily was well educated, and she was always scholarly inclined. She loved reading especially English literature and English novels. Her enthusiasm for literature easily transferred to her students at Hillsboro High. The students called her Miss Emily. Miss Emily used a dramatic approach to teaching English literature. She could impersonate a character from Shakespeare or Dickens realistically, and she held the complete attention of her students. She often used costumes and props from the period of the character's life, which was effective with her students. It was a most wonderful experience to hear her read poetry aloud. She could make you laugh or even put tears in your eyes whenever reading certain poetry selections. Some poems she read to her students would inspire them and other poetry would make students serious or more contemplative. Miss Emily was as much an actress as she was a school teacher.

Miss Emily was demanding and challenging as a school teacher. She expected the assignments and projects of students to be completed on time. She expected each student to put forth their best scholarly efforts. Miss Emily was most complimentary to students for good work or even their best effort, but she had no patience for inferior assignments by her students.

Miss Emily was a popular teacher and a most attractive woman. Her slim, tall figure, abundance of very black hair, light skin made her beautiful. She had a marvelous sense of humor and a pleasing disposition. She was destined to become an outstanding educator, and Hillsboro High School was fortunate to have her as a member of their faculty.

Miss Emily was considered progressive and modern in her approach to education. She attempted to determine the interests of each student and then make learning meaningful to them. Their individual assignments and projects could be centered around the particular interest of each student.

Miss Emily introduced several innovative projects for the students in her classes. She inspired several students to design and build a model of Shakespeare's Globe Theater. It was an outstanding project when completed. The model received much favorable attention in Hillsboro together with many other communities for its accuracy and details.

III

World War I

Some drastic and important changes were beginning to happen throughout the world in 1914. The Kaiser had become overly powerful and was threatening the free countries of Europe. A world war was starting. President Woodrow Wilson of the United States would not tolerate the aggression in Europe, and the neutral countries were asking for American help.

By 1916, the United States had become actively involved in the war. Robert Campbell received a notice from the Texas Draft Board that he would be inducted for military service and would be required to serve as a soldier. Robert did not want to be drafted, so he enlisted in the Officers' Candidate School, where he was guaranteed a legal position with the Army when he graduated from Officers' Training School. He was assigned to a military base in San Antonio for officer's training.

During training Robert wrote to Emily often. He invited her to his graduation from Officer's Training School followed by a weekend together in the historic city of San Antonio. Emily was excited about going to San Antonio because like every Texan she had heard about the Alamo. Lieutenant Robert Campbell met Emily at the bus station, where there were many soldiers waiting or meeting friends. Emily discovered Robert—she had never seen such a handsome soldier. Robert embraced her for a long time before they went to the Presido for the graduation. Emily was very impressed with the precision drill of the officers and their commander at the graduation ceremony. The saluting of the American flag, the firing of rifles, and the sound of the band playing "Stars and Stripes" and "Anchors Away" sent chills down Emily's spine. The military band played "Over There" which brought tears to her eyes.

Emily was very proud of Robert and felt so fortunate to know him. It was a happy occasion for all the officers, but Emily felt sad knowing that Robert would be sent overseas very soon. She knew that some of the soldiers would never return home, but she did not want Robert to know that she was pensive and held such thoughts. She would do everything to make him happy that weekend.

After the graduation, Lieutenant Campbell took Emily to dinner at one of San Antonio's best restaurants. Robert enjoyed a large sirloin steak while Emily had shrimp creole. They enjoyed two bottles of French bordeaux. It was a most wonderful time for them and Emily was elated that she had been invited to help Robert celebrate his graduation from Officer's Training School.

Their accommodations for the night were at the fabulous Menger Hotel near the Alamo. Although separate rooms had been reserved for them, they spent the night together in Emily's room and discussed their childhood together in Hillsboro. They also discussed their future because Robert would be sent to Europe shortly to serve in the war. Emily promised to wait for Robert until he returned from overseas. Robert then took Emily in his arms and kissed her many times before they fell asleep.

When Emily awakened the next morning, Robert was still soundly sleeping with his arm around her shoulders. She waited for him to waken. When he did, he smiled at her and returning his smile, she said, "I suppose I should feel guilty."

Sunday was their last day to spend with each other. They again discussed their future life together and enjoyed walking around the historic sections of San Antonio. They toured the Alamo, and they marveled at the story of the patriots who died there for the freedom of Texas and its people. Emily was hoping the day would never end but it did, and after a long tearful good-bye, Emily again promised that she would wait for Robert until the war was over.

Emily returned to Hillsboro by bus which was crowded with weekend travelers and soldiers in uniform. She was courteous to one particular soldier who attempted to be friendly with her, but she found the bus ride tedious. She would have preferred staying with Robert instead of returning to Hillsboro but she knew Robert would be sent overseas soon by the military.

After a pleasant but brief conversation with the soldier who was sitting across the aisle from Emily, she explained that she was sleepy. Emily accepted the soldier's address and promised that she or her students would write to him soon.

Emily closed her eyes and tried to sleep in the large comfortable seats of the bus but sleep would not come. She kept thinking about the life she would have with Robert when he returned from the service. Emily assumed they would be married when he returned from overseas. They had promised to wait for each other even though a marriage date had not been determined. She closed her eyes and continued to think about the wonderful life she would have someday with Robert.

When she arrived home in Hillsboro, she felt a terrible loneliness. She missed Robert, everything reminded her of him. Emily told her father about her loneliness. Dr. Blackburn told Emily, "Busy people are never lonely." Emily could hardly wait to resume her teaching of students at Hillsboro High School.

Two weeks later Emily received her first letter from Robert. He had arrived safely in France and was impressed with the beauty of the French countryside and the large chateaus. Robert mentioned that after a few days of indoctrination about the war, he would receive his permanent assignment in England. He hoped he would enjoy England as much as he did France. He told Emily how much he missed her and to write to him soon. Emily cherished each letter from Robert and she answered each letter immediately with all the news which might interest him.

Miss Emily, who was always innovative in her teaching methods, assigned her students a letter-writing project. She told her students about the soldier on the bus who wanted her to write to him. She managed to receive a list of names and addresses from Private Richard Keene of soldiers in his platoon who would enjoy hearing from Hillsboro students.

The letter-writing project to soldiers was popular with the soldiers and the students. The soldiers were lonely, and they enjoyed hearing about the events of a small Texas town. Some soldiers answered the letters sent to them and the students were highly pleased.

IV

Fiona McGill

Robert Campbell was unhappy when the weekend came to an end in San Antonio with Emily. He said good-bye to her and he had never liked good-byes. He felt sad when Emily boarded the bus for Hillsboro. Robert hoped he would see Emily again before too long. He knew it was unlikely that he would see her before being sent to Europe to serve as a legal counselor to the military.

The next day Robert said good-bye to his instructors at the Officer's Training School in San Antonio. Robert traveled to New York by train to board a troop ship to Le Havre, France. It was a long tedious voyage for Robert although he had a private cabin for the voyage. He passed the time by reading books and exercising with the troops on the ship.

Robert finally arrived in France where he was given additional training before he was sent to England for his permanent assignment. Robert was impressed with the French countryside and he would have enjoyed staying there. Some fellow officers had warned him about the English climate and the bland food, but when Robert arrived in London for his assignment, he was more impressed with the British than he had ever anticipated. He enjoyed the city of London with its beautiful parks, the double-decker buses, and the interesting streets with nice shops. He did not tell his buddies but he developed a fondness for English foods. He enjoyed the taste of fish and chips, the large English sausages, and the natural cheddar cheese and biscuits. Robert soon acquired a taste for the English style of living.

He was well pleased with his assignment in the British Isles. His duties involved expert legal advice on military matters for the United States Government, and he enjoyed the many places in the British Isles where his duties required him to go. On one occasion he was sent on an assignment to Scotland.

In Scotland the base commander, Field Captain John McGill,

was impressed with the young lieutenant from Texas. After a few days of working together, the captain invited Robert to his home for a visit and to meet his family. To Robert's surprise, the McGills lived on a large estate with a castle called Thornberry.

Castle Thornberry was a large baronial Scottish structure built of native stone to last hundreds of years. The color of the stone blended into the colors of the Scottish countryside. The rooms were large with tall ceilings and large stone fireplaces to curtail the dampness of the Scottish climate. Robert admired the plain but sturdy dark furniture with Scottish tartan on the upholstery. Robert was ushered into the great room of the Castle where he was introduced to Captain McGill's wife, Elizabeth, and his twenty-year-old daughter, Fiona. Elizabeth McGill, an attractive woman, was formally dressed for the evening. Robert was also impressed with her beautiful jewelry which was genuine. Fiona was lovely with her auburn hair, blue eyes, and pale complexion. Her soft Scottish voice was wonderful to hear.

After Scotch whisky was served to Robert and Captain McGill and Bristol Cream sherry for the ladies, dinner was served in the dining room of the castle. Robert had never seen such a large dining table with so much china, crystal, and silver on the table. The first course was a delicious Scotch broth followed by tender Scottish venison served with the national dish of Scotland, haggis. The haggis tasted similar to Texas cornbread dressing. The dessert was fresh raspberries and thick cream produced on the estate.

At the conclusion of the dinner, the McGills and Robert retired to the weaponry room of the castle, where Scottish shortbread and Drambuie were served. Robert had never tasted Drambuie before. He enjoyed the sweetness of the taste, a combination of honey and whisky. The furniture in the weaponry room was very comfortable and less informal than the dining room and great room. The large display of swords, daggers, and guns was amazing. There were many paintings and prints of Scottish heroes in battle with the English. A large painting of William Wallace hung over the large stone fireplace. Captain McGill told Robert interesting stories about Robert the Bruce, William Wallace, and Rob Roy. Robert Campbell listened intently. He then realized how hearty the Scots are and how proud they are of their country and their heritage.

The history of the castle was told to Robert by Captain McGill.

It had been in the McGill family for at least nine generations. It was built for the McGills from a grant given by King David II in appreciation of one of the early warriors at the battle of Bannockburn which took place near Stirling. Captain McGill promised Robert he would take him to the battle site just outside of the town.

At the end of the evening Robert Campbell thanked his host and hostess for the most unusual and wonderful evening of his life. He also thanked Fiona and said he hoped to meet her again. A coach was ordered for Robert which took him to his base. The wind and rain continued all night and Robert could not sleep. He pinched himself several times to determine if the evening at the castle had actually happened or had been a beautiful dream.

Robert was pleased that this assignment required several more weeks in Scotland. Captain McGill was fond of Robert and he invited him to play golf at Castle Thornberry and also to fish for salmon in the rivers of the estate. Fiona and her mother were always available to join the men afterwards. Fiona and Robert developed a good bond of friendship and rapport. Fiona invited Robert to Scottish dances and social affairs at the castle and at the large homes and estates of her friends. Fiona was charming and enjoyed dancing with the handsome Lieutenant from the United States. Fiona had never met a real Texan before. Robert was beginning to feel very much at home with this family and their hospitality.

One evening when they left the home of friends, the Scottish rain was falling furiously and fast. All umbrellas had been taken. But Robert gallantly put his rain coat over Fiona and helped her to the coach. She tripped as she entered the coach, and Robert caught her in his strong arms. It was like an embrace and they held each other closely for some time. Robert held Fiona close to him in the back seat of the coach while the chauffeur drove them home.

Fiona gave Robert a warm passionate kiss just before arriving at the castle. She also suggested that he should not return to his base due to the raging storm, emphasizing that it was a Saturday night, and there was plenty of room at the castle for Robert to spend the night. Robert insisted he did not want to impose but after a whisky, he decided to spend the night. His room was across the hall from Fiona and Robert did not sleep well because his thoughts were about Fiona.

Robert finally went to sleep but was awakened later in the morning with a short knock on his door. It was Fiona who greeted him with a kiss. She reminded him that it was Sunday and he deserved a day of rest from the American government. Fiona ordered a proper Scottish breakfast from the household servants, and ordered Robert to stay in bed and enjoy his breakfast. Fiona's parents had gone for the day to visit friends and to play golf. She sat on the side of the bed and observed that Robert had slept only in his undershorts. Fiona pretended to be embarrassed, but Robert explained that all the soldier slept in their underwear. Fiona teased Robert about his dark hairy chest as she softly rubbed his large shoulders with her hands.

Breakfast arrived. Robert was hungry, but the breakfast was larger than any breakfast he had ever seen in Texas. Robert was accustomed to large breakfasts in Texas which Ettie always prepared for him. There were kippers, Scottish ham and eggs and delicious morning rolls with homemade black currant jam from the berries grown on the estate. Fiona encouraged Robert to enjoy his breakfast. After Robert had consumed the enormous breakfast, Fiona asked him what he would enjoy doing today. Robert gently took Fiona in his arms and pulled her into his bed carefully and held her closely to him. He said, "This is what I would like to do today." She had never felt a body so warm and wonderful.

After an hour of ecstasy, Robert and Fiona dressed for the day. The rain storm had passed so they decided to take a long hike along the River Devon. The heather was beginning to bloom and it would be an enjoyable day. The servants prepared a basket of fresh sandwiches and a thermos of hot tea.

Robert had never seen such beautiful countryside. The Scottish mountains with purple heather were beautiful as well as the dark blue lochs in the valleys. The small villages with solid, stone houses lined along one high street appealed to Robert. There was an old castle every few miles. Some of the castles were in total ruins and others were still inhabited. The sheep grazing in the green fields added to the beauty of the countryside.

The day ended much too quickly for Robert and Fiona. It was time for Robert to return to the base. Robert's mission was nearly completed and he would be returning to his assigned base in England soon. Robert and Fiona had a few good evenings before he left for England.

When he arrived in England, he had several letters from Texas. He opened his parents' letters first, and they were both fine. He was not anxious to open Emily's letters. After some hesitation, Robert read her letters. They were always sweet and intimate. And she wrote much news about the people and events in Hillsboro. She ended her letter by telling him how much she missed him and loved him. She was anxiously waiting for his return from the war.

Emily's letters made Robert miserable. Robert and Emily had planned to be married when he returned to Texas. He was fond of Emily and he did not want to hurt her. It was a very difficult time for him. He could not concentrate at work, and his commanding officer advised him to take three days of rest and recuperation. Robert was glad of the short holiday because he must see Fiona again. He kept asking himself, "Do I really and truly love Fiona? Would I like to spend the rest of my life with her? The answer was yes to both questions. Robert took the very next train to Scotland. He could hardly wait for the train to arrive in Scotland.

Fiona met Robert at the station in Stirling. They went immediately to Thornberry Castle and Robert was impatient to ask the important question. He suggested a walk along the River Devon. When they were a safe distance from the view of the castle, Robert took Fiona in his arms, kissed her, and proposed marriage. Fiona did not answer. Robert kept nervously telling her that he loved her and that he would like to take her to Texas to live and be his wife. She finally replied, "I have always wanted to visit Texas, and I think I would enjoy living in Texas."

The happy news was related to Captain McGill and his wife, Elizabeth. With tears of joy in her eyes Elizabeth McGill said the war will soon be over, and we must have a large wedding for Fiona and Robert. Captain McGill said, "You must invite your parents from Texas for the wedding here at the castle."

Robert returned to England and his base by train. He closed his eyes and thought of his love for Fiona. But someone else kept coming into his mind. It was Emily in Hillsboro, his childhood girl friend he had left behind. Emily was sweet and kind and she was waiting for him to return. It would hurt her, but he must write her a letter. He wrote her the following letter:

May 10, 1918
Military Base
England

My Dear Emily,

I never thought I would ever write you this letter. I feel terrible that I will inflict hurt and disappointment upon you. You have always been special and important to me since I was a small child.

This is not pleasant for me, and I never dreamed it would happen to me. But I have fallen madly in love with a beautiful lady who lives in Scotland. I have asked her to marry me, and we will be married next month at her family's castle in Scotland. She and I will return to Texas where we will live, and I will practice law.

In closing, I hope some day you will understand and hopefully forgive me. I will always remember the good times we had together.

Sincerely,

Robert Campbell

The wedding took place in the gardens of Castle Thornberry in June 1918. Fiona was a beautiful bride in her white wedding gown which was trimmed with lace. She looked magnificent. Robert looked handsome in his officer's uniform. The rhododendrons were in full bloom, and the sunny dry day added to the glory and beauty of the occasion.

Five hundred guests were invited to the wedding—dukes and duchesses and other important people, many high-ranking officers of Captain McGill and several of Robert's army colleagues. Robert was elated just before the ceremony when he learned that his parents had come from America for the wedding.

The ceremony was beautiful and the local minister officiated. The groom and bride repeated the words after the minister and swore to love and cherish each other to the end of their lives. Fiona's bridesmaids were beautiful. They wore bright tartan skirts with white blouses and dark green velvet jackets. The bridesmaids each carried a bouquet of pink roses with white heather. Robert's best man was his commanding officer, Colonel John Morris. He looked wonderful. Other officer friends of Robert escorted the bridesmaids.

After the wedding ceremony was over, there was a reception followed by a buffet dinner. Every imaginable food Scotland produces was on the buffet table. There was Scottish salmon, roasted lamb, roast beef, and many vegetables and salads. The large wedding cake was finally cut and served to the company. It was magnificent—white except for borders of blue thistles on each layer with Robert and Fiona's names in the center surrounded by red roses. There was also a line of poetry from Robert Burns, "My Love is like a red, red rose that's newly sprung in June." Later in the great room of the castle, Scottish dancing began. Many traditional Scottish country dances including the "Gay Gordon" and many quadrilles were performed by the guests.

When the wedding was over and the festivities ended, Robert and Fiona went on their honeymoon to the continent of Europe. Fiona had visited most of the countries with her parents but Robert had not seen them. They toured Switzerland, Spain, and Italy. They never dreamed that Venice could be so romantic, and they thought Switzerland was like a picture postcard with the gorgeous mountains and beautiful clear cold lakes made from the melting snow of the Alps. Italy was one of their favorite countries. Robert and Fiona both loved fine art and they were delighted by the art treasures of the city of Florence.

When the honeymoon was completed, Robert was most anxious to take his new Scottish bride to Texas. They would sail soon from Southhampton in England to New York on the *Mauritania*. They had many trunks of wedding gifts; Fiona's parents had given them a complete setting for twelve of Royal Crown Derby china. It was priceless and they prayed for its arrival safely in Texas.

Robert's parents had taken a long tour of Scotland while Robert and Fiona had been on their honeymoon. R. W. had always known that his ancestors had come from the Highlands of Scotland. They enjoyed the Highlands with their beautiful lochs, and the green valleys with stone cottages. They also enjoyed a sail to the holy Isle Of Iona where Scottish kings are buried. At the end of their visit, they visited the city of Edinburgh with its large castle overlooking the city. They loved the stores and shops on Princess Street where they shopped for their friends in Texas. The Campbells were enchanted with the beauty of Edinburgh with its lovely parks and the crescents of Georgian houses and buildings.

It was finally time for Robert and Fiona to say good-bye to her parents, friends, neighbors, and all the servants. And it was even more difficult for her to say good-bye to her West Highland terriers. The caretaker said he would always take wonderful care of them. With tears in her eyes, Fiona waved farewell to everyone at Castle Thornberry.

Robert, Fiona, and his parents sailed on the luxury liner from Southhampton to New York. The newly-wed couple remained in their staterooms most of the day, but they joined the Campbells for dinner every night in the ship's main dining room. Every one dressed formally for the long and lavish dinner each evening. The women wore a different formal gown each evening with beautiful fine jewelry and other wonderful accessories. Even their jewelry was rotated. Formal jackets and black-tie were necessary for the men. In his Texas style, R. W. Campbell said, "The value of the jewels and the original gowns in this dining room is greater than all the gold in Fort Knox."

The Campbells had requested a table for four in the dining room so they could become more acquainted with Fiona. R. W. constantly told Fiona about the good points of Texas. Of course, it was the largest of the forty-eight states. He was convinced that Fiona would feel at home and love Texas.

Rebecca was more cautious because she remembered the shock she had when she arrived in Texas as a young bride many years ago. In her singular way, she attempted to prepare Fiona for living in Texas because it had been good economically for her and for R. W. In fact, oil had just been discovered on some of their farm land. But Mrs. Campbell cautioned that after several glasses of Dom Perignon champagne every place sounds wonderful.

The captain's party on the last night at sea was elegant and a delight for everyone. Captain Ian Fraser invited all the Campbells to his table on several occasions. Captain Fraser was from Glasgow and he had been entertained at Castle Thornberry. Fiona and the captain had many mutual things to discuss about Scotland and their life there. In the course of the conversation, R. W. invited Captain Fraser to come to Texas as his guest. At the end of the evening, Captain Fraser presented a rare bottle of malt whisky and a gorgeous Edinburgh Crystal decanter to the Campbell family.

Even though the Campbells had enjoyed the crossing of the Atlantic on the luxury liner, they were happy to see the Statue of Liberty in New York harbor. After clearing customs, R. W. and Rebecca hastily made their way to the train station for their trip to Texas.

Fiona had asked Robert if they could spend a few days in New York before their train journey to Texas. Robert would have preferred leaving immediately for Texas with his parents, but Fiona had friends and relatives who had visited New York and she wanted to see New York for herself. Robert cautioned Fiona that it was not typical of all America and especially Texas. Robert decided a few days would be possible even though he was anxious to return to Texas and open a law office in his home town of Hillsboro.

Robert arranged for accommodations for him and Fiona at the Plaza Hotel in New York. The hotel reminded Fiona of one of the grand hotels of Europe. Fiona loved the stores and shops on Fifth Avenue and she thought the women's fine clothing and accessories were wonderful. She became fascinated with a dress and its ensemble of matching items in one shop. But Robert said, "I think you should wait until you get to Texas." He told her about some of the fine stores in Texas and particularly about Neiman-Marcus in Dallas. Robert did not tell Fiona but he was not keen on spending money on expensive clothing. He did not want to disappoint his new bride but there were not many occasions in Hillsboro that required expensive clothing.

Robert realized that a small town in Texas would be an adjustment for Fiona. She had been accustomed to wealth from her family. He hoped their love and his patience could help Fiona make the transition to the wife of a lawyer in a small Texas town.

Fiona enjoyed the famous restaurants of New York. They were so elegant and served marvelous food. Robert became concerned because Fiona was becoming overly enthused about New York City. He decided it was time to take her to Texas to begin their new life there.

On their last day in New York, Robert told Fiona we are going to have one last extravagance before leaving for Texas. He said, "So get prettied up tonight, and I am going to take you to the Wal-dorf-Astoria Hotel for dinner." Fiona looked lovely in a new dress for the last evening in New York. She was enthralled with the opulence of the Waldorf-Astoria Hotel. The long entry way and long hall of the hotel with its gold ormolu and art deco influence were beautiful to Fiona. Robert and Fiona had a marvelous dinner with many glasses of fine champagne from France.

When they had finished their last glass of champagne, Robert decided it was time to give his new wife a briefing on their life-to-be in Texas. Robert said to Fiona, "I know you are having a wonderful time and enjoying the pleasures of New York, but I must speak plainly about our future in Texas, and even plainer in Hillsboro. There are no expensive stores, jewelry shops, or restaurants in Hillsboro. Women do not wear expensive clothing and jewelry, and they seldom drink champagne or liquor."

"But Robert," Fiona asked, "what do women do for pleasure in Hillsboro?"

Robert Campbell said most affirmatively, "We consider plain living a pleasure," and added, "Most women of Hillsboro are married and they enjoy their family and their husbands."

Fiona detected a slight irritation in her husband's voice, and she began to realize her husband was a strong person. She was learning not to push him. Robert had a kind nature but he did not like to be challenged by anyone. Fiona loved Robert too much to upset him.

The next morning, Robert and Fiona arrived at Grand Central Station in New York to board their train for their trip to Texas. Fiona was fascinated with the beautiful architectural aspects of the station. She would have enjoyed more time to study the architecture but she had to board the train for Texas. Robert had booked a roomette for them. It was comfortable but small for two people. Robert spent most of the time reading law journals.

Robert had given Fiona a book on the development and history of Texas to read during the long train trip of two days and two nights. The book was not interesting to Fiona at the beginning but she became more interested in the historical events as she continued to read. She asked Robert to clarify some details for her which pleased him very much. She also asked about certain leaders like General Sam Houston and General Santa Ana. She was amazed at the long and difficult struggle for independence. She learned that many European settlers had come to Texas to begin a new life. She read about Fredericksburg where many German settlers had emigrated in the 1840's and continued their German traditions of food, clothing, and lifestyle. Fiona asked, "Were there Scottish people who emigrated to Texas?" Robert mentioned that the Campbells originally came from Scotland. Robert also told Fiona that many Czechoslovakian families had settled in Hill County near Hillsboro.

Fiona could only absorb so much Texas history at this time. She spent a lot of time looking at America through the train window, and she secretly wondered what the future would be like for her in a small Texas town. She hoped the future would be good for her.

V

A War Bride in Texas

The new bride from Scotland arrived in Texas on a hot July day. Her enthusiasm for Texas was somewhat lessened when she left the train in Hillsboro and experienced the extreme heat and humidity. The town was much smaller than she expected even though the town square was interesting with the court house in the center.

Fiona had never seen men in overalls and women wearing gingham sun bonnets before. Robert explained that they were cotton farmers and their wives had come into town to do their weekly shopping. Fiona began to feel ill with the heat, and Robert suggested a glass of cold ice tea at Bob's Cafe. Fiona had never tasted iced tea. It was an adjustment since she had always drunk only hot tea in her native Scotland.

Robert suggested a bowl of hot Texas chili and crackers which he had not had for such a long time. Fiona declined the chili and slowly sipped her glass of ice tea. She had never been in such a plain and stark restaurant. She was also shocked at the familiarity of the people who came up to Robert and patted him on the shoulders and said, "Howdy do. Welcome home, Robert."

Fiona was relieved when Robert suggested they would go to Hillsboro House where they would be staying with his parents. They arrived on Craig Street and Fiona was pleased that the house was large and not a small cottage, although it was much smaller than Castle Thornberry.

A large group of people stood waiting in front of the entrance to Hillsboro House. The crowd included Robert's parents, Aunt Ettie, and daughter Bessie, and her husband Joe, who all worked for the Campbells. Many neighbors had joined the welcoming party. Robert looked among the neighbors but he did not see Emily Blackburn. Robert introduced every one to Fiona, his new wife. Fiona forced herself to smile even though she was feeling faint with the Texas heat. To her amazement, her father in-law invited everyone inside the house for iced tea, coconut cake, and lemon pie. Fiona got a quick lesson in Texas style hospitality. She had never met people so friendly to each other and so genuine and sincere.

Mrs. Campbell invited all the ladies into the drawing room for a visit. This would give them an opportunity to meet Fiona and get to know her. Mr. Campbell took the men and Robert to the large screened back porch where they could have a smoke and a strong drink to celebrate Robert's return from the war with his new wife.

The long celebration ended and Robert and Fiona retired to their living quarters which consisted of a large sitting room and bedroom on the second floor of the home with their own private bath. The rooms overlooked Craig Street with a pleasant view. Fiona now understood why the large white house was called Hillsboro House. However, the rooms were modest compared to Castle Thornberry and Fiona had stayed in many hotels in Europe with larger and more opulent rooms, but she would endeavor to accept Texas as her home and try to be a good wife to Robert. She loved Robert in spite of the intense heat of Texas. She unpacked some artifacts from Scotland which added a personal touch to their living quarters.

Within a short time, Robert opened his first law office in part of his father's real estate office on Elm Street. It was a good arrangement for both as Robert evaluated the legal abstracts of property which his father sold. He advised clients on their property rights and concerns. Life looked good for Robert with a bright future in the law business.

One day Emily Blackburn came into his father's office to check on her property insurance. Robert had not seen Emily since he and Fiona had arrived from England to begin their married life in Texas. Emily looked striking. She was tall and thin with the most perfect posture of anyone Robert had ever seen. Her clear complexion and dark hair made her most attractive. Robert's heart skipped a few beats when she came into eye contact with him. He was speechless. Emily spoke first. She said, "Hello, Robert. It is wonderful to see you." Robert's inclination was to hug Emily, but his instinct warned him to refrain as office workers would observe them.

Robert managed to say, "Hello, and I am so thrilled to see

you." He wanted to ask many questions and tell her many things, but he could only ask about her parents. Emily assured him they were fine. Before leaving, she courteously asked about his new wife, Fiona. Robert thanked her and Emily Blackburn left quickly.

Robert had difficulty working and concentrating that afternoon. He could not forget about Emily's visit to his father's office. She was so courteous and never revealed her true feelings to him. Robert kept remembering how close they had been and the last weekend they spent together in San Antonio when he graduated from Officer's Training School. He also wondered if Emily had found anyone else important to her. He decided to ask Miss Clarke, his father's secretary, who had been a classmate of Emily and Robert. Hazel Clarke did not know of any male friends of Emily Blackburn. Miss Emily was most engrossed in her teaching career at Hillsboro High School. This information was a comfort to Robert even though he had no rightful ties to Emily.

The intense Texas heat continued into late August and into the month of September. Robert noticed that Fiona was uncomfortable and sometimes irritable without a reason to be. Robert decided a week's vacation at the seashore would be good for Fiona. He took her to Galveston, where she enjoyed the Victorian seashore resort. The cool sea breezes were a relief from the severe heat. Fiona loved the gaslights and stately Victorian buildings. She and Robert enjoyed relaxing on the beach and swimming in the sea. They visited a different restaurant every night. Fiona enjoyed seafood which was plentiful. She was happier than she had been since arriving in Texas.

One special evening after several glasses of wine and a nice dinner in their hotel, Robert carried Fiona to bed and told her how much he loved her. Fiona became a better wife after the Galveston vacation. She would always cherish their last night in Galveston when Robert made love to her so intensely and so passionately.

When they returned to Hillsboro, Fiona tried to meet people who would be of mutual interest to her and Robert. She took a special interest in the redecorating of Hillsboro House. Robert's parents decided to give Hillsboro House to Robert and Fiona. Robert's mother knew something her son did not know. Fiona was sick almost every morning. Rebecca also knew that Robert and Fiona would soon need a nursery.

31

When Robert discovered the good news, his joy was unbelievable. He insisted on Fiona resting most of the time. Poor Fiona had no other choice. She had a most difficult pregnancy. Dr. Blackburn came every day to check on Fiona. Finally, the time arrived and Fiona was in labor for over twenty-four hours. The baby, a son, was stillborn. It was a great disappointment to Fiona, Robert, and the Campbell family. Robert cried gently for hours when he was not at Fiona's bedside. Fiona was very weak, and Dr. Blackburn advised no more children for the couple.

It took a long time for Fiona to recover. Her physical recovery was slow, but her mental state took a longer time. She was depressed and had no interest in anything. Robert was patient with her but he felt the depression had gone on too long. The first Texas winter was cold and bitter. Robert prayed that spring would come soon. Spring could be beautiful in Texas with many green plants, green trees, and wildflowers in bloom. When spring did arrive, Robert took Fiona for a long ride in the country in the new Campbell roadster. While enjoying the wildflowers in bloom, Fiona told Robert that she would like to return to Scotland for a visit with her family and friends. Robert agreed as long as it would make her happy.

VI

Fiona Visits Scotland

Fiona left soon for her journey to Scotland. She took a passenger train from Texas to New York, and from there, she sailed to England on the *Mauritania*, the same ship which brought her to America with Robert and his parents. The captain of the ship was the same Ian Fraser that she had met on her first trip.

Fiona was pleased that Captain Fraser was in charge of the ship. She was sailing first class, and she was given special treatment. Captain Fraser remembered Fiona and he invited her to have tea with him in his private quarters. Since her parents knew the captain, Fiona accepted the invitation.

The invitation was for 3:00 on the second day of sailing. Fiona dressed very well for her invite to afternoon tea. She was happy to wear her best jewelry and one of her most beautiful dresses which she had purchased in New York.

Just before 3:00, a first-class ship's steward came to escort her to the captain's quarters. Fiona admired the starched white uniform which the steward was wearing. The captain's quarters were on the main deck of the ship and were spacious. The natural wood of the furniture with the art deco design was appealing to Fiona.

Captain Fraser greeted Fiona cordially, saying, "You are looking wonderful, but a little pale and thin."

"Yes, I know," replied Fiona, "That is why I am going back to Scotland for a good rest."

The captain said, "Texas must be a big and strenuous place."

Fiona looked at Captain Fraser who had changed since she had seen him. He was now a man with a good physique. He was taller than she had imagined. His hair was dark red and he had a few tiny freckles on his pleasant face. He was now sporting a handsome moustache. Fiona had not remembered that the captain was so handsome. The captain invited Fiona to sit in one of his best club chairs. She could tell she was the only guest because the tea service was out, and the tea table was laid for two people.

The captain said, "Before serving tea, I suggest we have a gin and tonic. Would that please you?"

"Of course," said Fiona. Two gin and tonics were served by an orderly. Fiona said, "Captain Fraser, how do you ever have time to sail a ship? You have the most gorgeous view from the deck."

"Thank you Fiona. I don't have as much time to enjoy the view as I wish."

Tea was served shortly from the silver tea service. Fiona enjoyed the tiny, thinly sliced sandwiches and shortbread. Three musicians appeared and began playing current tunes of the nineteen twenties. Captain Fraser invited Fiona to dance with him. He was an excellent dancer. Fiona enjoyed the afternoon immensely. At 5:00, she thanked the captain, and an orderly appeared to escort her to her stateroom. The captain said, "Thank you for making a wonderful afternoon for me." The captain gave her a light kiss on the cheek, and said, "I will see you soon."

Fiona returned to her stateroom, feeling weak. But she had had a most beautiful afternoon. She lay on her bed for a while and thought about Robert for the first time that day. She wished he was with her.

The voyage continued to be pleasant for Fiona. Captain Fraser called each morning and each evening to see if Fiona was enjoying the voyage. She thanked him and invited him for cocktails in her stateroom. The captain accepted and came promptly the next day at 5:00. He said, "I can only have one whisky."

Fiona said, "It could only be scotch whisky." They had a pleasant conversation, and Fiona told him about her life in Texas. She then asked the captain about his family.

"I have a young son by my former wife. Our marriage did not last since I am away most of the time. I don't really blame her."

Fiona was very sympathetic. She said, "Captain, you must be very lonely even though there are hundreds of people on the ship."

He replied, "That I am but I am certainly not lonely now." After finishing his drink, he said, "I must return to my duties, unfortunately, yet I would prefer visiting with you."

The captain took Fiona's hands and held them tightly. Fiona felt weak in her legs, and the captain kissed her lightly on the cheek before leaving. She missed him when he left for his official duties.

Fiona could not help thinking about the handsome captain the remainder of the evening. "Well," said Fiona, "some woman is going to be lucky when she catches him."

The ship arrived in England. It had been an easy voyage; Captain Fraser had contributed to Fiona's pleasant trip. The ship arrived in Southhampton, where Fiona's parents had come to greet her. Captain Fraser invited Captain and Mrs. McGill aboard the ship where he served them morning coffee. The McGills enjoyed seeing the ship, and they appreciated his hospitality. As Fiona and her family were leaving the ship, the captain shook hands and thanked them, adding, "Fiona, may I see you in Scotland soon? I have a two-week holiday coming." Fiona invited the captain to Thornberry Castle for a weekend.

Captain and Mrs. McGill were concerned about Fiona's health. They took her immediately to Thornberry Castle in Scotland. She was happy to be at her ancestral home, where the large gray stones of the castle looked wonderful to her. The servants were pleased to have her home for a while.

Fiona went for a walk in the countryside every morning and every afternoon when the weather permitted. She loved the rich green countryside with the sheep grazing in the pastures. They were so gentle and she often stopped to pet them. The Scottish thistles were in bloom and the heather would soon follow. She especially enjoyed walks along the River Devon.

Fiona enjoyed afternoon tea each day at the castle. Her mother invited different relatives and friends to visit each day, and soon they noticed Fiona was looking and feeling better.

After a few days Fiona received a telephone call from a gentleman. At first, she thought it was Robert's voice in Texas, but that was not possible. It was the voice of Captain Fraser. He asked Fiona if he could come for a visit this weekend with her. Fiona gladly invited the captain to Castle Thornberry for the weekend.

She met the captain at the station on Saturday morning, where they exchanged pleasant greetings and she then drove him to the castle. His bags were taken up to a private room, and they had tea before she showed him his room. Fiona suggested that he change into walking clothes for a hike in the afternoon with her father. And then her parents would host a dinner party for him in the evening. Fiona showed him to his room on the second floor of the castle which had a view of the countryside. He said, "I can hardly wait for the walk in the country." She left to give him time to change into hiking clothing.

When she returned shortly afterwards, the captain was in the middle of changing his clothing. "Excuse me, sir," said Fiona.

"Never mind, I was admiring the view from the window, and I forgot to change my clothing until just now." He continued, "I remember the castle when I first visited it with my parents. I was only a small boy."

Fiona looked at the captain who was nearly nude. She said, "I am glad you are here, but you are certainly not a boy anymore."

The captain said, "You are going to make me blush."

Fiona and Ian enjoyed their walk in the countryside. The captain noticed everything. He admired every plant and shrub. The captain said, "I don't see many plants when I am crossing the ocean." They enjoyed their hike, and the fresh air made Fiona sleepy. She rested while her father and the captain had a game of golf in the afternoon. She wanted to be fresh-looking for the dinner party that evening.

The dinner party was a huge success. The captain enjoyed the roast sirloin of beef with roasted potatoes and green peas. He had cultivated manners and perfect social graces. Mrs. McGill was most impressed with him. After a glass of red bordeaux, Mrs. McGill said aside to Fiona, "He would have made a wonderful husband for you."

Fiona replied, "But I have a wonderful husband in America."

"Of course, my dear," said her mother, "we all love Robert Campbell."

Sunday arrived, and Fiona secretly dreaded seeing the captain leave. Fiona was inclined to agree with her mother that Ian Fraser would have made a good husband. She drove him to the train station in the late afternoon. The captain was sorry to leave, but he had commitments to his young son. Fiona was sorry to say good-bye to the Captain. As the train pulled away from the platform, Fiona decided it was time to return to Texas to her husband, Robert.

VII

Two Funerals

The next morning Fiona awakened to the ever-present rain falling, and she missed the feel and comfort of Robert's warm body. She longed to see her husband. She began to think about Texas and the heat and cold and the over-friendly people. Maybe she was the one who was wrong. Fiona wrote to Robert that she would take the next ship sailing to New York. When she arrives in America, she would come directly to Texas. Once again she said good-bye to her parents, the servants, the West Highland terriers, and her favorite friends and neighbors before embarking on the trip.

Robert was pleased to receive her letter that she was on her way home. He decided to surprise her and meet her in New York City. It was a pleasant surprise for Fiona. She looked vastly improved and healthier as a result of her visit to Scotland. They spent several days in New York City, enjoying the shopping, the theater, and the museums. Their suite at the Plaza Hotel was wonderful, and they enjoyed their meals in the Oak Room.

Before leaving for Texas, Robert received sad news. His father, R. W., had died suddenly of a heart attack. Robert had been close to his father, and was very sad over the loss. Fiona was sorry for her husband but she was glad she was with him at this sad time. Robert and Fiona returned to Texas.

The funeral for R. W. Campbell was Texas-style which meant a large funeral. Friends and relatives came from many areas of Texas. It took several vehicles to transport the flowers. The governor of Texas sent a delegation from Austin to attend the service. The Episcopal Church could not accommodate every one who wanted to attend the service, so a second service was conducted at the cemetery for those who were not admitted to the church service. R. W. was buried in the Campbell plot of the cemetery. After the services, Mrs. Campbell opened Hillsboro House for family and close friends to sign a memorial book and have coffee and cake.

After several weeks of mourning for her husband, Becky Campbell believed it was time to turn the management of Hillsboro House over to her daughter-in-law. Fiona gladly took charge of the house and quickly began redecorating it. She gave the house a new twenties look and began to entertain the important clients of Robert and the various business people of Hillsboro. She was an excellent hostess and she was becoming more attractive than ever to Robert.

The people of Hillsboro began to accept Fiona as if she belonged to their small town. Even Emily Blackburn came to afternoon tea with several other ladies. Fiona and Emily were cordial to each other. By this time, Fiona knew that Robert and Emily had planned to marry before he went overseas, but Fiona did not have this knowledge when she married Robert in Scotland.

Being a Scot, Fiona spoke plainly her point of view. Some times a sensitive guest could be offended by Fiona as she always spoke her mind. But Robert could always bridge the gap for Fiona. Robert had the art of explaining things without offending the person who was listening.

Fiona gave many wonderful dinner parties at Hillsboro House. She modified the Southern-style of cooking fried foods. All vegetables were simmered and beef was roasted with Yorkshire pudding. She introduced desserts such as blueberry fool, Dundee, bride's cake, Scottish shortbread, and fruit trifles.

Robert and Fiona gave a large garden party and invited everyone. Fiona hired a band and had an area for dancing. Champagne punch was served. The *Hillsboro Journal* gave it a very favorable review in the social column, but the next Sunday, the Baptist minister in his sermon mentioned that sinful parties where dancing and strong drink were served should be avoided.

One evening, Fiona gave a small dinner party for a few close friends and she served steak and kidney pie. The ladies did their best with the pie but the men only tasted theirs. Robert subtly suggested that Texas men would have preferred chicken-fried steak and gravy. Fiona maintained that Texas men needed to be introduced to a wider range of food.

Fiona's dinner table always looked beautiful. If she didn't use the Royal Crown Derby China they received as a wedding gift from her parents, she would use a set of Minton China or Royal Worcester bone china. Fiona loved fine china, and she owned many sets of fine English china. The silver and crystal were exquisite as well as her centerpieces of fresh flowers or plants depending on the season of the year. Fiona insisted that when dinner was served and finished, guests must be served coffee or tea in the drawing room. Another china coffee or tea set would be used.

One of Robert and Fiona's favorite parties at Hillsboro House was Robert Burns' night on January 25, the birthday of the national poet of Scotland. The invitations were designed with tartan borders and thistles. They asked guests to wear Scottish tartan which most Texans called plaid. The guests did not have to wear total tartan. A skirt, shirt, or tie would be acceptable. Fiona was dressed in the green McGill tartan skirt, a white blouse, and a black velvet jacket. With her auburn hair she looked gorgeous in her Scottish dress. After much persuasion from Fiona, Robert Campbell agreed to wear a kilt. It was the popular Royal Stewart tartan since they could not locate a Campbell kilt in Texas. Robert wore lacing shoes with knee socks, and a sporran hung in front of his waist. Over his shoulder he wore a plaid, a tartan sash. Robert was the hit of the party as most guests had never seen a man in a kilt.

The Scottish dinner was a gourmet meal. The first course was homemade Scotch broth followed by a small serving of haggis on a salad plate with relishes. It tasted like highly seasoned stuffing; Ettie had done her best with the haggis because Fiona had told her how to make it. The main course was roasted venison cooked in black currant sauce, roasted potatoes, Brussel sprouts, and a fruit trifle for dessert.

Fiona attempted to teach her guests Scottish dancing for a part of the evening's entertainment, but the guests made very little progress in learning the country dances. So Robert and Fiona danced several Scottish dances for the enjoyment of the party guests. Fiona sang several Scottish songs which the guests loved. Before the evening ended, Fiona insisted on several couples forming a dance quadrille for the final dance. The dancers did well, and the evening ended with Fiona reciting a few of Robert Burns' poems.

Life continued to be pleasant and enjoyable at Hillsboro

House for Robert and Fiona. Occasionally, she thought about the son who was born dead and was now buried in the Hillsboro cemetery. One evening she mentioned to Robert how happy life was for her but her life would be even happier if she could have a child. Robert reminded her that Dr. Blackburn had advised against more children for them. Fiona did not agree with Robert; she felt a child might bring much happiness to their lives. "If it is that important to you, you may have a child," said Robert.

Soon Fiona was carrying a child and she and Robert were so very happy. They preferred another boy but they would be very happy with a girl. The pregnancy was most difficult for Fiona just as Dr. Blackburn had warned. She had to spend most of the time in her bed. Robert stayed with her as much as possible. Mrs. Campbell and Ettie kept a close watch on Fiona since they were concerned about her condition. Ettie had seen many women in similar condition, and it did not look good for Fiona.

When the time came for the birth, Dr. Blackburn stayed at Hillsboro House and kept a close watch also on Fiona and her serious condition. Fiona went into labor, lasting many hours, but finally a healthy seven-pound boy was born. It was not an easy delivery, and Fiona was extremely weak afterwards. Her heart and blood pressure were so weak that Dr. Blackburn was gravely concerned. Robert suggested showing the new baby to Fiona who gave a big smile when she saw her new son. She tried to hold the baby, but she slipped into a coma. Dr. Blackburn called for the help of another doctor. Fiona never regained consciousness, and Robert Campbell was in a state of shock. He could not believe Fiona was gone. Robert Campbell would not leave her bedside until the Episcopal priest of the church came and said a prayer for Fiona.

All of his close friends were called to comfort Robert. Aunt Ettie was an old woman at this time, but she did her best to say the right things to Robert. Mrs. Campbell did her best to console her son. She did not want Robert to see her sadness. Robert's grief was unbelievable and he only spoke when someone asked him a question. In spite of his grief, Robert remembered that Fiona said she did not want an elaborate funeral like her father-in-law, R. W. Campbell. After a simple graveside service, Elizabeth Fiona McGill Campbell was buried next to her son in the Hillsboro Cemetery.

The tragic news of Fiona Campbell's death was relayed to Castle Thornberry in Scotland via the Trans-Atlantic cable. However, the cable did announce that a healthy seven-pound son named Clayton William Campbell had been born to Fiona before her death.

Many condolences and letters of sympathy came from near and far including letters from overseas from the family and friends of Fiona. Cables were sent by her parents from Castle Thornberry to Robert stating their love and sympathy. There were many local letters and cards including one from Emily Blackburn expressing her sincere sympathy to Robert. Robert decided he could not read the remainder of the letters and cards because each one made him more upset. He had his secretary at the office respond to the many expressions of sympathy.

Robert went to the Hillsboro Cemetery several times per day to visit Fiona's grave. He could not concentrate on any thing except the death of his wife, Fiona. He took fresh flowers in the morning, and in the afternoon he stayed beside the grave until the cold Texas air made him chilled and uncomfortable. His mother tried to persuade him to discontinue these constant visits to Fiona's graveside, but he was not receptive to suggestions from any person. Aunt Ettie said, "Poor Robert must do these visits to her grave because he is in deep grief, but time will ease his pain and suffering for Fiona Campbell." Aunt Ettie prepared Robert's favorite meals but he would only taste the food and eat small amounts. Ettie prayed for his appetite to return.

After a time, Robert's appetite returned. He discontinued the daily visits to Fiona's grave much to the relief of his mother and Aunt Ettie, yet he was not over the loss of his wife which he could not readily understand or accept. In his deep anguish and disturbed mental state, he could not rationalize why this dreadful misfortune happened to him and Fiona at such an early stage of their life together. Robert kept asking if this was God's punishment for something he had done, or was it the fate of some unknown God? Aunt Ettie said to Robert, "It was neither; it was an act of God." Ettie also said, "The good Lord gives, and the good Lord takes. "

VIII

Judge Campbell and His Son, Clayton

Robert Campbell thought he would never stop grieving over the death of Fiona who died after giving birth to a son. He blamed himself because it was not necessary for them to have had a child. Dr. Blackburn had warned them about the danger of having more children when their first child was stillborn. But Fiona had wanted a child. And before her death, she gave birth to a healthy son.

They had selected the name of Clayton William if their new baby was a boy. Robert became very emotional when he thought about the name they had selected if the baby had been a girl. He knew that a girl would never be possible now that Fiona was gone.

He had no desire to return to his law practice which was growing monthly, and he had even accepted a new junior lawyer to his firm. There was too much business for Robert to handle without another lawyer. The new lawyer must handle his cases until he could return to the law office.

For hours each day, Robert sat in the bedroom where Fiona died and stared out the windows. Aunt Ettie brought him meals which he never finished. This grieving continued for several days until his mother, Rebecca, decided to have a serious and long talk with Robert. She explained to him that many women have died in childbirth and it was not the husband's fault. She then asked Ettie to bring the new baby for Robert to hold. He wanted to decline but his mother insisted that he hold his own son. The blue-eyed, auburn-haired baby was cute and he resembled Fiona. It held on to Robert's hands and would not let go. Robert held his son until it was time for him to be fed.

Suddenly a miracle happened; Robert could not stay away from his son. His grief began to subside as he became more interested in his new son and he rationalized that a part of Fiona would live through their son.

Robert returned to his law firm, working harder than ever.

Work helped him to recover from the grief he had over his wife's death.

The new baby in the house kept Mrs. Campbell and Ettie busy. Some activity was constantly happening with the new baby. The infant was healthy and grew larger every week. Before and after work, Robert spent time in the nursery with his son, Clayton. Clayton began to grow and change. He could crawl and then, suddenly, he was standing in the crib, which brought great pleasure to Robert and his grandmother. When Clayton began to take steps and stumble and fall, his father would cheer him and encourage him to try again.

Clayton's bright blue eyes and blond hair reminded Robert of Fiona, and he was often sad that Fiona could not see the amazing growth of their son. But Robert was grateful that Fiona had given him a wonderful son.

The law practice of Robert Campbell continued to grow and expand, and Robert's reputation as an attorney was known throughout Hill County. The year was 1926, an election year in Hill County, with a vacancy for county judge. Many clients and friends encouraged Robert to become a candidate for county judge. He was not anxious to give up his law practice, but it was an opportunity for him and an honor he could not decline.

The campaign required much time and work. He had to drive over dirt roads to every small community in Hill County where potential voters always invited him for supper. It was a great year for black-eyed peas. Robert was served cornbread and black-eyed peas almost every night. He was anxious for the votes, and he continued to eat black-eyed peas. When he returned home to Hillsboro House he told Ettie not to serve any more peas until the election was over.

The campaign was costly because he could not spend much time in his law firm. His opponent made many critical attacks against him, but he could always answer him. One thing Robert had learned in life is that you should have an answer for anyone who criticizes you unjustly. Robert could take constructive criticism. He told the voters he was not perfect—admitted that he made mistakes for which he was sorry, but at least he was honest enough to admit his mistakes. He told the voters, "Ask my opponent if he has ever admitted to his mistakes and wrongdoings."

Robert wrote a note to Emily Blackburn seeking her help in the election. Robert suggested that she might join him on some of the campaign trips into other towns in the county. He received a quick reply written on one of Emily's expensive personal note cards. He read it anxiously.

August 10, 1926

Dear Robert,

Thank your letter requesting my help in your election campaign. I send my best wishes to you, and I hope the election will be successful for you.

I will ask my friends and neighbors to vote for you. It will not be possible for me to join you on election campaigns which are located out of town. It is necessary for me to be with my elderly parents who are not well at this time.

Sincerely,

Emily Blackburn

Robert continued his election campaign for district judge even more vigorously. He worked day and night on the campaign. The election was held in Hill County, Texas, and Robert Campbell became Judge Robert William Campbell.

A large celebration and victory party was held that evening in Hillsboro House. The most important supporters were invited, along with Robert's closest friends and neighbors. The celebration lasted all evening. Robert looked among the crowd to see if Emily was there. Judge Campbell asked his mother if she had heard from Emily Blackburn.

She answered, "Yes, Emily telephoned and sent her congratulations to you." She also added that Emily would send him a note the next day congratulating him on the election. Judge Campbell was not pleased and decided that he needed a strong drink. Several of the women supporters thought Judge Robert Campbell was a handsome man and many women thought he would be a good catch. Others thought it was a pity that he was a widower with no wife in prospect. Robert was aware of his popularity among women but he had little interest in them since the passing of Fiona.

Judge Campbell moved into the court division of the impressive Hillsboro Court House. He was pleased to go to his chambers in the beautiful court house each morning. He enjoyed serving as a judge, and found each case exciting. Some were very different and strange. Some cases were also ridiculous and even amusing while others were complex and difficult to resolve.

Young Clayton continued to grow and mature. The judge was proud of his son, and he often took him into town for an ice cream cone. Rebecca knew that Robert really wanted to show off his son to his many friends in the town.

Clayton entered school and became a good student. His report cards indicated A's in all subjects. He was a bright boy for his age. He did his homework every night with his father's help. One night Clayton asked, "Why do the older kids in school call me the Scotty?" This was painful to Judge Campbell. He explained to his son about how he fell in love with Clayton's mother when he was in the army overseas. He married her and brought her to America to live. He fetched a silver picture frame with his favorite photograph of Clayton's Mother. He encouraged Clayton to be proud of his Scottish mother.

"She was a beautiful woman and you would have loved her very much," he told his son.

The judge suggested that Clayton might want to go to Scotland for a visit when he was older. It would be good for him to see the homeland of his mother and her family. He told Clayton the Scottish people are proud of their beautiful country and its long heritage. He emphasized how brave the Scottish people had been over many centuries. He suggested Clayton read books on the history of Scotland and learn about the heroes of Scotland. He encouraged his son to read about Mary Queen of Scots, William Wallace, Robert the Bruce, James the First, and even Rob Roy MacGregor. He told his son that some day he must visit Scotland and see its beautiful mountains, valleys, and lochs. The judge said, "You will enjoy the beautiful and interesting old castles in Scotland." He encouraged his son to read the books of Sir Walter Scott and the poetry of Robert Burns.

After his father had finished discussing Scotland, Clayton would never regret if any one called him Scotty. He became very proud of his Scottish heritage.

Clayton began reading his mother's books on Scotland. When he had read all of her books, he wrote to his grandparents in Scotland to send him books on Scottish history. They gladly sent him historical books and literary books by Scottish authors. By the time Clayton was twelve years old, he had read most of Sir Walter Scott's novels. He had read numerous biographies of Scottish heroes and that of Mary Queen of Scots. All of his book reports in school were about Scotland or by Scottish authors.

One day the principal of Clayton's school telephoned Judge Campbell, who decided that it must be very important because the principal of the school had never called him before. When the court was in recess, the judge called Mr. Jones, the principal. Mr. Jones explained to him that Clayton was an excellent student but his teachers have a genuine concern. It seems they were worried that his grades in his history class were dropping because he was only interested in the history of Scotland. It was necessary for Clayton to study American and Texas history so that he could pass these classes with his usual grade of A on his report card. Judge Campbell was very relieved and he promised the Principal he would help Clayton balance his history reading.

When Judge Campbell went home that evening to Hillsboro House, he told Clayton that he had stopped at the city library and borrowed a book about the Alamo. The book told stories of the Alamo and of the heroes who perished there for Texas independence. The judge told Clayton as soon as he finished reading the book on the Alamo, he would take him to San Antonio for the weekend. Clayton and Judge Campbell went to San Antonio the next weekend. He was a fast reader.

Clayton's visit to San Antonio and the Alamo with his father resulted in an immediate interest in Texas history. The judge's plan had worked and he thought he would stretch it even further. He took Clayton to a popular old book store in San Antonio where he knew there would be many good books on the history of Texas. Judge Campbell encouraged Clayton to select several books on Texas, and Clayton took them home.

Shortly afterwards Clayton received his monthly report card from school with straight A's including Texas history. Clayton completed the school year with honors in his class.

He was looking forward to summer vacation—summers were a wonderful time in Hillsboro. The residents could be out of doors for ball games, picnics, and swimming in lakes and rivers. The mimosas were in full bloom, and the elms along Craig Street appeared as a green forest. The Texas summers were very hot, but the people of Hillsboro did not mind. It was a great time to visit with neighbors and friends. They could sit on the front porch and sip fresh lemonade. Gallons of iced tea would be served with the noon-time and evening meals.

Everyone in Hillsboro was looking forward to the Fourth of July. After Christmas, it was their favorite holiday. Clayton was excited. A large parade was planned for the town beginning at the town square and then circling around the court house, then proceeding down Elm Street to the Dallas Highway. Every one anxiously awaited for the parade to begin at 11:00 A.M. The mayor of Hillsboro led the parade in an open car followed by the fire brigade in their bright red fire trucks. The Hillsboro High School band came next playing patriotic American songs.

The Boy Scouts and the Camp Fire girls marched in the parade. Clayton and his best friend had recently qualified for Eagle Scout status. They were cheered by the crowds. Each boy carried an American flag. The Boy Scouts and the Camp Fire girls looked wonderful in their uniforms. It was a great day for a small Texas town. The Fourth of July parade was an important event in this community.

After the parade was finished, people had various plans for celebrating the big day. Some would have a picnic in the park. Others would celebrate at their homes. Judge Campbell had invited several lawyers and their families to Hillsboro House for a large Fourth of July celebration on his front lawn. He had sent Emily an invitation but she sent her regrets that she would be out of town.

Even though Aunt Ettie was an old woman by now, she had risen early to prepare the food for the holiday. It could not be the Fourth of July without southern fried chicken, potato salad, and baked beans. Ettie had baked several angel food cakes and her son-in-law had made several freezers of ice cream.

The dinner was to begin at 3:00, but Judge Campbell had some formal festivities planned before the feast. The mayor of Hillsboro led the flag salute. A tall flag pole with an American flag was al-

47

ways waving on good days in the front yard of Hillsboro House. The rector of St. Mary's Episcopal Church said the blessing. Then Judge Campbell using his most compelling voice read "The Declaration of Independence." He read it only as a good actor or lawyer would read. Even on a very hot afternoon, you could feel chills down your spine and a lump in your throat as the judge read the famous historical document. Clayton was proud of his father, and Clayton was happy to be an American. Everyone gave Judge Campbell a loud applause.

Martha Gates, the wife of his junior partner, had a good singing voice. The judge asked her to sing "God Bless America." Every one enjoyed her beautiful soprano voice. When she finished, she asked every one to stand and join her in singing the national anthem, "The Star Spangled Banner." By the time the guests had finished singing, they were all proud Americans. Judge Campbell thanked his guests for their cooperation and patriotic spirit.

The guests were also hungry. Southern people enjoy their food. And Judge Campbell said, "It is now time to celebrate with our food." Three buffet tables were covered with trays and bowls of marvelous and delicious food prepared by Aunt Ettie and her help. The tables looked festive with a theme of one table with a red table cloth, a second with a white cloth, and the third with a blue cloth. The guest tables were also covered with a similar theme, and in addition a small American flag in the center. The guests ate heartily, and they sent many compliments to Aunt Ettie for her outstanding food. None of the guests had eaten such delicious fried chicken. The freshly baked angel food cakes and the homemade vanilla ice cream were delicious. Some guests had seconds on the dessert.

Everyone enjoyed the picnic on the front lawn of Hillsboro House with the American flag flying above the breeze of the wind. Just before dark, the firecrackers and sparklers were brought out for the younger guests. The firecrackers were noisy but the sparklers were beautiful as they sent out hundreds of little sparks.

It was a wonderful day and a great celebration for everyone. The guests remembered that it was the one hundred and fifty-fifth birthday of America.

IX

Judge Campbell and Women

The summers of the late thirties passed slowly and most people of Hillsboro tolerated the heat by looking for swimming areas in lakes and nearby rivers.

On one very hot summer, Judge Campbell and Clayton went to Galveston for a few days to cool off in the Gulf of Mexico. Clayton enjoyed the Victorian city with its many gingerbread houses. They stayed in the same hotel where Robert and Fiona had stayed when they were there on a holiday before Clayton was born. Clayton enjoyed a daily swim in the sea.

Galveston rekindled many memories for Robert Campbell of his late wife. He did not tell Clayton but he was glad to return home at the end of the vacation. Clayton was also anxious to begin his senior year at Hillsboro High School. He was looking forward to seeing his special friends and some of his favorite teachers.

Clayton asked his father numerous questions about Miss Emily on the drive home from Galveston to Hillsboro. Robert was cautious and evasive about many of the questions which Clayton asked. Clayton knew that his father and Miss Emily were close friends when they were teenagers and students in Hillsboro. Clayton asked his father if he was ever in love with Miss Emily, and the judge replied, "I claim the privilege of invoking the Fifth Amendment to the Constitution." He also added, "That was a private matter between me and Miss Emily a long time ago." Clayton decided not to pursue the matter any further.

Father and son remained quiet for the remainder of the drive home to Hillsboro. The judge was thinking about Emily Blackburn who had lived most of her life on Craig Street. She had always permitted herself to travel during the summer. This summer she had been on a European tour.

Judge Campbell's thoughts were deep regarding Miss Emily. He accepted the fact that she had never forgiven him for marrying

Fiona when he was serving overseas during World War I. But he could not understand why they could not be friends since it had been more than twenty years ago. Before they arrived in Hillsboro, he had decided to confront Emily and would ask her to join him in renewing their friendship. He would wait for an opportunity to speak privately with Emily. He knew that she had returned from her European vacation. But each time he approached her for a private talk she excused herself by saying she had commitments to keep and errands to complete.

Judge Campbell was a leading member of the Hillsboro Board of Education. He wrote Miss Emily a memorandum that he would like to discuss an education matter with her, and he suggested that she come to Hillsboro House for a talk at 5:00 one afternoon.

Emily felt it was her duty to meet with a senior member of the Board of Education, and she arrived promptly at 5:00 P.M. on the appointed day where she was ushered into the drawing room. She had almost forgotten how opulent Hillsboro House was. It had been many years since she had been inside the house even though she lived only a few houses away and on the same block as Hillsboro House.

The judge appeared, greeted Emily warmly, and thanked her for coming to meet him. He asked about her European trip. Emily answered politely but remained very formal and stiff. He offered her a glass of sherry, but she declined, saying she had a dinner engagement and must leave as soon as their educational matter was discussed. He thanked her for the many years of successful teaching at Hillsboro High School and said he was going to recommend her as Teacher of the Year in Texas. Emily thanked him, but she felt he had omitted saying something else on his mind.

He confirmed her belief, by saying, "That is what I wanted to discuss with you, but I would also like to speak privately to you about our personal relationship."

Emily stood up abruptly, and said, "I came here only to discuss educational matters and I am afraid our personal relationship ended many years ago." Emily excused herself and prepared to leave.

Judge Campbell took Emily's hands and said, "Someday I hope you will forgive me because I have always loved you and I always will." Emily did not respond and left quietly.

Judge Campbell sat in his favorite chair for the remainder of the evening downing his best bourbon and thinking of the two women in his life; his late wife Fiona and Emily Blackburn who would not forgive him for his action many years ago.

With each sip of his fine bourbon, he reflected on his life. He had been fortunate and successful. His father, Robert Campbell, Sr. had been a sharp business man. His father's estate was large when he died. Robert and his mother were the only heirs. Judge Campbell had inherited an immense amount of property from his father's will and the need for money would never be a problem for him.

He had succeeded in his law career, with a reputation as one of Texas' most important lawyers. His knowledge of the ownership and transfer of property laws of Texas was unsurpassed. Many lawyers and legal analysts sought his advice on complicated property laws. He had received many honors from the state and local Bar Associations of Texas. He served on many committees of the Bar Association, where he was usually asked to be chairman. He was made an honorary member of many prestigious organizations.

With all his inherited wealth and his remarkable success as a lawyer, the judge had a void in his life. The beautiful Emily Blackburn could have filled that void. When the judge had his last swallow of bourbon, he mused aloud, "Damn it, why does Emily have to act like Scarlett O'Hara? Does she wish me to get down on my knees and beg for her forgiveness for renewed friendship?" He finished, "I am no Rhett Butler, and I do give a damn about Emily Blackburn."

He could not believe that Emily lived only four houses west of Hillsboro House. Her parents had built the two-story, pale-yellow brick house in 1910. It was small compared to his house but her home was impressive for a Texas home. It looked like a New England, Federal-style house. He remembered the large Victorian house which Emily's parents had built many years ago, which, unfortunately, had been destroyed by a Texas tornado. The judge was only a young man at the time, and Emily and her parents escaped the destruction of their home because they were in New Orleans visiting relatives and friends.

Judge Campbell knew that he had drunk too much bourbon that evening, but he decided he would call Emily and propose marriage to her. He wove his way into the hall to telephone Emily and tell her they would be married tomorrow morning in his office by another lawyer.

Ettie's daughter, Bessie, had been observing Judge Campbell since her living quarters were near the kitchen. She decided to have a talk with him and persuade him not to telephone Emily until the next morning when he would be himself. "Dammit, Bessie, you're like your mother and my mother, you are right again. I'll go to bed and sleep this bourbon off."

The judge wakened late the next morning. He had never been late to his office before, but he would be an hour late today as he would arrive about 9:00 A.M. Bessie had a large breakfast prepared for him—hot biscuits and homemade jam, bacon and eggs with fresh pork sausage, and many cups of black coffee to revive him. She stood by the table and watched him eat every bite of food she had prepared. He felt cranky that morning but he was not going to show it to Bessie. He did retort, "It is good that you are feeding me so well but you don't have to fatten me for the slaughter."

Bessie, who was inclined to be feisty in her conversation, replied, "Judge shut your mouth and eat your breakfast because I am going to talk to your mother today."

Judge Campbell asked, "How can that be possible since she has been dead for several years?"

Bessie replied, "I talk to your mother everyday and she gives me the directions for this here household."

Judge Campbell decided he had had enough breakfast and certainly enough of this type of conversation with Bessie. He would leave for his law office, and try to think of a reason for being an hour late if he had to explain to his secretary and associates in the office. He thanked Bessie for the good hearty breakfast, and for the fact that she kept him from making a fool of himself and calling Emily Blackburn when he had drunk too much bourbon. Bessie knew she was in charge and Judge Campbell knew she was in command of the situation. But he gave her a final warning, "Don't you dare pour out a drop of my fine bourbon today." Bessie shrugged her shoulders and walked out of the room.

The judge had difficulty concentrating at his office, and he frequently had to ask clients to repeat their questions or comments to him. His mind was giving him difficult thoughts, mostly about

Emily Blackburn. In his frustration, he could not understand why such a beautiful woman was so unyielding. The judge knew that Emily loved him before he went overseas to serve in World War I.

Robert Campbell decided he needed the good company of a woman. It might help him to forget about Emily Blackburn for a while at least. He asked Miss Clarke to move up the remainder of his appointments for the day and to cancel the unimportant ones. He explained that he was going for a drive in the country to inspect his tenant farms. He left his office in the early afternoon and he knew exactly where he was going. He drove out to the farm where Agnes Johnson lived. She had inherited the farm from her late husband, Tom, and his family. Agnes Johnson had been a widow for two years now since her husband died. He had a feeling she was lonely out there on the farm all day while her children were in school. He decided to go calling and say hello to Agnes.

The judge arrived early, before her children returned from school. Agnes greeted him warmly and invited him in for a glass of iced tea. He had represented Agnes when her husband had died, and he was successful in obtaining the full ownership of the farm for her from the other heirs who had claims against the farmland. Agnes had always been grateful to him for his help to her then. The judge and Agnes discussed the farm for a while, and then he asked her if she was ever lonely. Agnes admitted that she missed her husband very much and Robert told her how lonely he was since his wife had been gone.

Agnes made the judge a second glass of iced tea since she noticed he was beginning to perspire. She took a washcloth and gently wiped his forehead and he observed that Agnes still had a good figure. The judge put his arm around Agnes and Agnes did not back away. They continued to embrace each other passionately for a long time until he asked Agnes if he should leave. Agnes said, "I enjoy the touch of a good man after such a long time." Agnes then led the judge to her bedroom where they enjoyed a good hour together.

Just before he left the Johnson farm, he gave Agnes a long lingering kiss. He told Agnes that there are secrets that men and women must keep in life. He told her that their afternoon together must be a secret between them. Agnes invited him to stay for supper, but he declined and thanked her because he had a dinner engagement in Hillsboro. She told him she hoped he would come by often for a visit.

Judge Campbell drove slowly back into town while thinking about his afternoon with Agnes Johnson. He did not love her but she was a kind person whom he did not wish to hurt or disappoint. He was contemplative as he drove along the Texas countryside. He turned on the car radio, and Bob Wells the Texas crooner was singing a sad love song. The judge thought about his situation in life and his problems and he also thought about the many problems of his clients. The world seemed full of problems, but he made up his mind that he would overcome his own problems because he was made of the pioneer stock of his parents, Robert and Rebecca Campbell.

Robert Campbell returned to the big white house on Craig Street where Bessie had a nice fire burning in the fireplace and some refreshments of cakes and cookies on the table. The best sherry glasses and a new bottle of Bristol Cream sherry were on the piecrust tea table in the parlor, and two dainty white linen napkins trimmed in lace which his mother had made a long time ago.

Bessie could not wait to tell him that he was going to have a guest at 6:00 P.M. She had tried to call him at his office but Miss Clarke had told her that the judge was out of the office for the afternoon. Bessie continued, "Miss Emily Blackburn had called and said she would be pleased to join the judge for a glass of sherry at 6:00."

The judge replied, "Oh, hell, why wouldn't she have a glass of sherry last evening?" He dashed upstairs to freshen up since it was almost 6:00.

Emily Blackburn arrived promptly, looking beautiful. The judge greeted her and invited her into the parlor. He offered her a glass of sherry which she graciously accepted. As he served her, he noticed her beautiful jewelry and her expensive clothing. Her diamond earrings and a diamond and sapphire bracelet were exquisite. The jewelry looked wonderful with her navy-blue dress with its large white collar. Emily was very cordial and she apologized for her behavior the previous evening. She was very sorry if she had hurt his feelings because she respected him and valued his friendship. She also emphasized that she was not in love with him as she had been so many years ago. The judge told Emily he appreciated her sincerity and honesty even though he could not understand why she could not love him again as she did when they were very young. Emily emphasized to Robert that everything changes, including people and their feelings. Their conversation continued to be pleasant and enjoyable. Emily carefully changed the conversation to books and movies (these being among her many interests).

She stayed for an hour and the judge enjoyed her company. She thanked him for the visit, and she gave him a light hug and kiss when she left. The judge was pleased with her visit but he told Bessie that he did not understand women. Bessie said, "Judge, that is because you ain't no woman."

PART TWO

I

Ebenezer and Lucinda

Ebenezer Martin and his new wife, Lucinda, arrived in the state of Texas in 1860. They had taken the long journey on the Butterfield Stage from Tipton, Missouri. They had crossed the Indian Territory safely but not comfortably. Several times the stagecoach had difficulty crossing the numerous rivers which were often flooded. The Red River at Colbert Crossing was at flood-stage. The very red and muddy water covered many areas of land surrounding it.

Ebenezer and Lucinda were newly married, and they had decided to leave the stagecoach at the first station in Texas which looked promising to begin their married life together. They considered Sherman and Gainsville, but continued on the Stagecoach a few more stops until they came to Clear Fork on the Brazo River. However, because the air and the countryside did not look clear, they continued one more stop to Fort Belnap on the Brazo River where there were a few homes and stores.

Ebenezer was successful in securing a place to live on the ranch of a settler who permitted them to occupy a one-room cabin on his ranch. In addition to occupying the log cabin, Ebenezer was paid one dollar a week to help with the chores and tending of the cattle.

Lucinda expended great effort in creating a home for her and her husband in the primitive log cabin. She had brought a large trunk from Missouri with as many household items as would fit in it and still be able to close the lid of the trunk. She was glad that she brought cast-iron cooking pots, some pottery plates, and a tea kettle for heating water. Ebenezer was able to split logs and smooth them for a table top. The cabin had a fireplace where they did their cooking and heating.

Ebenezer made a good rope bed and they were comfortable with the wool blankets and handmade quilts which Lucinda had packed in the trunk. Lucinda also had packed a wood-framed oval mirror which they hung on the wall together with framed photographs of their relatives who lived in Missouri.

Lucinda had brought a wash basin and ewer in the trunk which had survived the long rough journey. Water had to be carried for the Martins. But they loved each other and their love compensated for the many inconveniences which they were missing.

Ebenezer worked hard and began to acquire a few possessions such as livestock and a wagon with a horse to pull it. Within a couple of years, he became a tenant farmer with land to cultivate for the growing of cotton and other crops. The couple were able to move into a three-room, wood-frame house. They managed to purchase good used furniture and an iron cooking stove. They bought an iron bed with metal springs and a cotton mattress.

The Martins grew and produced almost all the food they had to eat on the farm. They planted a potato patch, which produced enough potatoes to last them for many months. A vegetable garden produced fresh vegetables to enjoy during the spring and summer, and Lucinda preserved the beans and peas for the long cold Texas winters. Ebenezer selected good ears of yellow corn from the corn fields and took them to the grinding mill to make yellow corn meal. Their chickens gave them large fresh eggs each day, and their milk cow produced plenty of fresh milk and butter.

When freezing weather came, Ebenezer butchered a fat hog and their neighbors came for the day to help. Fresh hams were hung in a smokehouse after they had been salted for preservation. The women made fresh pork-and-sage sausages with a hand meat-grinder. The fat flesh of the hog was made into lard for cooking and the next day a kettle of homemade lye soap was made.

The Martins and their neighbors lived off what their land produced. They were content with life and they were grateful to God for his many blessings.

Soon a son was born to Lucinda and Ebenezer, and they named him James Ebenezer Martin. He was a good, healthy baby and he grew quickly. Lucinda was most pleased with her son, and she longed to show him to her parents and relatives in Missouri. Ebenezer promised Lucinda a visit to Missouri when little James became older. By that time he predicted the trains would be coming to Texas on the new railroads which were being built and it would be safe for his wife and son to travel.

The years passed quickly, and the time had come for the visit to Missouri. Little James was now ten years old, and he and his mother made a four months' visit to Missouri. James was immediately impressed with the lovely Victorian homes and their large porches with the light blue ceilings which gave the appearance of a cool blue sky. James vowed to have a better life when he grew older.

James enjoyed meeting his grandparents, uncles and aunts, and his many cousins. They made him feel special by cooking his favorite foods and taking him to special places to see and visit.

James enjoyed the beautiful city of Saint Louis which was on the Mississippi River. He enjoyed the fine stores and shops and the marvelous items that were displayed and sold in these most beautiful shops. His aunts took him to the Saint Louis Opera and to the theater, entertainment which Texas did not have at the time. Young James did not wish to return to Texas, but his mother told him they must return to his father in Texas where some day Texas would have theater, fine stores, and shops.

James and his mother returned to Texas and James swiftly grew into a young man. Texas also quickly became more populated with the new railroads which were built across it. The cities of Texas begin to stage more cultural events each year. As the railroads continued to expand, new merchandise and more products became available. Many private and public colleges began to form, and a university system was planned for the entire state.

An important economic influence on the state were the large and prosperous cattle ranches which developed. No other cattle ranch was as immense as the King Ranch in southern Texas. Many other large cattle ranches were dotted around the state of Texas. Beef was an important product and the cattle were sent by train to Kansas City and Chicago and later on to Fort Worth. Fortunes could be made overnight by a quick sale of cattle.

As a result of these ranches, the American cowboy originated, and other products originated with the cowboy. He could not be a cowboy without the famous leather boots commonly called cowboy boots or western boots. Western boots became popular for most Texas men, and many fine Texas boot companies originated such as Justin and the Nocona Boot Company. The cowboy helped introduce western blue jeans as well as western hats, fine leather saddles, and sometimes silver spurs. All the products contributed to the growth of the Texas economy.

Another important factor which had a great influence on the development of the Texas economy was a petroleum product underneath the vast ranch lands. It was the discovery of oil, the black gold of Texas, and it is still popular today throughout the world. It created thousands of Texas millionaires and unbelievable wealth for the State of Texas.

Unfortunately, not everyone in Texas enjoyed the riches of the state. James Martin's son, Jake, Jake's wife, Dora, and their two children, Millie Jean and J. D. Martin, lived modestly fifty years later on a tenant farm near the town of Hillsboro. The Texas economy had never trickled down to them.

Jake Martin's father, James, had married when he was a young man, and he and his new wife, Martha, decided to become farmers like their parents Ebenezer and Lucinda. Ebenezer helped his son locate a tenant farm in the Texas Hill County. James was a hard worker but it was difficult to get ahead financially as a tenant farmer. He and Martha had six children, five of whom lived to become adults. James and Martha did manage to own a ten-acre parcel of land and a small frame house when the time came for James to retire and draw his old-age pension of thirty dollars a month. The Martins had never had so much money before.

James and Martha were very pleased every Thursday when the grocery peddler came their way and they could purchase foods they had not been able to afford in the past. A loaf of light bread for ten cents was a special treat, and a jar of plum jelly was wonderful. Grandmother Martin often sold her hen eggs each week to the grocery peddler, which helped in the purchase of food.

James and Martha were very devout people. They were life-long members of the local country Baptist Church. They attended church twice on Sundays. They also knelt down on the floor every night and said their prayers. They thanked God for their blessings and they prayed for their children and neighbors each night. The Martins looked forward to the long summer revivals held outside during the warm evenings. They went every night to the revival, and Grandpa Martin would often testify for the Lord and express his most sincere sentiments about this life and the one in the here-after.

At the revival service, a song leader would lead the congregation in singing old hymns such as "In the Sweet By and By", "What A Friend We Have in Jesus", and "When the Roll is Called Up Yonder." The visiting preacher would give a long sermon usually about the life in the next world, and the preacher would urge all who had not been saved to confess their sins and believe in the Lord Jesus Christ. Each night several people would be saved and at the end of the long revival of two weeks, everyone who was saved would be baptized in the nearest river.

The Martins had several grandchildren, and it was a special treat when they were permitted by their parents to spend the night at their grandparents' home. Jake Martin lived closest to his parents and his children, Millie Jean, and J. D., often had the pleasure of spending the night with their grandparents.

Grandmother Martin was a kind and sweet person with a sparkling personality. She was loved by neighbors, friends, and most of all her family including her sons and daughters-in-law.

Grandfather Martin was stern by nature, and he could easily become displeased about small matters. People treated him with respect and were cautious about anything said which might be critical of him. Grandfather Martin did have a sense of humor and the family tried to keep him in a good mood by telling him amusing incidents or funny stories.

Jake Martin, their favorite son, lived near them. He had married a local farm girl when he was a young man and he and his wife, Dora, decided to remain cotton farmers because it was the only occupation they knew. It was also the only choice they had—most young couples had no alternatives. Texas farm life had improved from the days of the early settlers. The farm tractor manufactured by John Deere had become common with farmers, replacing the team of mules. Dora Martin was very sad when her husband got rid of a fine team of mules for a new shiny green John Deere tractor.

There was never much money available after the cotton harvest. Most cotton farmers had to repay the local banks for the numerous loans which they had taken up during the year prior to the cotton harvest. When the cotton crops did not produce well, many farmers had to renew old loans. It was difficult to stay out of debt, and many cotton farmers lived their entire lives indebted to the local bank.

But the Martins loved living on the land. A person would have had to live on their land to understand their devotion to it, and the joy in the planting of a new crop each spring. Their hopes and dreams were in these crops for a good harvest in the fall. A good harvest would make it possible to pay all their everyday debts, and allow them to live more comfortably.

Jake and Dora thanked God every day for their blessings. They thanked God for their two good children, Millie Jean Martin and J. D. Martin. The Martins believed in their family, their neighbors, and their community. They would gladly help a neighbor who was in need of something or who was ill and could not work.

The Martins had a genuine commitment to their way of life on the farm. They worked hard every day of the week except for Sunday. They grew and raised food. They made many items for their daily life. It was a practical, creative way of living. Dora knew how to sew and make clothing for the family. Jake raised livestock for food.

Early Texas farm families customarily had several children to help with the many chores that farm life required. The farm children had their daily task of feeding and caring for animals. The hen eggs had to be collected daily. Firewood had to be taken into the house each evening for heating and for cooking food. The kerosene lamps had to be filled with oil in the late afternoons.

It was a busy life for such families in the first half of the twentieth century. The days began early, usually at 5:00 and ended at dusk each day. The family spent the evening around the wood-burning stove, made of cast iron. Jake listened to his favorite radio programs. He especially enjoyed "Lum and Abner", "Fibber McGee and Molly", and "Mr. District Attorney." Dora often mended clothing and socks by the light of their best kerosene lamp. She often hoped for an Aladdin Oil Lamp with an inside white mantle which gave a very bright light for reading and sewing. The Little family who lived across the fields had an Aladdin Lamp, and it could be seen by all the neighbors for two or three miles at night. J. D. and Millie Jean did their school assignments in the evening.

The evening was the favorite time of the day for the Martin family. The responsibilities of the long day had been completed, and everyone could have freedom from duties for two hours before it was time to go to bed. Each person was free to do as they wished. Sometimes Jake Martin would play checkers or have a domino game with J. D. But J. D. did not like to play too often because his father always won.

II

Jake and Dora Martin

Millie Jean Martin could not go to sleep on this particular Sunday night, and her mother, Dora, had already asked her twice to turn the kerosene lamps out. Millie Jean was not sleepy because she was thinking about tomorrow when she would begin her senior year at Hillsboro High School. There were so many things she desired—some new dresses for school and a pair of new shoes. She was unhappy about having to wear the same coat she wore during her junior year at Hillsboro High. Many of her classmates would have new wardrobes for school.

The lack of money was a constant problem for the Martin family. The cotton crops of Texas were not the best for the fall harvest of 1938. Boll weevils and other insects had attacked the cotton fields because of the dry, hot humid summer. The pecan trees did not produce a good crop this year. Jake usually permitted his son and daughter to pick the pecans and sell them at various stores in Hillsboro for spending money. Millie Jean planned to buy her school clothes with her part of the pecan money.

The family had gone shopping on Saturday in the small town of Hillsboro. It gave them a pleasant outing and a relief from the farm labor of the past five days. They drove the eight miles into town in the old Chevrolet pick-up truck with the cotton which the family had picked that week.

Millie Jean and her brother, J. D., could hardly wait until they could go to Bob's Cafe on one of the side streets just off the town square for a large juicy hamburger and a bottle of Coca-Cola. Bob's Cafe was in a long narrow building with a long row of booths and tables and another long counter with red stools. J. D. wanted to sit at the counter but Millie Jean preferred a booth. The waitress served them the most marvelous hamburger that Millie and J. D. had ever eaten. The hamburger bun was the largest one they had ever seen. The hamburger buns were spread with French's Prepared Mustard and Kraft mayonnaise. The beef patty was wonderfully cooked with a large slice of a white onion, a large slice of a very ripe red tomato, and a generous supply of fresh green lettuce. Millie and J. D. thought the hamburgers were worth the cost of twenty-five cents each.

Jake and Dora did not go hungry for lunch. In fact, they enjoyed their plate lunch at Bob's Cafe. It contained chicken-fried steak covered with cream gravy, mashed potatoes, green beans cooked in bacon pieces, fried okra in corn meal, and a side dish of butter beans. It also included a large glass of iced tea, and a small dish of peach cobbler for dessert.

Millie Jean and J. D. loved Hillsboro. What could be more wonderful? The small town was built around a central square with a beautiful County Court House in the center. The Court House of Hill County Texas was the most impressive building in Hillsboro. It was the pride of the entire region, built in 1889 at a cost of $83,000.00 dollars. The magnificent building had four floors with a tall clock tower in the center which could be seen for several miles. The building was constructed with Texas limestone and ornamented with classical columns.

There were other interesting buildings and stores in Hillsboro. Of course, the drygood stores had wonderful clothing and was supplied with articles for the home. The five-and-ten-cent stores such as Woolworth's and Dukes-Ayre's were stocked with many fascinating items. But the Martin family purchased basic supplies—a large sack of Pur-A-Snow flour, a gallon of sorghum molasses, a gallon of Maxwell House coffee and a large sack of white sugar. Dora was happy with the cloth bag of flour because she could use the cloth material to make a new apron, or if she had two matching bags she could make a blouse for Millie. Jake Martin bought several yards of ticking to make new cotton sacks for the cotton-picking harvest.

A final item the Martins purchased before the end of the day was a large block of ice from the ice plant. They had brought an old quilt from home to wrap around it. They would use the ice for iced tea and cool aid drinks. Ordinarily they would use the ice to make homemade ice cream in their hand-turned ice-cream freezer, but this day they would go to the ice-cream parlor in the town square. It was called the Double Dip, and had white tile floors inside, small marble topped tables, wire chairs, and an ornate gray metal ceiling. The family ordered vanilla ice cream except J. D. who wanted chocolate. They saw several of their farm neighbors including the Littles and the Rudmans. Alice Little and Millie were in the same class as well as Jack Rudman.

Alice Little had several packages with her, and she was anxious to show Millie her new school coat that she had purchased at J. C. Penney's store. Alice opened the package holding the new coat. Millie tried not to be envious because the coat was the most beautiful red coat which she had ever seen. The coat even had a dark fur collar with large black buttons down the center. Alice was waiting to see Millie's new coat, but Millie explained that she had not made a decisions on one since Pullen's Clothing Store had two coats which she really wanted. Alice's new coat was upsetting to Millie, but she knew the Littles owned a large farm in the country and they could afford to buy Alice a new coat.

Jack Rudman was skinny and tall. He wanted to buy Millie a strawberry ice-cream cone, but Millie declined and Jack looked disappointed. Millie knew that Jack was fond of her. Jack was a very nice young man, and Millie's parents approved of him as a suitor for Millie. Millie preferred tall men, but Jack was too tall and thin. Millie thought his arms and legs were too thin. Everyone who knew Jack Rudman thought he was a nice boy. Millie felt sorry for Jack because most of her girl friends did not want to date him. Maybe Jack was too nice thought Millie.

When it was time to leave, Millie told Alice and Jack she would look forward to seeing them on Monday at Hillsboro High, the beginning of the new school term.

Millie's parents said good-bye to their neighbors and friends when they left. Dora invited every one to Sunday school and church for the next day. J. D. said, "Ice cream sure does make you feel good."

When they left the Double Dip Ice-Cream Parlor, the first person they recognized was Miss Margaret Rudolph. She taught the third- and fourth-grade classes at Boyd Elementary School in the country near the Martin's farm. Millie had been in her third- and fourth-grade classes several years ago. Miss Rudolph was from a local Czechoslovakian family which had emigrated to Texas many years ago. Miss Rudolph lived with her mother and father on their farm. She had never married. She greeted the family and embraced J. D. and Millie. She told J. D. that she was pleased that he would be in her class for the coming year. J. D. did not comment. Miss Rudolph wished Millie a wonderful year at Hillsboro High School.

The Rudolphs, who owned their own farm, lived near the Martins. They were considered prosperous by the people of the community. The Rudolphs were friendly when you met them but never very sociable. They mostly visited with two other Czechoslovakian family groups. Miss Rudolph was respected as a good teacher in the country school. The Rudolphs were most helpful if you needed them.

After saying good-bye to Miss Rudolph, Dora Martin saw the photography shop, Ruby's Studio. She asked her husband, Jake, if they had enough money to have a family picture made. This was Millie Jean's last year in school. Jake agreed that some of the cotton money could be spent for the photograph.

The studio provided a jacket and tie for Jake. J. D. was asked to remove his cap and put his arm on his mother, Dora. He was not pleased and it took much persuading from the photographer. Finally, he cooperated and the family photograph was taken at a cost of three dollars. The parents agreed it was worth the money.

On their way home, the family decided to make a visit to the grandparents of J. D. and Millie. The children were fond of their grandparents especially grandmother Martin. She was always kind and sweet to the children. Grandfather Martin was not so easygoing, but he would have a candy sack hidden some where, which he would pretend he could not find. When he located the candy, the children hoped he would be in a good mood because he was generous when in a good mood. J. D. tried to be on his best behavior which had a definite influence on his grandfather's generosity.

After a full day of visiting stores and seeing friends, neighbors, and grandparents, it was time to return to the Martin farm. The evening chores would have to be done. All the livestock would be waiting for their hay or corn. Every member of the family had their various duties. J. D. had to pump water in the wooden trough for the horses and mules while Jake fed the other animals. Some one had to prepare the firewood for the house in order to cook sup-·per and breakfast.

Another animal was waiting patiently for his one and only meal of the day, their pet farm dog, Old Sport. He was a fine pet and a good guard dog. Old Sport loved the family and watched after their livestock. His favorite place to stay was on the front porch but on cold nights he slept under the house. He greeted the family joyfully.

Supper was simple and plain that Saturday night—a pan of fried potatoes and a bowl of black-eyed peas together with fresh radishes and new green onions. The family lived on the fresh vegetables that Dora grew in her summer vegetable garden. She grew green beans, English peas, cucumbers, okra, yellow squash, and several other vegetables. She sometimes cooked new potatoes and green peas together with a cream sauce. The family was not very hungry after their big lunch, but J. D. was more excited about the loaf of light bread that his dad had purchased in Hillsboro. J. D. really hoped that it was the fifteen-cent loaf instead of the ten-cent loaf so that he could have several slices.

The Martin family had had a wonderful day. Millie Jean had enjoyed it, but she wished that she and the family lived in a nice white house or even a red brick home in Hillsboro instead of a three-room, tenant farmhouse with a lean-to enclosed for a kitchen. But her mother, Dora, always kept their farm house clean and neat. She took special pride in her furniture, and she was lucky to have married Jake because he had enough money to buy their household furnishings when they were first married. Many newly married couples during the twenties only had an iron bed, table, and wooden stove for cooking. Dora was proud of her oak library table which had an embroidered scarf in the center. She was pleased with the tall-back, upholstered rocking chair that J. D. and Millie loved to sit in and rock when their father was not in the house. The chiffonnier was also nice with a mirror, drawers, and wardrobe area for clothing. Her windows always had lace curtains with window shades. The floors were covered with new linoleum.

Jake and Dora were married in June 1920. With the money he had saved prior to the marriage, he went to Cheap-Jim's Used Furniture Store in Hillsboro to buy their furniture. Jake was twenty-nine when he got married. He had worked as a hired hand for several years, and being enterprising, he would cut men's hair for twenty-five cents. He also had a small blacksmith's shop, and on rainy days when he could not work in the fields, he did welding and sharpening of plows for other farmers to earn extra money.

Jake was a good tenant farmer, but he had always dreamed of owning his own farm. He worked diligently, yet he had never been able to save enough money to purchase his own land. Sometimes he had enough money saved for a down payment, but a cotton crop failure or an illness of his wife would take all the money saved. But Jakes' cotton crops were among the best of the many farms that Judge Campbell, his landlord, owned. In fact, Judge Campbell often complimented Jake when he made his monthly inspection to the eighty-acre farm.

Dora, Millie's mother, was a deeply devout individual. Even though life was never easy and at times difficult, she had a strong faith in the Lord. Dora was also a hard worker. She did the housework in the mornings and prepared a large hot meal at noon time. In the afternoons, she went to the fields and helped with the cotton picking.

Sundays were rest days and Millie Jean and her mother usually went to the country Baptist church. Sunday school and the long sermon by the minister was important for Dora. Millie was glad when the sermon came to an end. She tried to concentrate on the minister's words but it was not easy. For diversion, she looked around the church at various neighbors to see who had a new dress or a new hat. The people who attended church in the country were inclined to wear their best clothing. The men and the boys looked neat in their long-sleeved dress shirts with their khaki slacks and their new Sunday slippers.

Sometimes the minister and his wife came home with Millie and her mother for Sunday dinner, which would be a country feast because the preacher and his wife were the guests. There was always southern fried chicken with country gravy, steaming mashed potatoes with lots of cream and butter, fresh green beans which had been cooked for hours, okra fried in corn meal, fresh field corn cut from the cob and cooked in butter and cream, and freshly made hot biscuits and hot yellow cornbread. There would be several pies, either apple, berry, chocolate, or coconut-cream. There might be a large delicious cake with white frosting. The minister was always asked to say the blessing or offer "thanks". He reverently thanked God for the Martin family, Jake, Dora, J. D., and Millie. He asked special blessings for them. He asked God to let them always remember their Creator and be grateful for their many blessings. The minister and his wife enjoyed the big Sunday dinner. After much talking, they left for their home.

Dora told her husband Jake how much she had enjoyed the company of the Minister and his wife, Helen. Jake replied, "They were good company, and the preacher had a good appetite." Dora gave her husband a perplexed look.

The remainder of the Sunday afternoon was spent resting or just being quiet individually. Dora usually read her Bible for a few hours. It was the time of the week for meditation and private thought. Millie thought much about the life of her parents especially her father. She hoped he might be fortunate enough someday to own his own farm. She also felt sorry for her younger brother who had to work in the cotton fields constantly.

Millie Jean remembered the Great Depression of 1929 when her father had enough money saved to purchase a farm. The Depression caused a big struggle for her parents to survive, and her father had to spend the farm money to purchase food and the necessities or life. Her father had to work on the Works Progress Administration to earn money for his family. She was proud of her father, but she wished that life could be easier for him. She often prayed at night before going to sleep that life might be easier for him and that he and her mother would not have to always labor so hard in the cotton fields.

The Depression had also a terrible impact on many of her uncles and aunts, some of whom lost their homes and everything they owned. Her uncles could not find work, and their families were often hungry. All of her relatives had been affected by the Depression years.

Her relatives were poor people, but Millie remembered many good times with her various cousins. When Millie and J. D. were younger, their parents permitted them to visit some cousins and spend the night in their home. Her aunts and uncles would make them feel very welcome. They often made chocolate fudge candy at nighttime, or they might pop popcorn and make popcorn balls. Emily remembers one night they made fried doughnuts and J. D. became ill in the night because he had eaten so many.

Millie remembered once when she was visiting Uncle Jimmy

and Aunt Alice. Uncle Jimmy was often ill, and he believed that every one should take much medicine to keep well. She remembered on this occasion her cousins had a sudden attack of sneezing and coughing. They were ordered to bed immediately and Uncle Jimmy found the Vick's salve. He rubbed it on her cousin's face and chest. When Millie went to bed later, she had a sudden attack of sneezing. Uncle Jimmy came with the Vick's salve, but Millie covered her head and pretended she had gone to sleep.

Millie had already decided that she would leave the farm when she graduated from high school next June. She would like to go to college and become a school teacher at Hillsboro High School. But there was no money available for her, not even enough to enroll in Hillsboro Junior College. She would probably go to Dallas, the largest city near Hillsboro and seek employment. She was good in the typing class even though it was not her favorite class, but she might find a job as a clerk typist, and she could take secretarial classes in the evening. Many of the graduates next spring would go to Dallas to find jobs.

Millie finally did as her mother had requested and blew out the two kerosene lamps and crawled into her small bed in the front room of the house. Millie's parents slept in the only bedroom, and her brother J. D. slept in the dining room with the oak table and chairs her father had purchased when he was first married to Dora.

Dora loved the round oak table with a sturdy pedestal and six matching chairs. The chairs had dark vinyl seats which resembled real leather. The family had their three meals every day at the table. A hearty breakfast was served at 5:30 A.M. They woke up to hot biscuits and gravy with farm bacon or fresh pork sausage, fried eggs, and homemade jelly or sorghum molasses. Her mother Dora had a good appetite and she was inclined to add a few pounds each year. J. D. also loved his food. But her father, who was tall and thin, ate very sparingly. Millie took after her father. Food was not so important to her and she was glad to be thin and tall.

Millie finally felt sleepy. The patter of the rain on the tin roof of the small house helped her to sleep. She only hoped the occasional thunder and lightning would not create hailstones since the sound would be loud and frightening. She also thought about the black soil of Texas and how sticky it could be when it rained. Hopefully, the rain would stop by tomorrow morning for the opening of school. Just before falling asleep, Millie made herself comfortable by pulling a couple of handmade quilts over her. Her last thoughts before falling asleep made her feel more at ease. She was very pleased that Miss Emily would be her English teacher again this school year.

Millie fell into a deep sleep, and slept soundly all night. She could not believe it was morning when her mother was gently shaking her to awaken her. She must rise and get dressed for the first day of school and the beginning of her senior year at Hillsboro High School. Millie was glad that she had a new dress for the first day of school. It was bright blue with a large white collar. She had new black shoes and a pair of new light blue socks.

Millie was not hungry but her mother insisted she must have a good breakfast before the school bus arrived to take her to Hillsboro for the opening of school. The school bus arrived at 7:00 and Millie said good-bye to her mother before boarding the school bus.

III

Miss Emily Rose Blackburn

The school bus delivered Millie to the campus where she was pleased to see so many of her friends at Hillsboro High School. Alice Little, Jack Rudman, Betty Rowe, John Clarke, and sometimes a friend, Sarah Bankstead, greeted her cordially. Sarah Bankstead would greet you cordially when she was in the right mood. Her father was the President of People's National Bank, and she lived in a large red brick house on Corsicana Street with her parents. Sarah had a heavy crush on Clayton Robert Campbell, the handsome son of Judge Robert Campbell.

Millie Jean was a smart student, and she had been in the Honor Society with her classmates. She hoped that her grades would be high enough, mostly A's, to remain in the Honor Society for her senior year. All of her classes would be easy for her except for mathematics. She must take Algebra II or Geometry I in order to graduate next May. She decided to enroll in Mr. Talley's geometry class because she had heard he was very patient with his students.

Hillsboro High School was a three-story dark-red, brick building with a basement for gym classes and various other school departments. Millie loved it and was a little sad because this was her final year. She would endeavor to make it her best year of high school.

Millie would wait impatiently until her fifth-period class when she would enroll in Miss Emily Rose Blackburn's senior English class. Fifth-period English class began just after the school lunch ended. She went early to room 310 on the third floor which was Miss Emily's class room, and she felt privileged to be there since it was the Honor's English class. Emily Rose Blackburn was the head of the English Department. Every one called her Miss Emily instead of Miss Blackburn. Except for one year of graduate study, Miss Emily had spent her entire teaching career at Hillsboro High School.

Miss Emily would be the sponsor of the Honor Society for the school year of 1938. There would be a special field trip to Dallas for the honor students. There might be a trip to Austin, the capital of Texas, or to San Antonio to tour the Alamo. Miss Emily would also invite the honor students to her home for a dessert of cake and ice cream.

When the bell rang for fifth period to begin, Miss Emily entered the classroom. She was the most attractive and fascinating person that Millie had ever known. She always stood very erect with perfect posture. She was the best groomed of all members of the faculty at Hillsboro High School, with dresses which were usually floral and flowing, and her shoes and handbags always matched. Even on the warmest or coldest days, her hair was perfectly combed and totally in place. Her makeup was perfect and her cologne was never overpowering.

Miss Emily loved jewelry and she always wore beautiful jewelry to school for the students to admire. She often wore a string of genuine white pearls around her neck. Her watches were beautiful time pieces, and Millie loved an art deco white gold watch. Miss Emily's gold-and-diamond rings were exquisite. Some times she wore a Lalique brooch which the girls all admired. Her mother had purchased it many years ago on a visit to France.

Poetry was passion with Miss Emily. She read and recited Emily Dickinson, Sara Teasdale, Robert Frost, Carl Sandburg, and many others. Even the boys in the class were impressed when Miss Emily recited or read poetry to the class. All students had to memorize "The Pasture" by Robert Frost, but this year the emphasis would be on the English authors. Millie was looking forward to the study of English authors and she was so pleased that Miss Emily was the teacher.

Miss Emily greeted the students of her fifth-period English class warmly. She emphasized that all her students were special and important to her. She greeted personally Sarah Bankstead and Clayton Campbell. Everyone knew that Sarah Bankstead considered Clayton as her special boyfriend. Clayton was an excellent student in all of his classes. He was also a fine basketball player, and had been voted the most valuable basketball player during his junior year which helped Hillsboro High win the state championship.

There was something nice about Clayton Campbell. Once when Millie had dropped her notebook in the hall, Clayton picked it up and gave her a big smile. He was naturally polite to every one. Judge Campbell owned the farm that Millie's father was currently farming as a tenant farmer. Millie admired Clayton because he never mentioned that his father was the landlord of Millie's family. He often accompanied his father to the farm on inspection visits. Clayton remained quiet while his father and Jake Martin discussed farm matters that must be solved.

Millie was not jealous of Sarah Bankstead but she hoped that Sarah appreciated her special relationship with Clayton Campbell. All the girls thought Clayton was very handsome. He was almost six feet tall with wide shoulders, narrow hips, and a thin waist. He had lots of blond hair and beautiful blue eyes. His ever-present smile was wonderful. His sense of humor and pleasant personality made him even more wonderful to the girls of the class.

Miss Emily asked students to share their summer experiences with her and the class. Since there were no volunteers, Miss Emily discussed her exciting summer. She usually visited some important or interesting American city during the summer vacation but this summer had been even more special. She had taken a European tour. The class had never known anyone before who had been to Europe for a vacation. Miss Emily had taken the train from Dallas to New York City where she sailed on the luxury-liner *Queen Mary* to England. There was nothing comparable to this ship with its beautiful ball rooms and staterooms with burl walnut panels. After five days of sailing, Miss Emily arrived in England.

London was her favorite city. She stayed at the Ritz Hotel on Picadilly near Green Park with the elegant shops of the Mayfair section of London nearby. Miss Emily loved English bone china, and she purchased a set of Minton China from Thomas Goode's China Shop in Mayfair. She also loved the museums of London. The British Museum and the Victoria and Albert were her favorites. She also enjoyed afternoon tea at the Ritz Hotel, and the London theater was wonderful in the evening.

After London, it was Paris—such a beautiful city. It was worth the trip to see Leonardo da Vinci's *Mona Lisa* and the paintings of the French Impressionists. She loved the sidewalk cafes and the beautiful streets, always having had an affinity with French things. At home she often went to New Orleans because of its French influence.

Miss Emily acquired a small French poodle in France, and she invited the class to come to her home on the weekend and help her select an appropriate French name for it. Miss Emily neglected to tell the class how much she enjoyed French champagne.

After Paris she visited Italy and Switzerland. Both were interesting and beautiful. She enjoyed Venice with its romantic canals, churches, and bridges. She was greatly fascinated with the handsome gondoliers, and she asked the boys of the class to close their ears while she told the girls how really handsome the gondoliers were. After Venice her tour took her to Florence. Miss Emily loved the art and sculpture of Florence, in particular the marble statue of *David* by Michelangelo.

Finally, she visited Rome, the eternal city, and was overwhelmed with St. Peter's and the Sistine Chapel. The school bell rang for the end of the class and the students were disappointed because their vivid imaginations were in Rome instead of Hillsboro.

The week passed quickly and on Saturday afternoon several students went to Miss Emily's home on Craig Street to help her select a name for the new poodle. It vas a cute and adorable little black poodle who wanted to sit in the laps of the students. She was so tiny that you could hold her in the palm of your hand. No one could think of an appropriate name but it did not bother Miss Emily because she enjoyed the company of her special pupils.

Millie Jean was enthralled with Miss Emily's lovely home. She had never seen such a splendid one. The house was located on Craig Street among many large and beautiful homes. Many large green trees enhanced Craig Street. Miss Emily's home was a pale yellow brick of two stories designed in the Federal style. It was built about 1910 by her parents who were Dr. Benjamin Blackburn and his wife. Miss Emily, an only child, had inherited the house from her parents.

Dr. and Mrs. Blackburn had come to Hillsboro in 1890 before Emily was born. Her father had just graduated from the medical school at Tulane University in 1890 and had heard of the need for a new doctor for Hillsboro. Dr. Blackburn was a good and successful doctor for the small central-Texas town. Miss Emily had inherited considerable property from her father who had invested widely in local real estate, and it enabled her to afford the finer things of life because she was not dependent on her small teachers' salary.

The inside of the house had two floors. On the first floor, guests entered a nice hall with stairs on the left. On the right was a wood door with glass panes which led into a lovely drawing room. The entry hall was painted a Wedgwood blue with white trim. The house had lovely hardwood floors and oriental carpets. The entry hall had a long oriental runner on the floor. Millie Jean was in awe. She had never seen real oriental carpets before.

On entering the drawing room with its pink marble fireplace and large oriental carpet, Millie Jean was even more amazed. The walls were dark green with a white ceiling and white trim on the woodwork. The windows had green velvet drapes which hung splendidly. The oil paintings were beautiful landscapes in ornate gold frames. There were several paintings of animals as Miss Emily was an animal lover. She had fine ceramics and bronzes of dogs.

The furniture was exquisite in this room. The colors of the woods and their grains were more beautiful than dark oak and mahogany. A small round table had a silver tea service on it. From the drawing room you could look into the dining room. It had a superb round rosewood dining table with six matching chairs. A large silver candelabra with white candles was the centerpiece on the table. There were silver forks and white napkins to be used with the Minton dessert plates which Miss Emily had purchased in England. On a grand sideboard there was a large crystal punch bowl with many crystal cups together with a delicious and huge chocolate cake. The punch in the large bowl was made of orange sherbet, club soda, and fruit juice.

Beatrice, Miss Emily's maid, appeared and began to serve cake and punch. Beatrice had been with the Blackburn family for a long time. She wore a black dress with the neatest white apron. Millie Jean observed how perfectly Beatrice could slice a serving of cake.

When it was time to leave, Miss Emily asked Millie Jean to remain for a short time. After the other students had gone, she asked Millie if she might have permission to name the tiny poodle, Jeannette, after Millie Jean's second name. Millie Jean was honored.

Millie Jean, Alice Little, Sarah Bankstead, and Clayton Campbell were invited almost every Saturday afternoon to Craig Street. The elegance of Miss Emily's home had an important influence on Millie Jean who hoped that some day she would have a beautiful home in a nice setting with elegant furnishings. Each Saturday evening over supper Millie described in detail the artifacts and furnishings to her mother. Dora admired beautiful homes even though she could not afford one.

Millie learned many things in Miss Emily's English class for senior students. She enjoyed the plays of William Shakespeare especially *Hamlet* and *Romeo and Juliet*. She was introduced to the Romantic poets of England. Her favorite poets were Wordsworth, Keats, and Shelley. There was something amazing about Millie, a Texas farm girl, who enjoyed the great poets of the world. She was learning to think independently, critically, and analytically in Miss Emily's English class. Miss Emily was amazed at the great progress her students had made, but she privately knew that Millie Jean was her outstanding student of 1938 and 1939.

Miss Emily had arranged a field trip to Dallas, the nearest large city from Hillsboro. She took the students to the Fine Arts Museum in Fair Park to view oil paintings by famous artists of the world. Clayton Campbell and Millie Jean appreciated the paintings more than other students did. Miss Emily intended that her students should be introduced to the fine arts.

Most of the students were more anxious for noon time so they could visit the Neiman-Marcus department store in Dallas and have their special lunch in the Zodiac Room on the top floor of the store. The lunch was even more wonderful than they anticipated. Everyone had the famous chicken salad, iced tea to drink, and delicious rolls and breads. After lunch the students toured the famous store. Millie Jean was amazed at the way the merchandise was displayed. She really admired the ladies' gloves and handkerchiefs displayed in a bronze-and-glass cabinet. She had never seen such exquisite handkerchiefs. Could she afford to spend two dollars for a linen handkerchief for her mother? Millie counted her money and then purchased the handkerchief.

The tour of the store continued. Millie was most impressed with the stairs and elevators and the pink Italian marble which contributed to the elegance of this very famous and special store. Neiman-Marcus was the most famous store in Texas and its reputation for quality was known through the United States. Millie was even more impressed when in the ladies' department Miss Emily asked if Mr. Marcus was available. Within a few minutes, Mr. Marcus warmly greeted Miss Emily and asked her if the last dress that he had sent to her in Hillsboro was satisfactory. The girl students were amazed to learn that Miss Emily was an important customer of the famous Neiman-Marcus store in Dallas.

Before the day ended and it was time to return to Hillsboro, the class was scheduled to visit the Dallas Zoo. The zoo was in a fine setting with many large green trees and grass areas for the animals. There were several animals which the students had never seen before. Millie Jean loved animals as did Miss Emily, who thought all animals are special, cute, and adorable.

The school year of 1938 continued until Christmas. The students in Miss Emily's class exchanged names for a small Christmas gift. Several of the girl students had a party planned on the day before Christmas vacation began. Gifts were exchanged. Millie had drawn Clayton Campbell's name. She had a difficult time deciding on a gift for Clayton who had almost everything. Millie decided on a necktie with a lot of red for the holidays. Miss Emily was inundated with presents. She was going to New Orleans for the holidays to visit relatives and she often mentioned her special nephew, Louis Blackburn.

Millie Jean would have a quiet Christmas vacation with her parents and her brother, J. D. It was customary for the country people to buy a crate of apples and oranges for the holidays. They also had a large bag of English walnuts. A bag of bright-colored candy was in evidence. Before going to bed in the evening, every one could have a treat from the Christmas food. Sometimes a fresh coconut would be served.

The Christmas tree was simple and plain, and it was always green. The family had gone into the woods on Christmas Eve morning and selected a nice green cedar tree. They strung popcorn and red berries for the decoration of the tree, along with a few bright Christmas cards which the Martins had received from relatives and friends. The bright little tree was a pleasure for the Martin family.

Gifts were exchanged on Christmas Eve. There was an old custom of saying "Christmas Eve Gift" to the first person you saw on Christmas Eve. That person must give you a gift. It could be as simple as an apple or an orange. The Martin family exchanged gifts on Christmas Eve. Millie Jean received a new Parker fountain pen for her school work. J. D. received a nice pocket knife.

The Christmas dinner was a marvelous feast. Several relatives such as uncles and aunts and cousins would come for Christmas Day dinner which was served at noon. There would be a fresh ham and roast turkey or chicken with home made corn bread dressing and real cranberry sauce. Many vegetables would be served and a very large fresh fruit salad was necessary. Homemade fruit cakes and mince pies were the main desserts. Everyone was in a happy mood and they were thankful to God for his many blessings.

Millie Jean had enjoyed the Christmas holidays with her family realizing that it would be her last one while still living with the family. J. D. was only twelve years old so he would be with the family several more years.

Millie Jean was glad to return to high school in January of 1939. She studied hard in all of her classes but Miss Emily's English class was still her favorite. Miss Emily required her students to write a term theme on a famous author. She finally selected Robert Browning and Elizabeth Barrett Browning for her term paper. Millie went to the school library in the basement. The library was only opened before and after school hours. She looked at every book and publication which had biographical information on the Brownings. Miss Emily suggested that she write to a Professor Armstrong at Baylor University in Waco who was a Browning scholar. He gladly sent her much information on Robert and Elizabeth Barrett Browning. After much reading and research, Millie wrote her theme on the lives of the Brownings and their poetry. She read and studied many of their writings and sonnets. She emphasized the great romance between the Brownings and the influence it had on their poetry especially the sonnet, "How do I love Thee? Let me count the ways."

This was a romantic time in the lives of Miss Emily's students. It was their last year of school for many of them. They enjoyed the theme of love and romance. Alice Little gave an excellent report on Shakespeare's *Romeo and Juliet*, love and romance being a universal theme for the young.

Clayton Campbell certainly gave the most dramatic report. He selected the Scottish poet, Robert Burns, who died at the age of thirty-seven. Clayton emphasized the hard life which Burns had although he was a genius in his writings. His popularity was unequaled throughout Scotland and the world. Clayton selected January 25 to give his report, that being the birthdate of Burns. He gave an interesting account of the life of Burns, who was a farmer and received very little money for writing his poems. Clayton ended his report by reciting Burn's poem, "A Red, Red Rose."

Clayton began in a strong and fine voice, "Oh, my love is like a red, red rose, That's newly sprung in June. Oh, my love is like the melody, That's sweetly played in tune." After reciting the entire poem to the class, Clayton presented a large and beautiful red rose to Miss Emily and each girl of the class. The female students were astonished with the beauty of the red roses. How was it possible to find red roses in January in this cold central Texas town? Miss Emily knew that Clayton was the son of Judge Campbell, and Judge Campbell had many connections in Texas, such as the nursery in Tyler where roses were grown in abundance. Judge Campbell had represented this particular nursery in a court case most satisfactorily.

Springtime finally came after a long cold winter with much snow and ice. It was springtime in Texas and the trees and grass began turning green and wildflowers began to bloom. The sky was much brighter with large white cumulus clouds and more sunshine. Miss Emily decided the class should have a field trip to San Antonio. On the route through the hill country of Texas, the blue bonnets were in full bloom. A school bus was provided for the students. Miss Emily asked the bus driver to stop frequently for the class to view the wild flowers. The blue bonnets were spectacular with miles and miles of beautiful brilliant blue color. The red color of the Indian paint brush was also glorious.

When the class arrived in San Antonio, they were enchanted with the historic city and its traditions. Mark Twain had written that San Antonio was one of the five most interesting cities in America. They loved the colonial architecture and the San Antonio River in the middle of the city. The highlight of the visit was the tour of the Alamo where so many patriots had died in 1836 fighting for Texas independence, including Davy Crockett and James Bowie. Their defense of the Alamo was heroic to the class as it was told to them.

On the return home, the students visited the German communities of Fredericksburg and New Braunsfel where German settlers had arrived in the 1840's. Their businesses and homes looked prosperous. The students had enjoyed this field trip, on which they learned much about the history of their state of Texas.

After returning home, the class began to prepare for the final exams, the senior prom, and the graduation. Millie's mother made her a lovely dress for the prom. The dress was made from light green organdy material that she purchased at the dry goods store. The senior prom was beautiful, with the school gymnasium decorated from freshly cut green shrubs and bright flowers with large banners of blue and green crepe paper. Millie's date was Jack Rudman who looked smart in a blue sports jacket, white shirt and tie, and gray slacks. Millie wore the green dress her mother had made. Her shoes were white. All the students looked their best.

Miss Emily was a chaperon at the prom. She looked gorgeous in her emerald green gown from the Neiman-Marcus store in Dallas. The fine jewelry she was wearing far surpassed that of other members of the faculty. She wore a large emerald-and-ruby brooch with matching earrings, but the crown jewel was the necklace which matched the brooch and the earrings. The green velvet dress and the fabulous jewels worn by Miss Emily made her striking and beautiful. Students often wondered why Miss Emily had never married.

Millie Jean enjoyed the prom and she was asked to dance by most of the boys in her class. She so enjoyed the dance with Clayton Campbell even though Sarah Bankstead constantly kept a protected look at him. Clayton was ever so handsome in a navy-blue suit and white shirt.

Although the prom ended very late, graduation was the next day, and Millie's parents came to it with Millie hoping her father would not wear his farm overalls. Fortunately, her father came dressed in his best khaki slacks, a nice blue dress shirt, and his best slippers. Jake and Dora Martin thanked Miss Emily for the help and guidance she had extended to Millie Jean over the past two years. They also thanked other members of the faculty. Other parents expressed their gratitude to Miss Emily and the other teachers for their guidance and work with their sons and daughters.

The graduation began and the speaker was Judge Robert Campbell. He encouraged the students to continue learning and always to follow their dreams. Judge Campbell wished the graduating class of 1939 much success for the future. When he had finished speaking, the honor students of the class were announced. Millie Jean Martin and Clayton Robert Campbell were the two top honor students of the senior class. Millie Jean was most pleased with this special honor, yet disappointed that she could not afford to go to college, since Clayton and Sarah Bankstead would be going away to college. Sarah would be going to the Women's College in Denton and Clayton would go to law school at the University of Texas in Austin.

Miss Emily offered to help Millie Jean with her college expenses but Millie Jean preferred working for a while and earning some money to attend college. Miss Emily said she would speak to Judge Campbell since there was an opening for a file clerk in his law firm in Hillsboro.

IV

Millie Jean Martin

After graduation from high school, Millie Jean spent a few days at home with her family on the farm. She had a new status with her parents since she did not have to do farm chores anymore. A high school diploma gave children their independence from their family if they so desired. After a few days, Millie was becoming more anxious to leave the farm and seek employment.

One day a very special letter arrived from the Campbell law firm in Hillsboro, sent by Miss Clarke, Judge Campbell's private secretary. The letter stated that the Campbell law firm had a vacancy for a file clerk, and they were considering Millie for the position. If Millie was interested, she should come into the office for an interview within a week. Jake and Dora Martin were delighted for their daughter. They felt it was a great opportunity to be associated with Judge Campbell.

Millie Jean made an appointment with Miss Clarke. The law office was located on Elm Street in a large red brick building with large brass letters, spelling Campbell, Attorney-at-Law. Millie Jean arrived at the designated time and Miss Clarke asked her to complete an application form. Millie Jean smiled at Miss Clarke but Miss Clarke only gave her an indifferent look and said, "Please complete this form as soon as possible." Millie Jean felt uncomfortable but she quickly complied. After finishing the questionnaire, she returned it to Miss Clarke who only nodded her head. Millie Jean returned to the chair where she had been sitting. After a considerable time, Judge Campbell came out and invited Millie Jean into his office for the interview. Millie Jean was impressed with the beautiful book shelves and artifacts in Judge Campbell's office. The oak book shelves and law books behind glass doors looked expensive to Millie as well as his large desk. The walls of his office were decorated with his law degrees framed in black frames and glass-covered. Many other honors and photographs of the Campbells hung on the walls. Millie also observed the photograph of a beautiful woman on Judge Campbell's desk in a silver picture frame. She noticed that the woman and Clayton had a remarkable resemblance. Judge Campbell said, "The photograph you are admiring is that of my late wife and the mother of my son."

Millie Jean was impressed with Judge Campbell who was a handsome middle-aged man. He was dressed in a business suit and a tie. He kindly remembered her on the farm and asked about her parents. The judge had heard from Miss Emily about Millie's fine scholarship record.

Judge Campbell told Millie it would be necessary for him to ask her questions which are related to the nature of work in a law office. He asked Millie if she could listen to the concerns of clients who may be desperate and even angry without losing her composure. Millie Jean said she would certainly try to be attentive and would endeavor to be neutral when talking to clients. The judge also asked her if she could maintain silence on legal matters regarding his office clients. He also told her it was necessary to remain silent during a court case or until the resolution of a problem. The judge told her one comment or one suggestive look may result in a disastrous outcome for a client. By the time the interview had ended, Millie Jean felt that many secrets were kept within the walls of a law office.

She was asked to begin work on the following Monday so she asked Miss Emily to help her find lodging until she could afford an apartment of her own. It was the summer vacation, and Miss Emily suggested that Millie should stay in her home until September. Miss Emily would be away for the summer on her annual travels. Millie was given the narrow bedroom upstairs at the back of the house which overlooked the backyard where several large green trees grew. Beatrice prepared breakfast and dinner each morning and evening. Millie paid one dollar per day for room and board. Millie had always loved Miss Emily's home, and she considered it a fortunate arrangement for her.

Millie Jean would always remember her first day of work in the Campbell law office. She was introduced to the file cabinets which held hundreds of clients' folders. It would be her responsibility to keep the files in good order and produce them as Judge Campbell required. She was also shown the large office vault where wills and important documents were housed for safekeeping.

Millie was amazed at the many clients who came each day for a conference with Judge Campbell. Some would be in tears when they left the office. Others would be very stoic, but every one in the office was detached from the various clients and their problems, except Judge Campbell who always showed a genuine concern for all his clients. Millie was also amazed at how many of the important people in town who came to Judge Campbell's office seeking advice.

Millie enjoyed her work and took her responsibilities seriously. Miss Clarke never commented on Millie's work, but Millie felt that Miss Clarke was pleased with her. She did not see Judge Campbell often, but he was most cordial and greeted her kindly each time they met.

Later in the summer Clayton Campbell came home from law school for a few weeks' vacation. Judge Campbell required him to work a few days each week in his office. Clayton was most kind and friendly to Millie Jean. He told her all about law school at the University of Texas. The law school required a tremendous amount of work plus much reading of famous law cases and court decisions. Clayton read and checked law briefs for his father.

Sarah Bankstead was home from college for the summer, and she often stopped by the law office to check on Clayton. Sometimes they would go for iced tea at a nearby restaurant. Sarah considered Clayton as her very own special boyfriend. And sometimes, to Millie's disgust, Sarah would say that Clayton was her feller. Sarah often admonished Millie to keep her distance from her dear Clayton.

Sometimes Millie answered the telephone when Miss Clarke was having her lunch, and the telephone call would be from Sarah Bankstead with an unkind message for dear Clayton. It was always something critical about Clayton and she could not see him that evening. Millie was embarrassed to relate the message to Clayton but he never seemed upset or reacted to Sarah's criticisms. Millie was very sorry for Clayton and felt he deserved a kinder girl friend.

One afternoon Clayton asked to see a client's file which he could not locate. Millie and Clayton looked for a long while until they both discovered the missing file. Clayton was so enthused that he quickly hugged Millie. Fortunately, Miss Clarke did not see the embrace. Clayton thanked Millie and returned to his office with the missing file. Sarah Bankstead called and said to tell Clayton that her headache had diminished and he might come by her home on Corsicana Street for the evening and they would sit on the front porch in the big white wicker chairs and sip lemonade. Sarah would be returning to college soon.

Millie was pleased to hear that Sarah would be leaving soon for college. Millie felt guilty since she felt that she had no right to believe Clayton would become anything more than a close friend in her life. Sarah returned to the college she was attending in Denton. Even though Sarah and Millie had been friends in high school, Millie did not miss her.

One day Clayton appeared to be serious and sad. Millie Jean was sorry to see him look so sad. She asked Clayton what would make him happy? Clayton indicated that he wished to see a new movie in town called *Gone With The Wind*. Clayton asked Millie if she would join him. Millie was delighted at the invitation. Clayton and Millie went to see *Gone With The Wind* that evening and Millie thought it was the most wonderful evening of her life. They loved Vivien Leigh and Clark Gable. They had tears in their eyes during the performance and were shocked at the burning of the city of Atlanta. Clayton gently held Millie's hand after this scene. At the end of the movie, when Rhett Butler told Scarlett, "Frankly, my dear, I don't give a damn," Clayton said that he would like to say that to some person he knew. Millie thought she knew who that person might be. That moment was a turning point in Millie's life because she knew that she loved Clayton Campbell very much. Clayton escorted Millie home to her apartment, one which she had rented before Miss Emily's return, but Millie wisely did not invite him in for a visit.

Clayton returned to law school in the fall and Millie missed him very much. She received letters frequently from him and answered every letter promptly. She kept every letter from Clayton and photographs of him were displayed in her apartment.

Millie Jean continued her work effectively at the Campbell law firm. She enjoyed her work and made remarkable progress. Miss Clarke was helpful in her own way to Millie. One day she asked

Millie if they could have a private conversation regarding an office change. Millie agreed. Miss Clarke told her she had decided to retire after many years of service to Judge Campbell and his father. She wished to recommend Millie as Judge Campbell's new private secretary. Millie could hardly believe what she had heard since several other girls had been in the office longer than she had. Millie was most grateful and was very surprised that Miss Clarke would recommend her to Judge Campbell for such a position. She asked Miss Clarke if she really felt that she would be the right person for the job. Miss Clarke told her that she had the capability to become a private secretary and that she would discuss the matter soon with Judge Campbell.

Miss Clarke's retirement came at the end of the month. Millie was sorry to see her leave after a long career in the Campbell firm. Miss Clarke's roll as a private secretary to Judge Campbell was the most important thing in her entire life and it was coming to an end. Miss Clarke was not an easy person to have around but anyone could succeed if they followed her professional standards.

An office party was planned on her behalf on her last day at work. Cake and coffee were served, and everyone gave her books to read since reading was her main hobby. Judge Campbell gave her an autographed copy of *Gone With the Wind* by Margaret Mitchell. Several other lawyers and their secretaries came round to wish her well in her retirement. Judge Campbell gave an eloquent tribute to Miss Clarke, and told interesting incidents of her career. He congratulated her for the many years of service she gave to his late father and to himself. Miss Clarke's eyes were misty but there were no tears. When Judge Campbell finished his speech, he said that he had an important announcement to make. "One fine private secretary is ending her career while another one is beginning hers. I have selected a new secretary for myself, and that person is our office clerk, Millie Jean Martin. You may join me in calling her Miss Martin."

Millie Jean was not too surprised, but it was hard to believe that she was now Judge Campbell's private secretary. She preferred to be called Millie, but she realized that Miss Martin was more acceptable to the dignity and importance of the Campbell law firm.

V

A Legal Secretary

Millie Jean Martin was nervous when she began her first day of work as Judge Campbell's private secretary at the Campbell law firm. Miss Clarke had left her several pages of suggestions and information on certain clients with which Millie must become familiar. Her small office was adjacent to Judge Campbell's private office and law quarters.

She arrived at the law office earlier than 8:00, the time she was required to begin each morning. Miss Clarke had a copy of the Monday agenda for Judge Campbell and the original copy was on the lawyer's desk. Miss Clarke had emphasized that Judge Campbell considered his daily agenda of the utmost importance to him. Millie had been told that she must prepare his daily agenda at 4:30 P.M. each day, and then she must place the original copy on his desk no later than 5:00. Millie studied today's agenda and was overwhelmed with the number of appointments that Judge Campbell had for that particular day.

At 8:00 A.M. he would be counseling a client on a pending law suit; at 9:00 he must go to the court house and preside over a divorce hearing; at 10:00 he would meet with the executor of Mrs. Ferguson's estate; at 11:00 he would counsel the president of a local manufacturing company which was merging with a larger company; and at 12:00, he would attend a luncheon and be the guest speaker for the Lion's Club on Law Day.

Millie glanced at the appointment book and realized that Judge Campbell's daily agenda would be the same almost every day. The appointment book was crowded with appointments. The telephone rang often and she would have to slot in immediate appointments for special clients.

Two beautiful bouquets of flowers arrived for Millie, one from Miss Clarke and one from Miss Emily both congratulating her and wishing her well with her new position. Millie Jean could hardly believe her good fortune. She only hoped that she could meet the standards expected of her.

At 8:00 A.M. Judge Campbell arrived at his law building and greeted everyone cordially. He greeted Millie warmly and again told her how pleased he was to have her as his new secretary. Millie thanked him and she observed how tall and handsome Judge Campbell really was. He was wearing a nice dark gray suit, fine white shirt, and an expensive blue necktie. He had an excellent physique and carried his weight well. He smelled very good, probably of fresh soap and a good aftershave. Millie did not understand why he had never remarried since his wife had died so many years ago. She thought that surely he had had many opportunities from a nice and pretty woman. Millie often thought that Miss Emily would have made a good wife for the judge.

Judge Campbell entered his private office to look over his daily agenda. In a very short time the judge buzzed Miss Martin and said, "Please send in my first client for today." The judge called every few minutes for documents or files, and he always called her, Miss Martin.

The first day was very busy for the law office both morning and afternoon. Millie was glad that she had brought a cheese sandwich and an apple for lunch because she did not have the time for the thirty-minute lunch break to which she was entitled. Miss Martin could not believe when it was 4:30. Miss Martin knew it was time to prepare Tuesday's agenda and have it ready by 5:00 to place on Judge Campbell's desk for the next day. Millie met her deadline but she was still working at 6:00.

Judge Campbell came into her office. He was wearing his expensive Stetson hat, and carrying a fine leather briefcase. She was amazed that he would be taking work home. Judge Campbell said, "You have done well on your first day as my secretary, Miss Martin, but it is now time to close and lock the building and I'll see you at 8:00 tomorrow morning." Before leaving he said good night to Millie.

It was difficult for Millie to sleep that night. She thought about how well Judge Campbell could counsel so many people in a given day. She knew that it must take an enormous reserve of energy and self-control to handle so many clients in one day. He was a hard-working lawyer, and he deserved the large amount of money he earned each day.

Millie continued her work with enthusiasm and devotion to the Campbell law firm. She was amazed at the many law cases Judge Campbell was administering. Millie knew some of the clients personally or she knew members of their family. She was sworn to secrecy and could not discuss a case with friends or family. It was sometimes difficult when she visited her family and they asked her questions on legal matters, but she developed several evasive techniques in her conversation so that she would not divulge information regarding clients.

In the meantime, Judge Campbell often performed marriage ceremonies. Millie Jean was often the only witness and she was required to sign the marriage certificate. On one afternoon before Millie had typed the next day's agenda, Judge Campbell asked Millie to be a witness for the couple who were to be married the following afternoon in the judge's office. Shortly before three o'clock the next day, the nervous young couple arrived for the ceremony which would unite them in marriage. Millie Jean was shocked when she saw the tall skinny groom and the familiar face of a girlfriend. It was Jack Rudman and Alice Little. Millie had grown up with both of them. It was unbelievable since they had grown up as friends, classmates, and neighbors. Jack Rudman had had a crush on Millie when they were growing up, but she had never encouraged him to become her sweetheart. So Jack had selected Alice Little to be his bride. Millie heartily congratulated her long-time friends. She wished that she had known before hand that it was going to be the marriage of Jack and Alice so that she could have had a nice wedding gift for them. Somehow she felt sorry for them. Poor Jack was not handsome in his odd-fitting suit but he was a kind and good person which was more important than good looks. He would be a loyal and dependable husband for Alice. Alice was also pathetic and nervous. She was wearing her best light blue dress and white shoes. She had been brave with her makeup that day. Her cheeks were covered with pink rouge and her lipstick was a bit too red. But she looked proud and smiled happily at Jack while the judge read the marriage vows which Jack and Alice repeated. Jack had a tiny gold wedding ring for Alice. His shaky hands almost prevented him from placing it on her small finger. Millie remembered that she had a fresh bouquet of flowers which she gave to Alice.

When the ceremony was completed and Judge Campbell had pronounced them man and wife, Jack Rudman paid the usual five dollars. The judge and Millie signed the marriage certificate and he wished them many happy years of marriage. Millie gave Alice a big hug and shook hands cordially with Jack. Alice mentioned that they had rented a farm from her father and they would be moving into their own house soon. They both invited Millie to visit them in the country.

Millie was serious for the remainder of the day. She was somewhat sad when she went home to her small apartment that evening. She was happy for Jack and Alice Rudman. She could have married Jack but she did not want to be a farmer's wife. She immediately thought of her mother, Dora, and the hard life she lived as a farm wife.

Millie Jean's best thinking time was always before she went to sleep at night. She wondered what her future life would hold. She was thinking about Clayton Campbell who was totally different from Jack Rudman. Clayton Campbell's inheritance would be considerable some day. Millie continued to think about Jack and Alice who had no inheritance or large possessions to begin their married life. They seemed happy when they left the law office as a newly wedded couple. They had something greater than wealth; they had the love and devotion of each other. They had something that Judge Campbell and Miss Emily did not have even with their wealth.

Millie Jean wondered if she would ever meet anyone she really loved. It would not be a problem for her if she did not meet some one. She had a good and secure position with the Campbell law firm. She had her own apartment and a nice Chevrolet car. She had several friends including Miss Emily. She might be happy just being single without the trouble of a husband and children to rear. She had never wanted to be a farm wife like her mother even though she was most proud of her mother. She admired Miss Emily who had never married. Millie Jean was independent and she enjoyed her independence, which enabled her to afford many things for herself and her family.

VI

The Engagement of Clayton and Millie

Hillsboro looked beautiful during the Christmas season of 1940. The large elegant homes on Craig Street were beautifully decorated for the Christmas holidays. The Christmas lights at night were spectacular. Many visitors and residents would drive along Craig Street to enjoy and admire the holiday illuminations. Judge Campbell's home was unique and slightly different each year with its Christmas theme.

Millie was looking forward to the Christmas season because Clayton would be home from law school for the holidays. She also knew that Sarah Bankstead would visit her parents in their large home on Corsicana Street. Sarah caused Millie to be depressed at times since she knew Sarah had her influence on Clayton Campbell.

Clayton arrived home on schedule. His father encouraged him to work in the law office while he was on vacation. Clayton greeted everyone warmly in the office and was extremely pleasant to Millie. He referred to her as Miss Martin, but Millie would have preferred using first names. Millie realized that Judge Campbell wished Clayton to be called Mr. Campbell. Millie respected the wishes of Judge Campbell, her employer.

On one afternoon Sarah Bankstead came to the office to visit Clayton. Clayton embraced Sarah, and she reciprocated with a slight kiss on Clayton's cheek. She insisted on saying hello to Judge Campbell, and to wish him a `very, very, merry, merry Christmas.' Millie could hardly believe her sincerity. Millie strongly protested and said, "Judge Campbell is very busy with important legal matters and it is not possible for you to see him just now, but you can leave a little note for him."

Sarah ignored Millie and said, "You are a typical secretary who protects her boss too much." Sarah went into Judge Campbell's office unannounced. The judge greeted and welcomed her because he considered her as his future daughter-in-law. To Millie's annoyance, Judge Campbell invited Sarah and the Banksteads to his home for eggnogs and holiday treats. Sarah gave Millie a sly smile when she left the law office. Millie gave her a casual nod of acceptance. After Sarah had gone, Millie felt guilty because she did not really like her. Her mother had always taught Millie to love everyone. Millie thought, I suppose I must love Sarah, but I don't have to like her.

When Millie went to her home in the small apartment where she lived, she burst into tears. She felt it was unfair for Sarah to have such influence over Clayton. She was full of disappointment and frustration, and she decided that only a glass of milk and some cookies her mother had sent her would suffice for her evening meal. She decided to read poetry for the remainder of the evening. The poetry took her mind away from Clayton and Sarah. She began to enjoy the poetry as she read the sonnets of Elizabeth Barrett Browning. After reading for a considerable time, she selected the sonnet, "How do I love thee? Let me count the ways." As she was reading it, the telephone rang and the voice made her weak in the legs and her entire body felt weak. It was Clayton Campbell and he asked her if he could come to her apartment for a visit because he had something important to tell her. Millie protested that it was late, and she must be to work at his father's law office by 8:00 next morning. Clayton was persistent and Millie could not say no to him.

Clayton arrived shortly and he hugged and kissed Millie gently. He told her that he had some important things to tell her and asked her if she would be kind enough to listen to him. Millie consented. Clayton told Millie that he loved her very much. He told her that he wanted to marry her as soon as possible. Millie could not believe what Clayton had said to her. She asked about Sarah Bankstead because she thought Clayton would marry her after he graduated from law school. Clayton said he liked Sarah but he did not love her. He did not want to spend the remainder of his life with Sarah Bankstead.

Millie told Clayton she wished to think about the proposal for a while before giving an answer. Clayton said, "I will give you until the end of my vacation which is a week from now." He took Millie into his arms and kissed her many times. He continued to hold her closer to him and she felt a strong passion for him.

He glanced at Millie's bedroom, and Millie realized what Clayton desired. She enjoyed the feel of his strong body close to her. She cautiously said, "Clayton, you must wait until we are married."

Clayton released her and said, "You are right and I don't have to wait a week for your answer to marrying me."

Clayton stayed for several hours, and they made plans for their future wedding. It would be in the spring either at Hillsboro House or at St. Mary's Episcopal Church. They decided on Hillsboro House with Judge Campbell officiating.

When she arrived at work the next morning, Judge Campbell greeted her and said, "Miss Martin, you are a fine and loyal secretary and I am sure you will be a fine and loyal daughter-in-law. Welcome to the Campbell family." Millie replied that she would be proud to be a member of the Campbell family. The judge grinned, and said, "Make sure we have several little Campbells."

Millie had never been so happy in her life. Her Christmas gift from Clayton was a beautiful diamond engagement ring. The diamond was pear shaped and the band was of white gold. Millie decided to purchase Clayton a gold wedding band at Cheap Gem Jewelers in Hillsboro. Clayton was pleased with his wedding band and he invited Millie to Hillsboro House for Christmas dinner, which she accepted.

On Christmas Eve Millie went to visit her parents and J. D., her brother, who still lived on the farm where Millie had been reared. Millie had almost forgotten how primitive farm life really was but her parents were pleased to see her. They exchanged gifts and laughed and talked about the good times they had. Millie's mother had prepared a good Christmas Eve meal for them. Dora was disappointed that Millie could not stay for Christmas dinner because she was going to serve chicken and dressing and cook a new ham.

Millie then told them about her engagement to Clayton with a marriage planned for springtime. Millie showed them her new engagement ring. Dora cried and said, "I am losing my baby girl."

Her father looked serious.

J. D. said, "What are you going to do with all that money?" J. D. was at that awkward stage of life where he spoke without much thinking about the consequences. Millie Jean politely ignored her young brother.

After several hours of visiting, it was time to return to Hillsboro. The family all wished Millie well and a very, merry Christmas. They all went out to see Millie's new car, an almost new 1939 Chevrolet roadster. She had purchased it from Mr. Grimes who had a garage in Hillsboro. J. D. was most impressed and he had to have a short ride in the car before Millie left for Hillsboro.

Millie arrived at Hillsboro House for Christmas dinner at 3:00 on Christmas Day. She was greeted warmly by Clayton and his father. There were a few other guests including Hazel Clarke who was the former secretary to Judge Campbell, a couple of lawyers and their wives, and Father Anderson, the minister of St. Mary's Episcopal Church. Millie was hoping Miss Emily Blackburn would be there since she was a close neighbor.

After much polite conversation in the lovely drawing room, Bessie, Aunt Ettie's daughter, announced that Christmas dinner would be served shortly in the dining room. Millie had never seen such an elegant dinner table. The white Irish-linen tablecloth and napkins were beautiful. The sterling silver was admired by everyone as well as the Royal Crown Derby dinner service. Clayton proudly told everyone the silver and china belonged to his mother who was from Scotland. They only used it once each year and that was for Christmas dinner.

The menu consisted of roast turkey, corn bread dressing, and fresh cranberry sauce. A large smoked ham from Tyler had been ordered for the dinner. There were candied yams, fruit salad, and numerous relishes.

Judge Campbell asked Father Anderson to say the Christmas blessing. He was most eloquent as he mentioned the many blessings we enjoy today, the day of Jesus' birth. He asked the Heavenly Father for special blessings for Clayton and Millie in their future life together. After the blessing was said, Judge Campbell proposed a toast to his guests. Millie had never tasted claret before but it was pleasant and quite sweet.

All the desserts were marvelous. Bessie had made several pies—pumpkin, mincemeat, pecan, and apple, all from her mother's recipes. Judge Campbell reflected on Ettie and the wonderful service she had given to the Campbell family for so many wonderful years. Aunt Ettie had passed away last summer in her sleep. Clayton had tears in his eyes because Aunt Ettie had helped rear him since he was only a few days old. Bessie was very proud of the Campbell family and thanked them for their many kindnesses to her mother.

Dinner continued and Judge Campbell urged everyone to have extra helpings. Millie had tried a small serving of all the food which was served and she could hardly finish so many servings. The enormous and long dinner finally ended. Everyone was asked to return to the drawing room for a Christmas punch and the most delicious fruitcake in Texas.

The Christmas tree was large and totally covered with the most exquisite ornaments Millie had ever seen. Judge Campbell and Clayton had a gift for all the guests. The men received silk neckties, and the women received silk head scarfs from Neiman-Marcus in Dallas. Millie had never seen such exquisite and expensive scarfs.

As the evening progressed, Clayton suggested that everyone should walk along Craig Street and sing Christmas carols to neighbors and friends. Some guests were not too enthused but no one dared to say no to Clayton. Some guests thought it might be too cold so extra coats and scarfs were provided for the cold and clear night. The homes were beautiful and festive with their decorations, Christmas lights, and green wreaths with large red velvet ribbons on every front door. Many residents came to their door to wish the carolers a very Merry Christmas. They finished their caroling by singing "Silent Night" at Miss Emily's front door. Her large green velvet drapes in the drawing room opened sightly and Miss Emily waved at them. Millie quickly observed that she looked gorgeous in a red velvet dress.

It was one of the most lavish Christmas parties that Millie had ever experienced. Millie knew that her life would change tremendously after she had married Clayton Campbell. The Campbells had high social and financial connections throughout the state of Texas. She hoped she could live up to their standards and meet their expectation. She also believed in the values which her parents had taught her and she hoped that she would never have to modify the principles held by her mother.

VII

Lunch with Mrs. R. V. Metcalfe

After the Christmas vacation, Millie Jean continued her life in a most euphoric state of mind. The reasons were many but the main reason was because Clayton Campbell wished to marry her. She had never had a serious boyfriend and she had never been in love before. It was like walking on clouds and eating ice cream at the ice-cream parlor. She had admired boys before, but there were never any comparable to Clayton Campbell for his kindness, his intelligence, his sensitivity, and his assurance of everything in life.

Millie wrote to him at the University of Texas daily. She shared many private thoughts with him concerning their future life after they were married. Millie was thrilled with every letter from Clayton and she attempted to analyze every word, phrase, and sentence in each one. Clayton wrote weekly because his studies required so much time.

They had set their wedding date for the first Saturday in June. Clayton would finish his second year of law school in May, be home for the summer, and Millie decided to keep her small apartment until Clayton finished his four years of law school.

Millie found it difficult at times to concentrate on her work with Judge Campbell. She knew he could be demanding and she knew she must maintain her efficiency because he expected his employees to have high standards and dedication to their positions. Millie endeavored to do her very best as a secretary for the judge.

Millie met a large number of people who were clients of the law firm and, as she had lived a very conservative life, she was often fascinated with people who were different from her own upbringing. One of the judge's most unusual clients was Mrs. R. V. Metcalfe. Everyone called her Mrs. R. V. Metcalfe including the judge. Mrs. R. V. Metcalfe was certainly different from any other clients Millie had met before. She came into the office frequently to see the judge, who prepared leases for her large real estate holdings in Hillsboro. Mrs. R. V. Metcalfe was fond of Millie Jean and often stayed in the office to talk with Millie after she had finished her business with the judge. She was a large jolly woman, with a good sense of humor, and an independent thinker, a trait which annoyed many residents of Hillsboro. Millie had never known any one like her. Her attitude toward life was very positive and she never spoke badly about her tenants or her neighbors on Craig Street, but she could be very firm with tenants whenever it was necessary.

One day Mrs. Metcalfe came to the law office in a most jovial mood. Millie asked her if she wished a conference with Judge Campbell. "Oh, no," she replied, "I came here to invite you to Sunday lunch at my home on Craig Street." Millie accepted with pleasure, and she asked Mrs. Metcalfe if she should arrive after church service on Sunday. Mrs. Metcalfe said, "No, I only go to church once each year Easter Sunday." She smiled. Millie thanked Mrs. Metcalfe for the invitation.

Millie observed Mrs. Metcalfe's dress. Her dresses were all similar—large and flowing with short sleeves. Her dresses and shoes looked comfortable. Millie commented on her dress, and Mrs. Metcalfe said she made all her dresses from one particular pattern which she liked.

Sunday came, and Millie went to Mrs. Metcalfe's house for lunch. It was a large, white wood-frame house; freshly painted, with a fence around the house and an open back gate. Mrs. Metcalfe came out of the house laughing and greeted Millie cordially. She explained the fence with the gate which was always open, saying, "If an animal comes into the yard, it has a way to leave." Millie noticed several large mounds in the yard which Mrs. Metcalfe had built with her own hands. She said she never threw anything away. Millie did not ask anymore questions about the mounds.

Mrs. Metcalfe invited Millie into the house, and it was certainly different. She had never seen such a large collection of magazines, mostly *Life* and *Look* which were folded in half on low shelves along the walls of each room. She also noticed that every window was also a door to the outside. Millie thought it was amazing but Mrs. Metcalfe thought it was most convenient.

Lunch was certainly unusual. Mrs. Metcalfe had prepared it.

The meat course was little beef sausages cooked in a sauce, fresh corn, green beans, and dark bread. No tea or coffee was served because she only drank fruit juices. Dessert was also unusual. There were plain cookies made with honey instead of sugar. Mrs. Metcalfe did not believe in using white sugar. Dessert also included prunes stuffed with shredded coconut. Millie did her best to give a favorable impression of the luncheon. Mrs. Metcalfe laughed and talked constantly. She often mentioned her late husband. She referred to him only as Mr. R. V. Metcalfe. The telephone rang several times, and Millie noticed that she answered the telephone with a rather loud yes instead of the normal hello.

After lunch had been completed, the two sat on a side porch and enjoyed an hour of conversation and much laughter. Mrs. Metcalfe believed that laughter was good for the soul. Millie thanked her for the lunch and visit before leaving for home.

The next day Millie spoke with Judge Campbell regarding Mrs. Metcalfe. The judge smiled and said, "She is a most unusual woman." Millie knew she would receive no more information from Judge Campbell regarding her but she sensed that the judge had private opinions which he was reluctant to share with her. After all, Mrs. Metcalfe was a client.

Millie had met many interesting people who were the judges clients, but none as unusual as Mrs. R. V. Metcalfe. Although some clients could be disagreeable, Millie developed an approach that was positive in dealing with each one. She tried to determine the personal interests of each client which helped everyone.

As time passed, Millie Jean became a valuable secretary to Judge Campbell. The judge had many important clients and Millie worked at gaining their confidence and trust. She learned how to make them feel appreciated. She could easily give a suggestion to them if they needed a quick solution to a problem. Millie was learning many legal terms and had a good grasp of many legal codes.

It took considerable courage, but Millie asked Judge Campbell if she could borrow a few volumes of law books from his vast personal library. Judge Campbell was pleased that Millie had developed an interest in the law. Millie took at least one law book home each week to read and study.

PART THREE

I

Wedding Plans

Clayton and Millie had decided on a June wedding at Hillsboro House, the family home of the Campbells located on Craig Street in Hillsboro, Texas. The wedding was going to be on a Saturday afternoon with Judge Robert Campbell, Clayton's father, performing the ceremony.

Bessie, the Campbell's maid, was looking forward to the wedding because it was the first one at the big house on Craig Street. Many important events had occurred at Hillsboro House and there had been many sad occasions such as when the parents of Judge Campbell had died. Also, no one would ever forget the very sad time when Fiona Campbell died after giving birth to her son, Clayton.

Bessie had worked all her life for the Campbells, and her old mother, Aunt Ettiebelle, had worked at Hillsboro House from the time the house was built in the 1890's. Bessie knew every important thing that had happened in the house, but she did not share information about the Campbells readily, because she believed that secrets should be kept secret. Bessie said, "A secret ain't no secret when it has been told."

When it was almost time for the wedding, Millie Jean conferred with Bessie on the meal, which would be served in the garden after the ceremony. Bessie and Millie Jean agreed on the menu: honey-cured ham, southern fried chicken, potato salad, ambrosia, and other salads. Millie suggested ordering the wedding cake from the city bakery, a suggestion which offended Bessie who had already planned a large cake in four tiers with white frosting. Millie apologized and said, "Clayton and I will love the cake you wish to bake for our wedding day." Bessie and Millie became close friends as a result of their planning the food for the wedding day.

Millie was happy that Bessie was in charge of the food arrangements because Millie had many other things to do for her forthcoming wedding. She would be glad when Clayton came home for his spring vacation from college so that they could finalize their plans.

At present, Millie had her duties to perform for the law firm. Judge Campbell's schedule was constantly busy with legal cases, advising clients, writing leases, contracts, and numerous other legal matters. Millie had told Judge Campbell that she wished to continue her position as his private secretary after her marriage. The judge was pleased that Millie would remain as his assistant. She had learned quickly her responsibilities, and her grasp of legal terms and Texas real estate laws was amazing to him. She continued to study law books from his private library.

When Clayton came home for the Easter vacation, he was amazed at Millie's knowledge of law. He was deeply in love with Millie, and it was most satisfying to him that she was studying law from his father's library. Clayton was so pleased that he promised Millie that he would speak to the head of the law department at the University of Texas and possibly arrange for correspondence courses in Texas law. Clayton suggested that Millie might some time in the future take the law examination in Austin. If she passed the law examination for Texas, she could practice law. Millie protested that she only wanted to learn and understand enough law to be more effective at work. Clayton, who always had the last word said, "Father knows you are already as good a secretary as Miss Clarke and he needs two more lawyers in his office to help him with his expanding business. How would this sound, `Campbell and Campbell and Campbell?'"

Millie said, "It sounds fantastic, but you are such a dreamer, Clayton. I suppose that is why I love you so much."

Clayton replied, "No, Millie, I am not a dreamer, I am a believer, and anything I believe strongly will happen."

Millie retorted, "Yes, my love, and I believe in our June wedding, and it is time to make plans. This is the month of April, and June will soon be here."

At this time, Millie gave Clayton a large spontaneous hug and a kiss. She thought how fortunate and wonderful for her that she was engaged to marry him. He was so very good looking. She further thought, he is not only handsome, but he is so intelligent with a charming personality. Millie had observed that he had a very quick wit which many people did not have, and he was always forthright in his opinions. She often teased him about his wit and quick opinions.

Clayton kept reminding Millie that he had a Scottish background. His mother was a Scot who married his father during World War I. The Scottish people are known for their forthrightness.

Millie remembered a conversation she had had with Bessie about Clayton's mother. Millie had questioned Bessie about Clayton's mother who had died in childbirth after Clayton was born. Bessie had said, "Yessum, yessum, I'se remembers Miss Fiona even though it has been over twenty years ago when she died giving birth to little Clayton. Miss Fiona was a beautiful lady and no one in de whole town of Hillsboro had seen such a beautiful woman as she was."

Millie interrupted Bessie, saying, "Wasn't Miss Emily Blackburn a beautiful woman when she was young?"

"Oh yessum, yessum, she was a very pretty woman, but a different kind. Miss Fiona was blond-haired and she always said what she was thinking. You never had to guess what she meant and she could make you laugh and feel good all day long. I shore did miss her when she died, and I'se still miss her, but I'se never talks about her because of the judge—he took it real bad. The judge's mammy had a real hard time with him, and his mammy told me and my mammy to never mention Miss Fiona in front of the judge."

Bessie continued, "Something happened a week before little Clayton was born that almost scared me to death."

"Oh, goodness," said Millie, "What happened?"

"Well, one day, Miss Fiona, went for a walk down Craig Street, and when she was coming back a black cat ran in front of her, and the cat caused her to trip and fall on the sidewalk. I ran out to her, and helped her up. She hurt her knee and her arm, but she told me to never tell any one. I said, `Miss Fiona, a black cat ran in front of you and my mammy always told me that a black cat that passes in front of you was very bad, bad luck.' Miss Fiona then said to me, `Oh, no, no, a black cat in Scotland is a sign of good luck.' I replied, `I sure hope you is right, Miss Fiona.' " Bessie had tears in her eyes, when she said, "Poor Miss Fiona, she was dead within a few days.. This is a secret I have kept for over twenty years, and Miss Millie, don't you ever tell my secret!"

Millie replied, "Oh, Bessie, thank you for sharing your long secret with me, and I promise I will never tell anyone."

Bessie said, "You is welcome, Miss Millie."

Millie then asked Bessie, "Are there any more secrets?"

Bessie replied, "Oh, yessum, yessum, Miss Millie, I know a bigger secret, but my mammy said she would strike me dead if I ever told anyone, and I ain't going to ever tell anyone that secret."

That was the end of their conversation on secrets. Millie felt she would jeopardize her rapport with Bessie if she continued to question her because Bessie was adamant about not revealing anymore secrets about Hillsboro House and the Campbells. Millie respected Bessie's wishes and decided never to mention the big secret again unless Bessie brought up the subject. Millie was curious about Bessie's big secret, and she assumed it would probably be revealed to her sometime in the future.

Clayton and Millie continued to enjoy the Easter vacation together. Millie purchased a new pink silk dress, a new white straw hat with pink and blue flowers, new white leather shoes, and a white leather purse. They decided to spend Easter Sunday of 1940 with her parents, Jake and Dora, on the farm. Clayton, Millie, and her mother attended the local country church where Millie saw many of her old friends and neighbors. They complimented her on how beautiful she had become, and they were gracious to Clayton. Clayton enjoyed Easter Sunday in the country, and he told the family he hoped to own a ranch some day which was a surprise to Millie. She had assumed that Clayton and she would live in Hillsboro House some day. Jake and Dora enjoyed talking to Clayton because he had numerous questions to ask about the farm. Millie's younger brother also enjoyed the company of Clayton.

Dora Martin served a delicious ham dinner with new potatoes and English peas from their vegetable garden, cooked in a white cream sauce. Millie said, "It is just like the times I was growing up except we had an Easter egg hunt in the pasture after Sunday dinner." The entire family reminisced about the traditional Easter egg hunt.

Clayton was impressed and asked, "Why can't we have an Easter egg hunt this afternoon?"

Dora said, "We will have an egg hunt; I'll boil a dozen new eggs."

Millie said she would decorate the eggs.

Jake said, "I'll hide the eggs in the pasture where the new calves are kept."

Millie did an artistic job decorating the eggs with some old crayons she had located. She drew new baby chicks on some eggs and spring flowers on others. She also wrote Clayton and Millie on one egg and the other family names on the other eggs.

The Easter egg hunt was enjoyable for the Martin family and Clayton. The pasture was green with new grass, the trees had new buds for spring, and many wild flowers were beginning to bloom. A cool north wind was blowing, but the afternoon sun diminished the chill of the wind. Clayton found the majority of the Easter eggs; J.D. was second in finding numbers of eggs. Millie Jean found the Easter egg which was inscribed with Clayton and Millie. The Easter egg hunt was a great success.

When it was time for Clayton and Millie to drive back to Hillsboro, they said good-bye to Jake, Dora, and J. D., and Clayton and Millie drove slowly back to town. Clayton told Millie someday they would have a ranch with a large white house and a beautiful red barn with lots of farm animals. But Millie told Clayton, "You are dreaming again."

Clayton said, "No, Millie, this is my believing in the future."

They arrived in Hillsboro, and Millie was sad to see Easter come to an end. Clayton's vacation was also coming to an end since he would return to the university the following day. Millie could not believe the week had gone so fast and they had made very few wedding plans. Clayton said, "I will be there, and you will be there in June." He continued, "That is the most important plan, and I'll let you work out the other details."

Millie loved Clayton but she was beginning to realize he was not a person for detail. She had always believed in having an organized plan for everything. She knew she must make the wedding plans and, hopefully, they would please Clayton.

When Clayton said good-bye that evening, he apologized for not helping more with the wedding plans. He gave her authority to make all the plans for their wedding as long as he could be first to kiss the bride. Millie broke into sobs of crying because she had never loved anyone as much as Clayton Campbell. She told him that their June wedding would be the most important event of her life. Clayton asked, "Would it be more important than the birth of our children?"

Millie replied, "I will take the fifth amendment on that question."

Millie gave Clayton a long embrace while he stroked her hair, and said, "Millie we will have a long and wonderful life together."

After Clayton returned to law school, Millie made all the plans for their June wedding and took care of all the details.

She told Miss Emily about the wedding and Miss Emily volunteered to help. Miss Emily invited Millie to afternoon tea. Millie always enjoyed going to Miss Emily's home. It was only half the size of Hillsboro House, but it was just perfect in size for one person. Millie liked the plain Federal style of the house with its dark olive door and wood shutters on the plain yellow brick. The entry hall was always pleasant with a stairway at the left. On the right side of the hall was a wood door with glass panes which led into a lovely drawing room. Millie admired the large oriental Saruk carpet on the wood floor. Miss Emily's parents had brought it from New Orleans when they first came to Hillsboro to live.

The tea table, a round mahogany piecrust table, had the tea service on it. It was most beautiful and elegant to Millie. Miss Emily offered Millie a small glass of sherry before taking tea. Millie gladly accepted the warm thick sherry, but she hoped she would not feel giddy as she was not accustomed to any kind of alcoholic drink. She thought surely a tiny glass of sherry in such a pretty crystal glass could not harm her.

Miss Emily was very pleased about the wedding, and she reminded Millie that Clayton and she were among her favorite students at Hillsboro High. The afternoon tea continued to be enjoyable with the tiny thin sandwiches and cookies freshly baked by Beatrice, Miss Emily's maid. After a long pleasant conversation, it was time for Millie to leave, and Miss Emily asked her how she could help her prepare for the wedding. Millie said, "I would appreciate if you would help me select a wedding dress." Miss Emily was delighted and they made plans to look at wedding dresses the next week.

Millie and Miss Emily visited the local shops to view and consider various wedding gowns. They made a motor trip into Waco the next day where they visited several shops. Again, they did not succeed in finding a suitable wedding dress for Millie. On the drive home, Miss Emily said to Millie, "I want to show you a wedding dress I have, and never had the opportunity to use it." Millie did not understand why Miss Emily had never married, but Millie had a feeling why she had never used the wedding dress. Miss Emily did not volunteer anymore information about this wedding dress.

When they arrived home, Miss Emily took Millie upstairs to a clothes closet which was seldom used, where she located a large blue box with BRIDAL GOWN on it in white letters. She opened the box and inside neatly folded was the most beautiful wedding dress that Millie had ever seen. Miss Emily insisted that Millie try it on for size. It fitted Millie perfectly, and Miss Emily said, "You look beautiful in the dress, and you may have it for your wedding." Millie looked at herself in the mirror; she adored the dress.

Millie said, "The dress is gorgeous, but I couldn't possibly accept your wedding dress."

Miss Emily replied, "There was never a wedding. I want you to have the dress on one condition."

Millie asked, "What is that condition?"

Miss Emily told Millie very strongly, "You must never reveal where you got this wedding gown, not even to your husband." Millie agreed that she would never reveal the secret of the wedding gown to anyone.

Miss Emily insisted that Millie take the wedding gown, and Millie hugged Miss Emily and thanked her for the gown before leaving.

Millie did not sleep well that night. She thought about Miss Emily and the secret of the wedding gown. She wondered why Miss Emily had never had a chance to wear it. What would she tell Clayton, where she found the wedding gown? After a long sleepless night, Millie got up and dressed. She only wanted a cup of coffee. She decided to write Clayton a brief note and tell him that she had found a beautiful wedding gown.

May 6, 1940
Hillsboro

My dear Clayton,

After several days of shopping and searching, I found a beautiful wedding gown. I can never tell you where I found it, but I know you will think it most gorgeous. I am so busy with our wedding plans, and the finding of a suitable wedding gown pleases me and relieves me of a big worry.

I hope you are fine, and I love you very much.

Affectionately,

Millie

II

The Wedding at Hillsboro House

The day in June of 1940 for Clayton and Millie's wedding finally arrived and it was a beautiful day on Craig Street in Hillsboro. The sun made the day warm and bright and the large white house on Craig Street never looked so splendid. The judge had all the outside walls and the nine large Grecian columns painted with a fresh coat of white paint. The green grass had been manicured for the occasion. A white trellis hanging with baskets of red roses had been erected in the back yard. A banner on the trellis had the following inscription, MY LOVE IS LIKE A RED, RED ROSE, a quotation from Robert Burns. The marriage would take place in front of the white trellis.

Guests were seated in folding chairs underneath two enormous elm trees. Judge Campbell and Clayton arrived first, both looking handsome in their dark blue suits, white shirts, and tartan ties, which indicated their Scottish heritage. Next came the best man Stephen Anderson, Clayton's school friend, who wore a dark blue suit. Two bridesmaids came next dressed in pale pink satin dresses and large pink straw hats.

The musicians began playing the wedding march. After a seemingly long time, Millie Jean was escorted by her young brother, J. D., to the wedding trellis where she was acknowledged by Clayton. The guests were in awe with the beauty of the bride. Millie had never looked so beautiful in her life. There were tears in Dora's eyes when J. D. returned to his seat next to his parents. The wedding guests had never seen a wedding gown so beautiful. The dress was made of white satin with beige lace at the top and a collar of lace in the shape of a cape. The upper part of the dress fitted tightly but the skirt was very full. The dress gave the appearance of a southern belle.

Bessie sat in the back row but she had an aisle seat so she could observe the marriage ceremony. She was wearing a red and black plaid dress and a black hat and black shoes. Bessie said a silent prayer for the judge because she sensed he was sad that morning because Clayton's mother was not alive and present for the wedding. The judge spoke well and his voice never faltered. Clayton and Millie spoke strongly and clearly with their I do's. They were finally pronounced man and wife, and Clayton gave his new bride a kiss.

The music began and they made their departure from the white trellis and garlands of red roses when a large black cat ran across the garden passing in front of the bride and groom. "Oh, my God, not again," cried Bessie. The guests were stunned with Bessie's outburst, but the band played louder and began singing some popular songs.

Soon a reception line was formed. The entire wedding party stood in the shade of the largest elm tree in the garden. All the closest friends, the neighbors, the relatives, and the most important clients of Judge Campbell came through the reception line to greet the bride and groom. Jake, Dora, and J. D. were invited to stand in the receiving line. Millie was proud of her parents and her brother J.D., who was proud of his sister marrying Clayton Campbell.

Millie was pleased to see Miss Emily who always looked so lovely. She was wearing a floral dress with many colors and a large red hat and red shoes. Miss Emily was accompanied by a handsome young man who was very well groomed. She introduced him as her nephew who lived in New Orleans; his name was Claude Louis Blackburn. Millie felt she had met Claude before but she could not recall the time or place. Claude was very pleasant and he complimented Millie and Clayton on their beautiful wedding. Millie liked Louis immediately since he asked her to call him Louis, but she was curious when and where she had met him.

Millie and Clayton were relieved when the last guests had come through the receiving line. The guests were served a sumptuous meal prepared by dear old Bessie. Millie and Clayton did not eat much but they pretended to be eating food so Bessie would not be disappointed.

The time came to cut the large wedding cake which Bessie had baked. The white four-tiered cake placed in the center of a table with a sparkling linen table cloth was most beautiful. There were two large bouquets of red roses on each side of the cake. Each bouquet of roses had an inscription on a white satin ribbon. One was Millie and the other was Clayton. The peak of the cake had two red roses and the word "l o v e s." Depending on which side of the table you were facing, it would read, "Clayton loves Millie" or "Millie loves Clayton."

Mr. and Mrs. Clayton Campbell cut the first slice of cake for themselves and they received a large applause from the guests. One of Bessie's helpers continued to serve the cake.

It was now time to propose toasts to the newlyweds. Judge Campbell made the first toast to his son and his new daughter-in-law, wishing them good health, happiness, and a long and happy married life. Dora Martin spoke for her family and gave the young couple her sincere wishes and blessings for a wonderful future. Miss Emily toasted two of her favorite students. There were many more toasts from neighbors and friends, and the last toast by Stephen, the best man, who shared the numerous amusing incidents concerning Clayton.

Just before sunset, it was time for the newlyweds to leave for a brief weekend honeymoon. Millie had gone upstairs and changed into a dress for traveling in her roadster which Clayton would drive. The guests did not know where they were going on their honeymoon. Even the bride did not know because she had decided to allow Clayton to make that decision. She had assumed it would be in one of the large hotels in Austin. She had even hinted to wedding guests they would probably be spending the weekend in Austin.

A big *Just Married* sign had been put on the car. Stephen, the best man, drove the car along the side portico of the house. Guests threw rice and waved to them as they drove away. Millie noticed in the mirror that Bessie was crying and waving both arms in the air. She could see J. D. waving his arms and her parents looking sad.

When they reached the main highway, Clayton turned north on to the Dallas highway. Millie said, "I thought we were going to honeymoon in Austin." Clayton only smiled and patted Millie on the shoulder. She gave him a quick kiss on his cheek while he was driving.

They arrived in Dallas an hour later, and Clayton drove directly to the Adolphus Hotel, where they were expected and the honeymoon suite had been prepared for them. It was located on the top floor of the hotel and Clayton gallantly carried his bride over the threshold. Millie had never seen such luxury. There was a large entry hall which led into a beautiful sitting room furnished in the French style. There was also a well-appointed dining room, with the table beautifully set with fine china, crystal, and silver for two people. Two bottles of fine French champagne were being chilled in coolers.

A gourmet dinner had been prepared for them. It would be served whenever they were ready, but Clayton said they must sip and enjoy the champagne before they had dinner. A silver tray of hors d'oeuvres had been prepared for them which included fine caviar on tiny fingers of toast. Millie had never tasted caviar and such high quality champagne.

Dinner was served at 8:30, starting with Scottish smoked salmon followed by a delicious onion soup. The main course was beef tenderloin cooked in a burgundy with small white onions and mushrooms. Millie said to Clayton, "I am afraid I can never cook or produce a meal comparable to this."

Clayton replied, "This is my wedding night, and I want it to be very special."

Two musicians played romantic music during dinner and Clayton and Millie danced several times. The evening ended at 11:00. The musicians, the waiters, and other helpers said good-night to the newlyweds.

Clayton said, "It is time to go to bed together." Millie had tears in her eyes and Clayton did not understand.

Millie said, "I do not want the evening to end."

Clayton replied, "This is only the beginning."

Clayton helped Millie to undress and then carried her to their bed. Clayton undressed himself and then joined Millie in bed. Millie relished the feel of his marvelous body, and enjoyed its wonderful masculine scent. Millie and Clayton became as one being during their passion. Millie cried aloud in her ecstasy. The rest of the night was a contest to determine who could say I love you the most number of times. Millie and Clayton did not want the night to ever end. The night ended when the morning sun rose. They lay close to each other as they thought about their future, their many plans, and their wonderful dreams.

Meanwhile at Hillsboro House Bessie Mae and her husband, Tom Johnson, cleaned up after the wedding party. Judge Campbell had gone away for the night with friends. Bessie was still upset over the black cat which had run in front of the newlyweds. Tom said, "That is an old superstition, and you must get it out of your mind." But Bessie said her mamma had taught her about the bad luck of a black cat crossing your path.

Bessie said, "I will pray that nothing will ever happen to them kids."

Bessie then said, "Let's look at the wedding presents." They went into one of the rooms upstairs to look at the wedding gifts. Bessie had never seen so many wedding presents. The room was filled with so many gifts, that Bessie could not count them. Bessie said, "I'se never seen the like of it." Bessie continued, "I shore didn't get many gifts at my wedding."

Tom replied, "You got something better than gifts; you got all of me that night."

Bessie said, "That is enough from you, Tom Johnson."

Bessie and Tom decided to walk out on the second floor veranda to look at the beautiful moon and stars that evening. They stood and looked over Craig Street. It was a most beautiful night until Bessie saw a small creature on the front lawn. "Oh, dear," said Bessie, "It is that damn black cat again." Tom told Bessie that she must learn to like all animals including cats and even black cats. Bessie said, "I love all of God's creatures including cats and even black cats, but I'se just don't want a black cat to cross my path." Bessie continued, "My Aunt Delila had two pretty black cats. I use to hold them in my lap and pet them. I loved those cats and they loved me, but they never ran in front of me."

Tom looked at Bessie and commented, "I don't understand you, but I love you."

117

III

The Honeymoon

Clayton ordered breakfast in their room for Millie and himself on Sunday. He served Millie breakfast in bed, but chided her not to expect breakfast served in bed during their marriage. Millie questioned him, "What if I am ill, or if it is a special occasion?"

Clayton said, "Darling, that is an exception, and you will be served breakfast in bed."

Afterwards, Clayton and Millie went to Fair Park in Dallas to enjoy the rides in the amusement section of the park. Their first ride was on the ferris wheel, which Millie enjoyed. Although, it was somewhat frightening when their seat took them to the top of the wheel. After a couple of rides, Clayton suggested a ride on the big roller coaster. Millie was not very enthused about having a ride on it, but Clayton was persistent. Millie said, "The tracks sound very noisy to me."

She reluctantly went for the roller coaster ride with Clayton. She had never been so frightened in her life. She prayed to God to let her finish the ride safely. She would never ride on another roller coaster, and was most relieved when the ride ended. She announced to Clayton that she would never ride a roller coaster again. Clayton apologized to Millie, and he suggested they visit the museums in Fair Park. They enjoyed the Natural Science Museum because they both loved animals. They also enjoyed the Fine Arts Museum especially the decorative arts and oil paintings.

When Sunday had ended, they decided to return to their hotel suite at the Adolphus for a quiet evening together. They enjoyed the evening by discussing and planning their future life together. Clayton had two more years of law school at the University of Texas before graduation. They both agreed Clayton would finish law school. Millie would continue working for Judge Campbell. They also decided to retain Millie's apartment until Clayton became a lawyer and began earning a salary. Clayton also reminded Millie that he was very pleased that she was reading law books from his father's law library. He mentioned again that he had arranged with the head of the law department to send her a correspondence course on law from the university. Clayton would work the summer in his father's law office.

The honeymoon weekend passed quickly. Clayton and Millie returned to Hillsboro, arriving home on late Monday afternoon. They stopped by Hillsboro House to thank the judge and Bessie for their help. Clayton had a long talk with his father and Millie had a visit with Bessie. Bessie was so relieved that the newlyweds were home. She was so pleased that they were safe and no harm had come to them on their honeymoon. Bessie said, "But you will always be little Clayton to me. I'se helped raised you since you was in diapers."

Clayton said, "That is correct, and I still love you and I always will."

Millie and Bessie went upstairs to check on the wedding presents. Millie was overjoyed at the large number of wedding gifts. She asked Bessie about Louis Blackburn, Miss Emily's nephew. "Oh, yessum," said Bessie, "Louis is a fine gentleman."

Millie said, "I was not aware that Miss Emily had any brothers or sisters. Are you sure Louis is her real nephew?" Bessie was confused because she had never met his parents. Millie continued, "You have never met his parents, but yet, you have known Louis for a long time.

"Oh, yessum, my Aunt Delila worked for the Blackburns."

The gifts were stored in Clayton's bedroom. Millie looked at the bedroom carefully. The furniture was interesting and the artifacts were unusual. She looked at several photographs of Clayton when he was a small boy. One photograph in a silver frame was unusual with a close resemblance to Louis Blackburn. Millie said to Bessie, "This photograph resembles Louis Blackburn."

"Oh, no, Miss Millie, "that is little Clayton, and I would swear on de Bible it is," Bessie said.

"I agree with you Bessie, but I just thought there was a close resemblance to Louis Blackburn, Miss Emily's nephew." Millie observed that Bessie was not interested in discussing the photograph. When Bessie did not want to discuss a topic or if she was displeased about something, Bessie became very quiet on the subject under discussion. Bessie seldom talked about things that did not interest her. Millie was beginning to think that Bessie kept many secrets to herself.

When Millie and Clayton returned to her apartment that evening, they opened their wedding gifts and cards which took most of the evening. There was a wide range of gifts with many nice pieces of silver, china, beautiful towels and bed sheets, good kitchen items, decorative items, books, and many other useful articles. Miss Emily's gift was most unusual. It was a lovely painting of historic Saint Louis Cathedral in the old French Quarter of New Orleans, which they both loved. "Where shall we hang the painting?" asked Millie.

Clayton said, "1 think we should wait until we get our very own home before hanging it."

They decided that they would go to New Orleans on a belated honeymoon in the near future.

Millie said, "We might discover other paintings of the old French Quarter which we would enjoy."

Clayton agreed, "That's true, and we might find some wonderful French furniture which we would love but could not afford to buy."

Millie mentioned Louis Blackburn, who came to their wedding with Miss Emily, and how pleasant he seemed. Clayton had met him a few times when he came to visit Miss Emily during the summer vacations. He said, "Miss Emily usually visited him during her summer vacations in New Orleans. I had never met his parents, but I knew that Louis lived in New Orleans with them. Miss Emily never discussed him or spoke about him unless asked," said Clayton. He then asked Millie, "Why are you interested in Louis?"

Millie replied, "I don't really know, but he reminds me of someone I have known."

Clayton admonished Millie, "Louis is a charming and a very handsome man, but so am I." He continued, "Remember, Millie, you married me two days ago."

Millie retorted, "My goodness, Clayton, I think you are jealous." She then gave him a big hug and a long kiss.

Clayton responded, "Thanks, a kiss and a hug is always good for a jealous husband."

Millie said, "I think it is time for a jealous husband to go to bed."

"I agree," said Clayton, "and I am going to sleep in your bed tonight." Clayton added, "I am most sleepy tonight."

Millie replied, "I am surprised because you have not been sleepy the past two nights."

IV

Two Dinner Parties

The summer of 1940 was an enjoyable and pleasant time for Millie and Clayton. They both worked almost daily in Judge Campbell's law firm. Millie accepted more responsibility in the office since she was now a part of the Campbell family, and she sensed that Judge Campbell expected a higher sense of loyalty and a higher degree of performance in her duties and responsibilities to him. Judge Campbell expected promptness from all of his employees, and he expected exactness on all contracts including minor details. On the other hand, Millie would never in her own nature take advantage of her new status as a member of the family. She made special efforts to please Judge Campbell and he appreciated her efforts. The judge did not compliment often, but Millie overheard a compliment about her when the judge told a client, "I have the best legal secretary that a lawyer could possibly have."

She told Clayton about the compliment she had heard that day when they were dining at home. Clayton said, "My father has always demanded high standards of work, and he also appreciates good work and efficiency in his office." Clayton continued, "I think we should invite my father to visit us and serve him dinner."

Millie said, "Clayton, I am only learning to cook; he would think my food would be awful compared to that of Bessie."

Clayton said, "You are missing the point; my father would be honored as long as you don't serve black-eyed peas."

"What is wrong with black-eyed peas?" asked Millie.

"Nothing is wrong with black-eyed peas, and my father always eats them on New Year's day because Bessie won't cook New Year's dinner unless she can serve black-eyed peas with the New Year's ham," said Clayton. Clayton continued on the black-eyed peas, "Bessie says that you will have good luck all year long if you eat black-eyed peas on New Year's Day. When father was campaigning to be elected county judge, the country people served him black-eyed peas, but this is not an unkind joke because these people elected father county judge during the Depression era."

Millie admitted that her mother always served black-eyed peas on New Year's Day. Millie then said, "I will not serve black-eyed peas to the judge when we invite him for dinner."

Clayton said, "Father would love chicken-fried steaks, mashed potatoes, and cream gravy."

Millie admitted, "I am sure your father would, but I want to serve him something different because he can get chicken-fried steak in every cafe in town."

"My dear," replied Clayton, "you are the chef, and the choice is left to you."

Millie stayed awake most of the night trying to think what she could prepare that would be original and yet delicious to taste. While Clayton was sleeping, she slipped quietly out of bed so he would not awaken. They had received three large cookbooks and also a set of cookbooks as wedding gifts. Millie went through the volumes. She read about soups, meats, vegetables, casseroles, and desserts. Several items were possible, but none of the menus gave her inspiration for something that she would enjoy serving the judge. She wanted a recipe that would be a total success without any possible failure. She was inclined to be a perfectionist, and she continued to think about the menu for several days. Clayton had suggested inviting his father on a week night. Judge Campbell was usually busy on weekends, and Bessie always cooked a big meal for Sunday dinner as he often entertained friends then.

A Wednesday night was agreed upon, and Millie was some-what nervous because she did not have a menu planned. Clayton kept asking her if she had made a decision and she was either vague or indecisive about her answer. Out of desperation, she called Bessie and asked what she should cook for the judge. Bessie said, "You fry a big skillet of chicken, and when the chicken is fried and cooked, make a big pan of cream gravy, boil potatoes, mash them, add real cream and real butter, and the judge will love them. And don't forget to put a lot of salt and pepper on everything." Millie thanked Bessie but she was not positive about the fried chicken dinner.

The next day Miss Emily came into the Campbell law firm on a business matter. Millie often confided in Miss Emily and she told her about her predicament. Miss Emily immediately suggested cooking beef burgundy but Millie did not understand. Miss Emily said, "Oh, my poor child, I will tell you how to prepare it. We always had beef burgundy in New Orleans, which my mother served. Try this recipe. Flour two pounds of top round beef, cut into one inch squares and brown in frying pan with oil. Salt and pepper. Transfer to a sauce pan. Add a cut up onion, water, half a cup of tomato ketchup, and half a cup of burgundy wine. Simmer for an hour. Then add two diced carrots, some fresh mushrooms, and twelve small white boiling onions. Simmer forty-five minutes more on the stove. Serve with mashed potatoes and green beans." Miss Emily then said, "I will make you an exotic dessert, but you must keep this a secret."

Millie felt good about the beef burgundy menu. She decided she would keep it a secret until the dinner was served. She began preparing for the dinner three days ahead of time, and she hoped the judge would permit her to leave an hour early on that day so she could begin cooking in good time.

Clayton kept asking about the menu she planned to serve but she said it was a secret. Clayton said, "There are a few secrets in our life together."

"Yes," said Millie, "our honeymoon was a secret to me."

"And your wedding dress was a secret to me," said Clayton.

Millie said, "I am only one secret ahead of you." She gave Clayton a large hug and kiss, and promised him there would be no more secrets between them.

The next Wednesday arrived, the day for Judge Campbell's invitation to dinner at Millie and Clayton's apartment. Millie gave the judge his agenda at 4:00 that day. The judge thanked her and said, "Millie, you may leave an hour early today; I understand you are having a dinner party tonight." Millie was so pleased as this would give her three and a half hours before the judge's arrival.

She had all the ingredients ready for the beef burgundy. Miss Emily had given her two good bottles of burgundy wine. When Clayton arrived home, he could not believe the aroma from the kitchen. The table was set attractively, and wine glasses were available for the dark red burgundy. Clayton was very impressed, but he said, "I suppose it is a secret where the French burgundy was purchased."

Millie said, "It was a gift, and it is something for you and your father to enjoy this evening."

Judge Campbell arrived at 7:30 in a relaxed and cordial mood. The conversation was congenial, and Millie felt the judge and his son had a wonderful relationship. They respected each other and enjoyed each other's company.

Millie served dinner at 8:00. The first course was a green salad which they all enjoyed. Next came the main course of beef burgundy, mashed potatoes, and fresh green beans served with hot dinner rolls. The judge and Clayton enjoyed the food immensely and were impressed with the fine wine. The judge was curious about the wine but Millie could not divulge where she got it. The judge was also amazed at the delicious flavor of the beef burgundy. He asked Millie, "Where did you learn to cook so well?" Millie replied that she received several cook books as a wedding present.

The evening was a great success, especially for Millie. The judge had several glasses of wine, and Millie had never seen him in such a relaxed mood. He stayed until 10:00 P.M. He thanked them for a delightful evening. Before leaving, he told Millie to put on the next day's agenda a conference with Clayton and Millie at 10:00 Friday morning.

They cordially said good night to the judge, and he thanked them for one of the best evenings he had ever had. After he was gone, Clayton and Millie were curious why he had scheduled an appointment at 10:00 on Friday with them.

On Thursday afternoon at 4:00, Millie put the Friday agenda on Judge Campbell's desk. He was on the telephone with a client, but he gave a nod and smile as he glanced at the agenda. Millie and Clayton were still most curious why they had been scheduled for an appointment with the judge. Clayton said, "It must be very important."

Millie said, "Maybe he does not need us; maybe we are going to be fired."

Clayton said, "Well, at least, tomorrow we will know."

Friday came, and the judge's schedule was normal for a Friday morning. There were several appointments before the scheduled one for Clayton and Millie. Millie kept hoping for some clue to the reason for the scheduled conference with her and Clayton.

At 10:00 they knocked on the judge's door, both very nervous.

Judge Campbell greeted them cordially, invited them to be seated, and told them how pleased he was with their wedding, and he wished, at this time, to bestow a special wedding gift on them. Clayton said, "Father, you have already given us wonderful wedding gifts."

"That's true," said the judge, "but this one is special because I am so pleased with you." He then handed them an envelope which contained a deed to a house on Corsicana Street. Both of their names were on the deed and there were two shiny keys to the house. Clayton and Millie were speechless. They never expected such a gift. The judge clapped his hands and said, "It is time to return to official duties at the Campbell law firm. Millie knew the judge did not enjoy affection, but she hugged him and thanked him for the gift of the house. Clayton thanked his father and shook his hand before returning to his office.

Clayton and Millie were thrilled with the nice house on Corsicana Street. Corsicana Street was a beautiful street with many large green trees and many large old houses. Many of the large houses were built in the Victorian style.

The gift house was a white frame house with a large front porch. It was not new, having been built in the 1920s; certainly not as large and grand as Hillsboro House. The house was spacious enough even though it was a single-floor structure. Millie liked the large living room and the large fireplace, and it had a nice dining room off the living room. A pleasant kitchen was at the back of the dining room. The other section of the house had three adequate bedrooms with one large bathroom.

Millie and Clayton were anxious to move into the house, but in their enthusiasm, they had practically forgotten about furniture for the house. Millie's apartment was furnished and she had almost no furniture of her own. They certainly could not expect the judge to furnish the house; they would somehow manage to acquire enough furniture to move.

Dora, Millie's mother, gave them a nice chiffonnier which Millie had used when she was a young girl. It was a beautiful old chiffonnier, finished in a light wood instead of the usual dark oak wood. Millie felt sad about taking the chiffonnier, but she knew her mother would be disappointed if she and Clayton did not accept it.

Miss Emily had an old dining set in the garage with six chairs and a pleasant oriental carpet which she gave to her favorite students Millie and Clayton. The dining table looked exceptionally well in their dining room with the oriental carpet.

Millie had saved some money from her salary, so she invited Clayton to go with her to Cheap Jim's furniture store where there was new and good second-hand furniture. She and Clayton purchased a new bed, a gas stove, an electric icebox, and some living room furniture.

Their white house on Corsicana Street took shape with the basic furniture they had acquired. They could hardly wait until 5:00 each day to go home in order to do improvements on the house. Millie was most impressed with how enthusiastic Clayton was in doing the projects and repairs for their home.

It was a wonderful time. They loved their house, and each week the house looked better. They decided to postpone a belated honeymoon trip to New Orleans; they were most content to stay in Hillsboro and enjoy their house and continue to make improvements on it.

Millie told Clayton they could go to New Orleans in a couple of years when he finished law school. Clayton said, "We should invite Miss Emily and Louis Blackburn for dinner and they can tell us about New Orleans.

The next day Millie was in the Hillsboro library looking for a special law book for Clayton. Clayton had constantly to review what he had learned in law school. Millie observed Louis Blackburn who was looking at books on Texas history. They had a pleasant conversation and Millie invited him and Miss Emily to dinner. She mentioned that Clayton was an expert on Texas history. Millie said she would like to know more about his home city, New Orleans. Louis thought the next Sunday night would be fine for a visit. He and Miss Emily were not leaving town that weekend.

Millie decided to serve beef burgundy again. Clayton said, "It is wonderful that we know how to cook one dish."

Millie gave him a perplexed look and said, "I don't think Miss Emily and Louis are the chicken-fried-steak type."

"Darling, you are always right. Let's serve the famous beef burgundy," said Clayton.

Millie added, "We will serve egg noodles instead of mashed potatoes."

The dinner party was a great success, and Miss Emily and her nephew, Louis, were pleasant guests. Millie told Louis that Clayton could explain Texas history to him. Clayton said, "Well Louis, I could talk five hours straight on Texas history but I am only going to take a few minutes tonight.

"Texas has a very long and interesting history. The ancestors of the first Texans are believed to have migrated from Asia fifteen hundred years ago when they crossed the Bering Strait. There was a long Indian era in Texas before the European explorations with missionaries who came in 1519 and stayed until 1690. The next period was the Spanish domination which lasted to 1793. Then we had a Mexican era and Anglo-American up to 1835. There were many problems with the Anglo settlers and the Mexican government. There were differences in language, cultures, and religion. The people wanted their independence from Mexico, and they drew up a constitution to present to Santa Ana, the President of Mexico, in 1833. Sam Houston and Stephen Austin were head of the Committee.

"The first battle for independence took place in Gonzales in October of 1835 and the Mexicans were defeated by the Texans. The news spread and more volunteers came to Gonzales.

"Santa Ana who was alarmed about the events in Texas came to San Antonio on February 23, 1836. Colonel William Travis had 157 men at the Alamo. Colonel Travis appealed for aid, but only thirty men were able to break through Santa Ana's Army on March 1, 1836. This small band of men held the Alamo for five days against great odds, and on March 6, 1836, four to five thousand Mexican soldiers charged the Alamo and killed the Texans who died fighting. Only a few women, children, and slaves survived."

Clayton continued, "The Texans were defeated several more times at San Antonio, San Patricio, Agua Dulce, Golliad, and Victoria. Despite all these reverses, the Texans kept fighting and resisting.

"Santa Ana believed the Texas War had been won for him and Mexico, and he swept eastward with his army. On April 21, Santa Ana was taking a siesta at San Jacinto. General Houston's army which had been bypassed attacked Santa Ana and his army. Houston reported 630 killed, 280 wounded, and 730 captured. The entire force of the Mexican army was either killed, wounded, or captured. The Texans only lost nine men and thirty men were seriously wounded. The significance of this Battle at Jacinto was that it led to the independence of Texas and its later annexation into the United States."

Clayton said, "I think that is enough Texas history for tonight." Miss Emily, Louis, and Millie thanked Clayton for the account of Texas and its struggle for independence.

Miss Emily said, "Clayton, you should write a book on the independence of Texas."

Clayton replied, "I must finish law school before I write a book."

Louis said, "I can hardly wait to have another lesson in Texas history and could we not hear some more?"

Clayton said, "Well, I suppose you should know some of the symbols and mottos of Texas before you return to New Orleans. Let's have a quiz on the state flower, bird, tree, motto, and state song of Texas."

Miss Emily said, "I am not a native Texan, but I know the bluebonnet is the state flower, and I don't know what the Texas tree is?"

Clayton said, "You have the state tree in your backyard."

Miss Emily said, "Is it an elm, a mimosa, or a pecan tree?"

"The pecan tree is the state tree of Texas," said Clayton.

Millie said, "Clayton, please tell us the other state symbols."

Clayton replied, "The state bird of Texas is the mockingbird, the state motto is "Friendship", and the state song is "Texas, our Texas."

Miss Emily said, "I thought the state song was "The Eyes of Texas."

"No," said Clayton, "The Eyes of Texas" was adopted by the University of Texas as their song, and it is also a popular song throughout the state."

Louis said, "I thought the state song would have been "The Yellow Rose of Texas."

Millie said, "Well, the state dish of Texas must be chicken fried steak."

"Sorry," said Clayton, "the state dish of Texas is our famous chili."

Millie then said, "After this long lesson on the state of Texas, I am going to serve a dessert, and it should be the state dessert because Miss Emily made it."

"Oh, no," said Miss Emily, "it is a gateau from a New Orleans recipe." The dessert was enjoyed by everyone and the evening ended happily.

Louis Blackburn and Miss Emily thanked Clayton and Millie for the lovely evening. Louis was pleased with the lesson on Texas history, and Miss Emily always enjoyed the company of her two favorite Texas students.

When Miss Emily and Louis had gone, Millie said, "Why do you think Louis Blackburn is so interested in Texas history?"

Clayton said, "I think everyone should be interested in Texas history, because Texas helped make the United States a world nation. Without the large state of Texas and the Pacific Coast of the Northwest, the United States of America would have been a lesser nation in the world."

Millie was astounded at how much Texas history Clayton knew and remembered from his history classes. Texas history was a required course in the Texas public schools. Millie remembered many important facts about Texas history but certainly did not remember as many details and important events as Clayton did. Clayton told Millie that his father gave him many books to read on Texas history when he was very young.

In the short time Millie had been married to Clayton, she was learning many amazing things about him. His knowledge of so many subjects was remarkable. His interest and understanding of so many things were exciting to Millie. Millie believed her new husband would be a very brilliant and successful lawyer. She respected the skills and knowledge of Judge Campbell, and she believed that Clayton had inherited the same skills and knowledge from his father. Millie was looking forward to the time when Clayton would graduate from law school and become a lawyer with his father in Hillsboro.

V

Summertime in Hillsboro

Summer was coming to an end, and Millie would have preferred the long summer days to continue because Clayton would have to return to law school in Austin when it ended. She reflected about the events of the wonderful summer. She had gotten married to Clayton Campbell, and it was a lovely wedding at the beautiful home of Judge Campbell. Her brief honeymoon with Clayton at the Adolphus Hotel in Dallas had been wonderful. She further thought about the lovely home her father-in-law had given them as a special gift.

But the proudest and most important thing in her life was her husband and love, Clayton. Millie did not need wealth to enjoy life; she would love and enjoy life even if Clayton had been poor. She was planning a long wonderful married life with Clayton.

The summer time was enjoyable in Hillsboro. The residents enjoyed the outdoors with picnics, ball games in the park, swimming in the lakes and rivers, and fishing. Many people enjoyed barbecues in the evening, and many residents went to the ice-cream parlor, the Double Dip, during the warm evenings.

Millie and Clayton often went to the Double Dip in the evenings. It was like a social event because they saw many friends and neighbors from Hillsboro making it a most pleasant way to spend an evening. On one occasion they saw Sarah Bankstead and her parents sitting at a small marble-topped table enjoying bowls of fresh frozen ice cream. Clayton felt he should go over and say hello to Sarah and her parents. Millie did not feel it was necessary to make this gesture because the Banksteads were not invited to their June wedding. Millie stayed at their table while Clayton went over and spoke to them. Clayton returned in a few minutes and said, "Sarah and her parents were most pleased to see me, and Sarah said she would stop by to say hello to you before she leaves." Millie did not feel comfortable because she knew Sarah Bankstead had a big crush on Clayton when they were in high school. Everyone expected Clayton and Sarah to get married when they finished high school and college.

When Sarah and her parents were ready to leave the Double Dip, they stopped by Clayton and Millie's table. Clayton introduced Millie to Mr. and Mrs. Bankstead, who seemed kind and courteous. Sarah said to Millie, "Congratulations on your marriage to Clayton, and I hope you will both be very happy."

Millie said, "Thank you, Sarah; that is kind of you." Millie continued, "What are your future plans?"

Sarah replied, "I have no future plans since Clayton decided not to marry me. Some people think it is smart to finish college before they get married."

Clayton turned white with anger and said to Sarah, "Please don't be unkind to my wife because she is a wonderful person."

Sarah replied, "I am sure she is and best of luck to you." Sarah and her parents left quickly.

Clayton noticed tears in Millie's eyes. Clayton said, "Please don't be upset, Millie, because Sarah did not mean to upset you."

Millie replied, "She does not like me because you married me instead of her." Clayton said nothing more about Sarah or their encounter with the Banksteads, but Millie was frustrated because Clayton did not make comments or discuss the behavior of Sarah.

Millie did not sleep well that night. She thought about the rudeness of Sarah Bankstead all night. She did not like unpleasant situations. Her mother had always told her to be nice and act nicely at all times. Millie spoke with her mother the next day, as she liked to talk to her mother when something bothered her. Dora invited Millie and Clayton to come out to the farm, and they would all go to the Brazo River for a picnic and fishing on the river. Several uncles and aunts and many cousins would be there. It was a Saturday picnic held each August for the Martin family, and sometimes it was a fish fry if the men were fortunate enough to catch several fish. Millie agreed to bring some angel food cakes and she volunteered Clayton to bring cases of sodas and soft drinks. Millie could count on Clayton since he was always a good sport with her family. This was one side of Clayton that Millie really appreciated.

The Martin picnic was enjoyable and a happy occasion for the whole family. It was held in one of the parks on the Brazo River near Whitney. Millie introduced Clayton to all of her cousins and aunts and uncles on the Martin side of the family. Clayton had a clever way of greeting people that made them feel comfortable after they had met him. Clayton liked most people whom he met.

Most of the men had their fishing poles and lines in the river in order to catch fresh fish for the evening supper. The women spent most of the time talking and preparing the picnic lunch. There was a lot of southern fried chicken, potato salad, and baked beans. Some of the family members had gotten to the park early and selected a good spot for the family gathering. Bright red-and-white-check tablecloths covered each table. The food was delicious and there were ample foods for everyone to have second and third helpings.

Conversation was related mostly to the Martin family. Clayton was impressed by the warmth and friendliness of the Martins to one another. His family was so small, and he had never really met the McGill family in Scotland, the family of his mother who died when he was born. The family was friendly to Clayton and Millie was so pleased that Clayton was accepted fully by her parents. The day was spent relaxing, and talking when one felt the urge to talk.

Millie and Clayton went for a walk along the river. Even though it was a long hot day, a cool breeze came from the river which was refreshing. Clayton became very quiet at one point while he looked across the river at the large hills. Millie said, "Your life would have been different if you had married Sarah Bankstead."

Clayton said, "That is true, but look at the nice day I would have missed today with your family." Millie regretted that she had mentioned Sarah Bankstead.

When Clayton and Millie returned from their stroll along the river bank, they saw that the men had caught several fish, which they were cleaning and preparing to fry in corn meal. Several women were peeling potatoes and dicing them for the big frying pans which would be put over the two campfires to cook. The smell of the fresh fish frying in the lard and the fresh potatoes made everyone hungry again. When the food was cooked, it was a feast for everyone. Clayton had never tasted fresh fish so delicious. A huge thermos of iced tea had been made by some of the women. Texans love iced tea in the summer months.

After the delicious fish fry, everyone was quiet except Millie's Uncle Jimmy who began singing some camp fire songs. He asked everyone to join in. Some singers were off-key, but it made no difference to the Martin family because they were enjoying their family reunion. They sang country, popular, and folk songs. Millie knew her father loved "She'll Be Coming Around the Mountain when She Comes." Another popular song was "Home on the Range", and they all enjoyed singing "The Yellow Rose of Texas." After many more songs, the Martin family decided it was time to end the family reunion. So Dora Martin was asked to say a prayer for the family. Millie was proud of her mother who always prayed eloquently and spiritually for the family. Clayton and Millie said good-bye to all her family before leaving, and they promised they would come to the reunion again next year. Millie and Clayton drove silently back to Hillsboro because they were both in a contemplative mood after a full day with her family.

The next day, which was a Sunday, Judge Campbell had invited Clayton and Millie to attend church service at St. Mary's Episcopal Church and then have Sunday dinner with him at Hillsboro House. Millie was impressed with the small red brick church and its beautiful old colored stained-glass windows. The order of service was different from that of other churches which Millie had attended, but she listened attentively as the minister gave his weekly sermon to the parishioners and guests. When it was concluded, the worshippers and visitors left quietly. Millie recognized many of Judge Campbell's clients whom she spoke to cordially.

As they were leaving the church, Millie was surprised to see Sarah Bankstead with her parents and Louis Blackburn among the congregation. The Banksteads and Judge Campbell exchanged pleasantries, and Sarah said loudly, "Hello, dear Clayton and dear Millie." There was nothing quiet or serene about Sarah Bankstead.

She started to introduce Louis Blackburn, but Clayton interrupted and said, "We have had the pleasure of meeting Louis." Louis smiled and greeted everyone cordially.

Sarah said aside to Millie, "He's just a big darling of a guy!"

Millie said, "He is a very nice person."

Sarah whispered aside to Millie, "When you really get to know him, you will use a different word than `nice' to describe him." Millie was beginning to blush and she hoped to leave soon because she was not enjoying this conversation.

The Banksteads were going to the Country Club of Hillsboro for Sunday lunch, and they invited Judge Campbell, Clayton, and Millie to join them. Judge Campbell declined, and Millie was most relieved. Millie said good-bye to the Banksteads, Sarah, and Louis. But before Millie could leave, Sarah whispered in Millie's ears, "I must tell you this about Louis. Well, WOW! He's wonderful." Millie had never known anyone so persistent as Sarah Bankstead. Millie was relieved when Sarah finally said good-bye.

Millie could hardly enjoy her lunch at Judge Campbell's home because of her unpleasant encounter with Sarah. Clayton said, "You must forget about Sarah and enjoy the good meal Bessie has prepared." Bessie had cooked one of her large Sunday dinners, and Bessie would be disappointed if you did not try everything she cooked. Bessie would not have only two or three vegetables, but she often served ten vegetables for the big Sunday dinner. Millie commented on the large number of vegetables.

Judge Campbell said, "It began with my parents and Bessie's mother, Aunt Ettie. They served the main meal in the middle of the day, and we ate leftovers for supper." Judge Campbell continued, "I have tried to change Bessie, but that is like trying to dam up the Brazo River. Once when I spoke to her about serving so many dishes at one meal, she said to me, `Judge, can you not afford as much food as your father did in this house?' Why, of course, I can afford the food," I replied. `Then we is going to have plenty of food as long as I am the cook in this here house,' she said. I backed off because I did not want to lose the best cook in town."

The long meal ended at Judge Campbell's home and the guests thanked Bessie for the delicious meal. Bessie said, "You is all welcome because you got to eat to live. And I see to it that the judge has plenty to eat."

And Judge Campbell said, "Amen, Amen to that." Bessie gave the judge one of her special looks, and the judge said, "Bessie, we love your food."

When they arrived home on Corsicana Street, Millie told Clayton about the conversation with Sarah just after church. Clayton was obviously unhappy that Louis Blackburn was dating and seeing Sarah. Millie said, "My mother has a name for girls like Sarah Bankstead."

Clayton inquired, "What does she call girls like Sarah?"

"My mother calls them 'fast' girls," replied Millie.

"I don't understand what she means by a `fast' girl," said Clayton. Millie suggested to Clayton that he should look at the various meanings of fast in the dictionary. "Never mind," said Clayton. "I think I know the meaning of a `fast' girl."

Clayton told Millie that he was glad he married a nice girl instead of a "fast" girl. "Some guys date `fast' girls, but they usually marry nice girls." Millie accepted Clayton's way of thinking, but she would be very glad when Sarah returned to her college in Denton. Of course, she would miss Clayton at the same time because he would be returning to law school in Austin. She assumed Louis Blackburn would be returning to New Orleans in the fall to attend school.

The telephone rang later in the evening, and Millie answered the telephone. The telephone call was from Miss Emily, who called to invite Millie and Clayton to a special dinner party on the next Saturday evening which was the last weekend before everyone returned to college for the fall term. The dinner party was to be at Craigview the lovely home of Miss Emily on Craig Street. Miss Emily said, "It is going to be a very special occasion with an important announcement to be made by my nephew, Louis Blackburn. Miss Emily continued, "I would be most disappointed if you and Clayton cannot come to the party." Millie thanked Miss Emily for the dinner invitation, and she promised that she and Clayton would do their utmost to be present on the Saturday evening for the special occasion which seemed so important to Miss Emily.

When Millie had finished speaking to Miss Emily, she was curious about the special occasion at Craigview. She told Clayton about her curiosity, but Clayton replied with indifference, "Curiosity killed the cat."

Millie said, "I have never understood that expression."

Clayton said, "Well, ask Bessie, and she will explain it to you, my dear."

Millie replied, "Thanks, dear Clayton, but I'll work this out for myself."

VI

The Engagement of Louis and Sarah

The special party pending at Miss Emily's home was constantly on Millie's mind during the entire week. She told Clayton about her anxiety, and that she was not really looking forward to the dinner party. She was fond of Miss Emily and her nephew, Louis, but her concern was that Sarah Bankstead would have a big part in this special dinner party.

If Clayton was concerned about the dinner party, he did not show it openly to Millie. Millie admired Clayton's self-control in not showing his private thoughts and emotions. Clayton reminded Millie, "It is because of my good Scottish background."

Millie said, "That is wonderful, Clayton, but I really wish at times I knew what you were thinking."

"If I am going to be a good lawyer, I have to conceal many of my private thoughts," said Clayton.

"Well, I do want you to be a good lawyer," said Millie.

Saturday evening finally arrived, and it was time to go to Miss Emily's home on Craig Street. Millie and Clayton decided to dress in their very best clothes for this special occasion. Clayton wore a summer jacket, a crisp white shirt, and an attractive necktie. Millie selected one of her best silk dresses together with her best jewelry and accessories.

When they arrived at Miss Emily's home, they noticed many cars parked on the street. Millie knew it was not going to be a small intimate party which she always preferred. James, the husband of Miss Emily's maid, welcomed and greeted guests at the door. James was formally dressed for the occasion in a black suit, white shirt, and a white bow tie. There were many guests that Millie and Clayton did not know when they were ushered into Miss Emily's lovely green drawing room. Millie did recognize several of her classmates from Hillsboro High, and she recognized the parents of Sarah, Mr. and Mrs. Bankstead. Judge Campbell was there, and in a most happy and wonderful mood. Millie had never known of Judge Campbell attending a party at Miss Emily's home because their relationship had been largely business over the past twenty years. Millie also recognized several of Judge Campbell's clients and neighbors. Millie was impressed with the attractive way the guests at the party were dressed. She was pleased that she and Clayton had chosen their best outfits for the party.

Tall glasses of sparkling champagne were served to guests who wished it, and a refreshing bowl of orange-sherbet punch was also available for guests who did not care for champagne. Lovely silver trays of hors d'oeuvres were passed and served by Beatrice's helpers. It was a most elegant party and the many guests were enjoying it.

Miss Emily, who looked radiant, greeted Millie and Clayton warmly. She was wearing an emerald-green evening dress. Her lovely black hair was nicely styled, and her jewelry, which was largely diamonds, sparkled. Her diamonds, which included earrings, a brooch, a bracelet, and other rings, were admired by the guests. Clayton and Millie complimented Miss Emily on her beautiful appearance which pleased her.

Clayton asked Miss Emily, "Where is Louis Blackburn?" Miss Emily replied, "Almost any moment, he and Sarah will be coming down stairs. Louis and Sarah have a special announcement to make this evening, and I am so pleased that you are here to be a part of this special occasion."

When Miss Emily had finished speaking with them, she asked the guests if she might have their attention. She said, "The two special guests are now coming down the stairs, and they have a special announcement tonight for everyone." Louis Blackburn, dressed in a dark suit, and Sarah Bankstead, dressed in a pretty white gown, came down the stairs and said good evening to everyone.

Sarah said, "This is a special evening for us, and we want to share the good news with you."

Louis continued, "Sarah and I are announcing our engagement to be married sometime in the future. We hope you are enjoying the engagement party my Aunt Emily has given for us tonight." Louis continued, "I have always enjoyed your warm friendly small town, and now I will enjoy it even more."

Sarah laughed and said, "Isn't he marvelous and sweet? I just can't tell you how thrilled I am tonight!"

Judge Campbell said, "Let's toast Louis and Sarah tonight, congratulate them, and wish them much happiness." He raised his champagne glass and said, "A toast to Louis and Sarah." Everyone gladly joined in toasting the young couple and wishing them much happiness for the future.

Clayton and Millie joined the toast, and Millie pretended she was happy for Louis and Sarah. Most of the guests were exclaiming what a beautiful young couple. A reception line was formed with Sarah and the Banksteads and Louis and Miss Emily.

Millie said to Clayton, "I would like another glass of champagne before I go through the reception."

Clayton said, "All right, Millie, but you have already had one glass of champagne."

When Millie had finished her second glass of champagne, she and Clayton decided it was time for them to congratulate the new couple. Sarah was first in line followed by her parents and then Louis and Miss Emily. Millie shook hands with Sarah and her parents and wished them much happiness. Clayton was going to shake hands with Sarah, but Sarah said to Clayton, "I want a big hug and a kiss from you."

Even though Millie was speaking to Louis, she observed that Sarah hugged Clayton longer than necessary. Millie also noticed that Sarah whispered something into Clayton's ear. Clayton's face immediately turned red, and Clayton said to Sarah, "You are probably right." Millie gave Clayton a signal to finish his conversation. Clayton finished by wishing Louis much happiness in the future, and he gave Miss Emily a light kiss on the cheek.

A sumptuous buffet table was ready for the guests in the dining room. There were many wonderful salads, a large ham, and Miss Emily's famous champagne meatballs, which people asked about only to be told the secret of the meatballs is in the sauce. Sarah Bankstead said, "Just pour a bottle of expensive champagne over them, and that's all there is to it. Isn't that right, Miss Emily?"

Miss Emily said, "No, my dear, it is not that simple."

Sarah said, "Well, you will give Louis and me the recipe when we are married."

Miss Emily gave Sarah a firm reply: "There are some secrets

in food and in life we must keep." Sarah retreated to her parents for the remainder of the evening.

When it was time to leave, Clayton and Millie said good night to Miss Emily, Louis, and Sarah. They thanked them for being included in the engagement party. Sarah said to Millie, "Isn't this engagement just wonderful for me? I could have ended up being an old maid for the remainder of my life because you married dear old Clayton."

Millie replied, "Sarah, I don't think you would ever have stayed a spinster for very long." Sarah continued to laugh and giggle like a young school girl.

Millie was relieved when it was time to leave the party. When they arrived home on Corsicana Street, Millie's first question to Clayton was, "What was your opinion of the engagement party?"

Clayton said, "The champagne meatballs were delicious."

Millie countered, "Oh, Clayton, how could you think about food when poor Louis is going to be married to Sarah Bankstead? I suppose you know the secret of the sauce for the champagne meatballs."

"I certainly do," said Clayton, "and I will make them for you when we have something special to celebrate."

Millie said, "I suppose it is a secret how you discovered the sauce recipe for the champagne meatballs."

"Yes," said Clayton, "and it is time for you to go to your bed and sleep." Millie went to bed but before going to sleep, she privately thought there were many secrets on Craig Street.

Maybe the two large glasses of champagne which she drank at the party helped her to go to sleep, but in the early hours of the morning she woke up suddenly. Clayton was soundly sleeping and she thought he looked handsome when he was sleeping like a child. She would liked to have asked him some questions but she was not sure if he would have given her the answers she wanted to hear. Clayton had an evasive way to avoid answering questions. Millie realized that her husband was not perfect but she loved him too much to be critical. She lay awake for a long time, curious to know what Sarah had whispered into Clayton's ear that made his face turn so red. Millie had never really liked Sarah and she had good reason now to dislike her. Sarah was always flirting with Clayton. Why did Sarah continually remind Millie that Clayton did not marry her? The entire situation of Sarah and Clayton was upsetting.

Millie never set a trap for Clayton even though she admired him in high school. It was Clayton who asked her to marry him when Sarah treated him so badly. Millie could not believe how mean Sarah had been to Clayton, and she could not understand why Clayton never showed any animosity toward her. Millie's true feeling about Sarah was that she was spoiled by her parents and they had always given in to her for all her wishes.

Millie looked at Clayton as he slept, and she determined that she would not spoil their last weekend together before he returned to the university. She moved closer to him, put her arms around him as he slept, and silently thanked God for her good fortune in marrying him. Millie would be glad when the time came for them to begin their family. She hoped for a son for Clayton, and a daughter for herself, but she knew that Clayton must finish law school before they had a family. Clayton would be returning to his university before long to continue studying for his degree in law.

Millie finally fell into a deep and peaceful sleep for several hours. Clayton awakened at his regular time of 7:00 but Millie continued to sleep soundly. Clayton slipped out of bed quietly in order not to disturb her. He decided to surprise her with breakfast in bed. After all, they had been married all of three months. Clayton remembered how Millie enjoyed breakfast served to her in bed on the first morning of their honeymoon at the Adolphus in Dallas.

Clayton had Millie's favorite breakfast prepared by 8:00, took it on a tray to their bedroom, and awakened Millie by hugging and kissing her. The breakfast tray was wonderful to her. The food consisted of a small glass of orange juice, a pot of black coffee, a small plate of toast with grape jelly, and a breakfast plate of scrambled eggs with fried, link pork sausages. The food was served on a white linen cloth and there was a large red rose with a card with writing on it. Millie smiled and read the card which said, "To Millie, my love, who is like a red, red rose," signed Clayton. Millie said, "Thank you, Clayton, I will love you until the seas go dry, my dear."

Clayton replied, "Isn't poetry wonderful especially when it is by Robert Burns?"

Clayton was so amazing to Millie because he was not always predictable. She enjoyed the frequent surprises from him. His kind gesture of serving her breakfast in bed was so appropriate this Sunday morning, because it would probably be several months before they would have a chance to have breakfast together. Millie hoped she would be able to wait for his first vacation either at Thanksgiving or the long Christmas vacation.

After breakfast, Millie and Clayton lay side by side with their arms around each other. Clayton said, "We deserve this time together. It is our third anniversary."

Millie replied, "Clayton, we have only been married three months. How could it be our third anniversary?"

"That's easy," said Clayton, "we were married three months ago, today."

"My husband is always right," said Millie.

Clayton moved closer to Millie and said, "Since you think your husband is always right, it is time for me to have some real romance with my wife." Millie had never felt such ecstasy in her whole life as Clayton made love to her, and Clayton felt the same rapture while he made love to Millie.

When they had finished their lovemaking, the couple lay still and quiet for a long time. Millie finally said to Clayton, "What are you thinking about, and why are you so quiet now?"

Clayton's reply was, "I am thinking we are now really husband and wife, and I love my wife very much." Clayton then asked, "What are your thoughts, Millie?"

Millie replied, "I am thinking about how much I love you while I am looking at the beautiful red rose on the breakfast tray. The red rose will always be a symbol of our love, and that's our secret for the rest of our life." Millie kissed the red rose, and then she handed it to Clayton who kissed the rose which sealed the secret.

Clayton said, "The red rose is now our symbol of love."

"And our own very precious secret," added Millie.

The remainder of Sunday was spent packing clothing and school supplies for Clayton to take to the university. He would be an upper classman this year, his third year of studying law. He would be given privileges which he had not had during the first two years at the university. One of the main privileges would be his own private room in the men's dormitory, with a nice view of the campus with its many elm trees. He could take personal things, and he opted to take a radio, a record player, and a coffee pot. Clayton reminded Millie about the electric fan which he wished to take along with him. Millie said, "It is almost time for fall weather."

Clayton replied, "You know how hot I often get."

Millie commented, "I certainly do." Millie was skeptical about how many more items she could pack in her small car. She kept urging him to finish packing, and warned him that not one more law book would fit in her car. But Clayton reminded her they had to go by Hillsboro House on their way to Austin. Clayton wanted to say adieu to his father and to Bessie.

Millie was very glad Craig Street was the next street and parallel to their Corsicana Street. They had a pleasant and short visit at Hillsboro House. His father wished him well, and gave Clayton a large stack of yellow legal pads to use in his study of law cases. Clayton hugged his father before leaving, and Bessie who was standing in the doorway of the entry hall suggested that she deserved a good hug from the little boy she helped rear since the time he wore diapers. Clayton hugged Bessie and told her to keep well. Bessie said, "What do you mean, my boy, I ain't never been sick in my whole life?"

"That is right," said Clayton, "because you are so mean and tough." "Now look here, boy," said Bessie, "you watch your talk. I'se got two big boxes for you and they're full of your favorite cookies made by me this morning. Nothing like fresh cookies."

"Oh, thanks, Bessie, but you know I am sweet enough."

Bessie said, "You hush your mouth and get going. You'se better learn to be a good lawyer like your own daddy."

Millie and Clayton enjoyed the long drive to Austin. It was a pleasant Sunday afternoon, and there was only a hint of fall with a slight chill in the air. Some of the trees were beginning to turn their leaves from green to brown and orange. The cotton fields were beginning to turn white with large bolls of cotton on each stalk. The cattle and the horses coats of fur were beginning to get heavy and thick for the cooler months ahead. The sun was not quite so bright, and it was located more southerly than in the spring months when it set each day in the west. A south wind was also blowing, and the weather would definitely change soon. Autumn was an interesting time in the hill country and the central part of Texas.

After a three-hour drive, they arrived in the beautiful city of Austin, the capital of the state of Texas. They arrived at the University of Texas campus which was impressive to Millie. She thought the campus was most beautiful with its fine large buildings, and the campus grounds with the many elm and oak trees which dotted it.

The men's dormitory was comfortable and the large room Clayton was assigned pleased Millie. He would be most comfortable with his own privacy for studying or listening to the radio or his record player. Millie helped him unpack and move his personal items and clothing inside. When everything had been removed from the car and was inside, Millie indicated she must start on the long drive back to Hillsboro. Clayton glanced at his three-quarter size bed and said, "There is enough room for both of us to sleep together tonight."

Millie said, "We would not get much sleep or rest tonight. I have to work in the office tomorrow, and you begin law classes tomorrow."

Clayton said, "Unfortunately, my wife is always right. But Millie promise me that you will drive at a slower speed going home than the speed you drove on the way here."

Millie said, "Oh, Clayton, you know I don't drive fast because I am not a fast girl. Give me a big hug and a long kiss, and I will be on my way home."

Millie drove cautiously on the road home, her thoughts constantly on Clayton. She would naturally miss him very much. She not only loved him; she also enjoyed his company. They had been together everyday for the past three months, and it would be three months again before they would be reunited for the Christmas holidays. As she was thinking about Clayton, she wished she had accepted his invitation to spend the last night with him in his dormitory. She could have left at 5:00 A.M. and gotten to work by 8:00 the next morning. It was against the rules for women to spend the night with men students but Clayton would have taken the chance. He could have explained that he was a married man, and his wife was spending the last evening with him before classes began the next term.

A light rain began to fall, and she had to switch on the windshield wipers which helped her see the Dallas road more clearly.

The rain did not enhance her state of mind or mood, and she was longing to arrive home to Corsicana Street. She had lived alone before and really never minded it.

Millie had neglected to check her gas gauge in the car, and she suddenly discovered that the gas tank was on empty. She was ten miles from Waco. She reduced her speed and the car made it into Waco, where she stopped at the first gas station. Fortunately, the filling station was still open even though it was after 6:00 P.M.

Millie made it safely home, but the house had an empty feeling without Clayton. The beautiful red rose was still on the tray in the bedroom. She put the red rose in a crystal vase that they had received as a wedding gift. She located a good framed photograph of Clayton, and she placed the photograph and the crystal vase with the red rose on a table in the hall so that she would see them as she moved about the house. She rested the note card from Clayton which said his love was like a red, red rose on the crystal vase.

Millie prayed to God for Clayton and herself when she went to bed that evening. She thanked God for her blessings and she prayed for Clayton's welfare. It was not in her nature to be sad and lonely. She had a philosophy that life is wonderful and that each day should be enjoyed. She always said a prayer of thanks every night before going to sleep. Her mother had taught her to pray. She thought about her parents, and she said a prayer for them. She hoped they were well, and that the cotton harvest would be good this year. Millie thought about the rain and knew the rain would not be good for the cotton crop.

VII

Holidays and the Echoes of War

Millie returned to work on Monday morning, where Judge Campbell had a very full schedule. Many clients had waited until summer was over to do legal business, instigate law suits, and update or make additions to their wills. Millie did not mention it to Judge Campbell, but she thought how wonderful it would be when Clayton could be a full-time lawyer. He could relieve his father of some of the work load. Millie was amazed that Judge Campbell could maintain such heavy work loads. The judge was not older looking, but he was no longer young.

Millie was still studying legal codes and law cases and continued to get encouragement from Clayton and his father. Millie was uncertain whether she could pass the long and tedious bar examination of Texas. It took place twice a year in Austin at the state capitol, and it lasted three days. She was unsure if she wanted to become a lawyer. There were not many women lawyers in Texas in 1940. Millie felt it was her duty to continue studying law and learn as much as possible in order to help everyone in the Campbell law firm.

Clayton wrote her every two or three days and she was pleased with his loyalty to her. He had a difficult schedule, and was required to do much research in his studies. He had to spend long hours in the law library researching famous and important decisions in court cases. Millie hoped he would not neglect his studies by writing letters to her. She wrote frequently to him and she tried to keep her letters cheerful and positive.

But there were things happening in the world which were disturbing and upsetting especially in Europe. The German armies under the command of Adolf Hitler had invaded Holland, Belgium, and Denmark. No country was safe from the German army, and Britain was preparing to defend itself against the Nazi powers and the Third Reich.

Millie received most of her news from radio reports and she had recently subscribed to the *Dallas Morning News*. The newspaper was full of the account of the beginning of the war in Europe. The foreign correspondents sent daily reports to the newspapers.

Most Americans were concerned about the war as the reports of bombing in London continued. One report indicated that Prime Minister Churchill estimated that the German Air Force flew an average of four hundred bombers a day over London from September 7 to October 7, dropping an estimated five million pounds of bombs which killed about seven thousand civilians and wounded ten thousand others. Coventry, England was attacked next for eight hours on November 15 by at least four hundred bombers. Entire city blocks were destroyed and many people were killed. Other midland cities of England came under attack by the German planes.

The Royal Air Force did its best despite the Luftwaffe having more aircraft than the RAF. Many German planes were destroyed during the day, and the Germans changed from day bombing to bombing at night.

During 1940, there were constant attacks on British ships and port facilities. It was difficult for British shipping since the Germans controlled most of the ports of Europe. The British often lost sixty thousand tons of shipping a week due to the enemy. The Irish government would not permit the British to use their ports which made an additional hardship on the British war efforts.

All these reports were disturbing to Millie and many other people in Hillsboro. Judge Campbell was concerned in case America should enter the war because Clayton was at the draft age. Many people in America did not want to become involved in a European war. American observers had been sent to Europe to look at the war effort. The American government helped the British government by sending aircraft to Britain.

The three months passed quickly for Millie; it was time for Clayton to come home for his Christmas holidays. He took the train from Austin to Hillsboro and Millie met him at the train station. She immediately noticed a change in him. He was changing physically. He was losing his boyish look and his body was developing more into manhood. They greeted and embraced each other.

Millie was pleased to have Clayton home for two weeks. They

had no big plans for celebrating the holidays like most people due to the uncertainty of the war in Europe. Even Judge Campbell decided on a smaller Christmas dinner with only Millie and Clayton and possibly two more guests. Bessie seemed more somber as she served the traditional feast at Hillsboro House. The food was just as delicious and plentiful as ever. Clayton had second helpings of the mince and pecan pies.

After the big meal had been consumed, the judge and guests retired to the large and elegantly furnished drawing room. Eggnog and cranberry punch were served and Judge Campbell had a small gift for everyone. Millie was pleased to see the good rapport between father and son, but she had some troublesome private thoughts which she kept to herself. Those private thoughts were fears, one being in case the United States became involved in the war and Clayton would be required to serve in the military to help defend the country.

When they went home that evening, Clayton sensed that Millie was preoccupied with some inner thoughts. "Millie, something is disturbing you." said Clayton. "What is the matter?"

"Nothing, absolutely, nothing," she said.

"Millie, are you afraid that we will have a war, and I might have to go to the war?"

Millie replied, "Clayton Campbell, you always read my mind."

Clayton jokingly said, "Don't worry Millie. If I had to go to the war, I would come home to you as a hero."

Millie said, "I am sure you would be a hero, and I admire heroes, but I would rather have a husband than a hero."

Clayton said, "You would love both."

Millie changed the subject, and thanked Clayton for the lovely Christmas gifts. He had given her a variety of things: a box of stationery with red roses on each page, a bottle of expensive perfume, and a book of Edna St. Vincent Millay's collected poems. Millie gave Clayton a Parker fountain pen, a shaving kit, and a bottle of fine French champagne. He asked, "May I make champagne meatballs on New Year's Eve? I want to tell Miss Emily that I have her secret recipe."

New Year's Eve was delightful for Clayton and Millie. They decided to stay at home for the evening even though they had several invitations to some of the parties in Hillsboro. Clayton was in the mood for cooking. He had inherited his mother's recipes that she had brought from her native Scotland. Clayton decided to make Scottish shortbread. Millie and Clayton had shopped that day; they had to drive to Waco for the rice flour. Clayton insisted that his mother only used four ingredients for the shortbread: regular flour, rice flour, real butter, and sugar. Millie could not believe the work involved. Clayton gradually mixed the ingredients and slowly kneaded them together before baking in the oven at a moderate heat. Millie could not believe the wonderful taste of the shortbread.

Millie also helped Clayton cook the meatballs. She made the ground beef into medium-sized balls, and Clayton cooked them in a pan over a medium heat. After they were all cooked, Clayton said, "It is time to make the champagne sauce which is Miss Emily's secret sauce for the meatballs."

"Should I leave the kitchen while you make the sauce?" asked Millie.

"Of course not," said Clayton. "You may stay here and watch me make the sauce for the meatballs." Millie noted that Clayton mixed an equal part of grape jelly and tomato ketchup together in a sauce pan. He heated them together, and then added a cup of champagne to the sauce. The sauce was then poured over the meatballs.

The champagne meatballs and the Scottish shortbread were gourmet treats for Millie. She had never tasted shortbread before and she loved the taste. The champagne meatballs were delicious. Clayton observed that the new year would be in soon. Clayton said, "Louis Blackburn will stop by as our first guest of 1941."

"I didn't realize Louis was in Hillsboro," said Millie.

"He is visiting Miss Emily for a few days. I asked him to be 'the first foot' for us," said Clayton.

Millie said, "I don't understand 'first foot.'"

Clayton explained that first foot was an old Scottish tradition for the new year. The person must have dark hair, and he will usually bring a gift and some money. The dark-haired person will bring good luck to the home for the remainder of the year. Millie said, "It is like our serving black-eyed peas on New Year's Day here in the state of Texas."

Clayton said, "You are correct, but the first foot must not be by a person of light complexion."

At 12:00, Louis Blackburn knocked on their front door, and they invited Louis into their home. He wished them a Happy New Year and presented them with a bottle of chilled champagne and a five-dollar bill.

The three of them had a pleasant visit. They opened the champagne and sipped it in champagne glasses that Miss Emily had given them. Louis apologized because Sarah Bankstead could not join them. Sarah's college sorority was having a New Year's Eve party, and she returned to college early. Louis and Clayton discussed college and shared some of their amusing collegiate situations. Each one had some unusual professors and fellow students to talk about. Louis left about 2:00 A.M. He shook hands with Clayton and he hugged Millie and wished them both a healthy and happy New Year. They thanked Louis for being the first foot in their home.

Clayton and Millie had a long sleep and rest the next morning. Clayton would be taking the train on January 2 for Austin to finish his third year of law school. When Millie awakened, she said a prayer for herself and Clayton, and she prayed the world would be a safer place in 1941.

Millie slipped out of bed in order to serve Clayton his breakfast in bed. She made her way quietly to the kitchen, and she fried a pan of J. C. Potter's country sausages. Then she mixed milk and flour to make a pancake batter. She fried a large plate of pancakes, and then she pored a pitcher of dark Karo syrup. She had a red rose hidden on the service porch for the occasion. She arranged the breakfast neatly on the tray and took it to Clayton, who was still asleep. She called his name gently but he continued to sleep very soundly.

Millie touched and rubbed his big shoulders and said, "Happy New Year, Sir Clayton, my handsome knight." Clayton opened his eyes and smiled.

He said, "Happy New Year to my Lady Millie." She gave him the freshly cooked breakfast which he could smell already. He saw the red rose on the tray, picked it up and smelt it. Clayton then said, "Can I have breakfast later?"

"You may have your breakfast later, but it will be cold," said Millie.

"Darn it, Millie, you are always right on everything, but I think I will have a cold breakfast this morning because I have something else I need to do." Clayton gently pulled Millie into bed with him.

Clayton had his breakfast an hour later, after Millie rewarmed the country sausages and the hot cakes. Clayton devoured the food quickly and Millie praised his very good appetite. Clayton said, "I am looking forward to a pot of black-eyed peas later today." Millie gave him a strange look because she had forgotten to cook a large pot of black-eyed peas. Clayton reminded her that it was a tradition among southern people to serve black-eyed peas on New Year's day. It is suppose to bring good luck for the remainder of the year.

Millie developed a plan of action to secure the black-eyed peas. She telephoned Bessie at Hillsboro House to see if she had cooked black-eyed peas for New Year's day. "I shore did," said Bessie, "a whole big pot full. They're the best ever cause I cooked them with salt pork and onions." Millie told Bessie of her predicament. Bessie said, "Don't you worry; I'll send you a lot of black-eyed peas right now."

Millie said, "Thanks, Bessie, you have saved the day for me, but please keep this a secret between you and me."

"It's a secret; I have a whole bunch of secrets to keep," said Bessie. "The good Lord made me to keep secrets."

Shortly after the conversation with Bessie, Millie heard a gentle knock at the back door. When she opened it, there was Bessie's husband Tom with a large pot of freshly cooked black-eyed peas. Millie thanked Tom, and he said, "You is most welcome, Miss Millie." Tom left quietly and Millie put the pot of black-eyed peas on the kitchen stove. Bessie had also sent several pieces of hot corn bread to have with the black-eyed peas.

Millie then went to the living room where Clayton was reading a book, and she announced that the black-eyed peas were ready. Clayton was surprised as he did not think Millie had cooked black-eyed peas for the New Year. Clayton went into the kitchen to look at the freshly cooked peas. Clayton said, "They look and smell delicious, but I have never seen this cooking pot before."

She said, "I don't use that pot very often."

There were black-eyed peas and cornbread for lunch. Clayton wanted seconds so he would double his chances for good luck. As he was eating his second bowl of black-eyed peas, Clayton exclaimed, "These are the best black-eyed peas I have ever had, but don't you tell Bessie what I just said about the peas."

Millie said, "Let's keep this a secret."

The next morning Millie took Clayton to the station to catch his train for Austin. They hugged and kissed each other good-bye and told each other to keep well until the spring break when Clayton would return. After he had gone on the train, Millie felt that she was always saying good-bye to Clayton.

PART FOUR

I

The Dangerous Situation of the World

The conflicts among the nations of the world were disturbing to most people of the world at the beginning of the forties. There was much tension within nearly every family in America during the year of 1941 due to the Selective Service Act created by the government. President Franklin Roosevelt had signed the first Selective Training and Service Act on September 16, 1940. The Act called for the annual training of not more than nine hundred thousand men at any one time in the land and naval forces of the United States. The Selective Service Act also provided for the classification of millions of other men on the basis of their availability and general qualifications for use in military and civilian endeavors in times of emergency. The Act also provided for a reserve of men trained in the various branches of the service.

President Roosevelt issued a proclamation fixing October 16, 1940 as the first day of registration. Over sixteen million men registered for service, the first group of men being inducted in November 1940. By January 1, 1941, about one million American men were inducted into the armed forces through the Selective Training and Service Act.

The dangerous situation of the world continued to spread to many countries during 1941. Many American mothers were upset and concerned about the possibility of a World War II for America. Almost every family in America would have one or more members that might be drafted by the Selective Service Act.

Dora was concerned about her son, J. D., even though he was only sixteen years of age. Various sources including magazines, newspapers, and the radio implied that eighteen-year-old men would have to register and serve in the military if a world war should spread.

Jake and Dora Martin still came to Hillsboro on Saturdays for their weekly shopping. They usually visited with Millie Jean before returning to the farm later in the day in order to do the evening chores. Millie was close to her family, and she shared her concern with her mother regarding the possibility that her brother would be drafted in the future if the war continued. Millie served her parents lunch almost every Saturday and sometimes the family would stay for an early supper. However, they always left early for the evening care of the farm animals.

Dora Martin usually brought some items from the farm for Millie such as a dozen fresh eggs or a pound of freshly churned butter. Millie's favorite item was freshly ground pork sausage with lots of sage added to the meat. Dora brought fresh vegetables in the springtime.

Jake Martin felt that a good meal must consist of a pan of hot fried potatoes. Her father judged every meal by how delicious the fried potatoes tasted. Millie had learned from her mother how to fry potatoes in a cast-iron frying pan with a lid on it. The Crisco shortening must be hot when the peeled and sliced potatoes were dropped into the hot pan. Millie added salt and pepper, and she turned the potatoes often with a spatula. When they were half cooked, she put the large iron lid on the frying pan and let the potatoes cook slowly until they were completely cooked. It was all so very simple. Millie knew that if she pleased her father with his plain and limited taste, the meal would please her mother.

J. D. usually went to the Plaza Theater on the square in Hillsboro to see a new western film. It cost twenty-five cents to see a movie on Saturdays during the daytime. J. D.'s favorite western star was Gene Autry. J. D. loved to hear Gene Autry sing "Back in the Saddle Again" and that "Silver-Haired Daddy of Mine." J. D. never missed any of Gene Autry's films. Every Friday, J. D. studied the skies and clouds of Texas to see if it might be raining on Saturday. If it rained considerably on Saturday, the family could not drive the pick-up truck over the mud-filled dirt road which led to the paved highway into town. J. D. prayed that Saturdays would always be dry and clear of the frequent rain storms in Texas. Of course, there were some rainy Saturdays, and J. D. felt bad about that.

On the rainy Saturdays, his mother suggested that he read books. J. D. replied, "Mom, I can read books the other days of the week. I like to go to town on Saturdays so I can buy some things and see a good movie." J. D. wished that he lived in town like his sister, Millie. He was beginning to think he might like a job in town when he finished high school provided the army did not draft him. His father often reminded him that he was the only son on the farm, and if he remained on the farm to help with the work, the draft board might excuse him from military duty. This was frustrating to J. D. who was not anxious to become a soldier, nor was he anxious to continue living on the farm for the rest of his life. J. D. realized he would be confronted with danger if he went into the military, but deep down in his mind, he would love to see different parts of the world. He kept these private thoughts a secret from his father and mother.

J. D.'s parents did not say openly too much about the future but he could sense their concern. He could observe the worry on their faces and he could feel the somber mood of his mother. He felt his mother was quieter and more serious than normal for her. He did not enjoy seeing his mother worried about anything.

The Martins were not alone with their serious concern for their son. There were many Texas families who were anxious about their sons. Some families had several sons who might be required to serve in the army. Families and their members became closer and tried to comfort each other. They all secretly knew that in case of war not all sons would return home safely and some sons might never trod the Texas soil ever again.

Dora prayed every night for the welfare of her son, her son-in-law Clayton, and several of her nephews. She prayed to God every night to keep and protect the young men of her family safe from harm.

Dora looked at the clock each day at 3:30 when the big yellow school bus brought J. D. home from school. He was now a sophomore at Hillsboro High School. On one particular afternoon, the school bus arrived shortly after 3:30, and Dora pulled the lace curtains apart so that she could peer out the glass window and see J. D. exit from the school bus. On this certain afternoon, she could not believe the size of her son. He seemed to be growing and getting taller with wide shoulders everyday. She had tears in her eyes because he was at the dawn of manhood. Dora had found several notes from girls in his shirt pockets. She realized that some young lady would soon put her claim on him, and if not, the army would be after him. She knew that she and Jake would be alone before long. The years had passed so rapidly with her two children.

Dora thanked God for her children because they were good children; they had never given her any problems. She was grateful to God that her two children did not smoke cigarettes or drink beer. She knew about one or two young men in their community who had beer parties on Saturday nights. Dora did not believe in drinking liquor of any kind. She believed the Bible taught against strong drink, and she believed the most awful thing in life was to see a person drunk on liquor.

Jake smoked tobacco, and she was not totally happy about this. Jake was a smoker when she met him many years ago. He rolled his own cigarettes and she had become accustomed to his bright red tins of Prince Albert tobacco. Most of the men in the country smoked cigarettes made from Prince Albert tobacco. Dora was glad that Jake did not smoke cigars as she did not like the smell of them. Dora was also glad that he did not drink liquor. If Jake drank whisky, it was such a small amount that she had never noticed. Dora was aware that most country men kept a bottle of whisky hidden in the barn. When visiting neighbors, Dora was often suspicious when the men spent all the time visiting at the barn. She hoped they were discussing farm matters. Dora would sometimes question Jake on the way home about the topic of conversation in the barn between the two men. Dora could determine by the tone of Jake's conversation if he had taken a swallow of whisky from the bottle.

J. D. knew how opposed his mother was to drinking liquor. He used to tease his mother about Millie and Clayton drinking champagne. Dora denied they were drinkers even though champagne was served at their large wedding. J. D. persisted, "I don't think Clayton and Millie are teetotalers." Dora Martin would change the subject which she often did if something was distasteful to her.

II

Last Wills and Testaments

Millie Jean continued to work devotedly at the law firm. Judge Campbell had many clients which he saw almost daily and many more whom he saw weekly. Millie was concerned about the pressure the judge was constantly under and she was amazed at his stamina. She wrote to Clayton telling about her concern for the amount of work the judge was doing. Clayton wrote in his letter to Millie that the Campbells were a strong and hearty clan, and they could cope with work and responsibility.

Millie continued to study law in the evenings, utilizing the library of the judge. She read all the books which were available, but she did not feel competent that she could pass the Texas Bar Examination. She decided to take the correspondence course in civil law. Clayton was able to arrange an extension course in law through the Department of the University of Texas. The first three or four lessons were easy, but the following lessons were more difficult. Millie decided that she must continue to do more research.

The months went very quickly for her. She tried to keep abreast of the world situation by reading various news magazines and daily newspapers. She hoped world conditions would improve. Unfortunately, each month seemed to worsen in the European conflict. There were also reports about trouble with the eastern countries such as Japan which was creating problems for the western world.

Due to her busy schedule, Millie did not see Miss Emily as much as she would have enjoyed visiting with her. Miss Emily did come into the law office one day and asked Millie if she would do a special favor for her. Millie and Clayton had always been most fond of Miss Emily Blackburn. Millie was very curious as to what the favor might be and she mentally prepared herself for this special request.

Miss Emily began, "I am not as young as I used to be; I would like some changes in my last will and testament."

Millie glanced at her, and said, "Miss Emily, I think you are in your prime of life. You do not look old, and I think you are only middle age."

She replied, "You are correct, Millie, but I often have chest pains in the night. Please keep this a secret between us. I would not want Louis and Sarah to know. She continued, "Millie, would you be the final executor of my will?"

"Of course," said Millie, "I would be honored, but you know, you may outlive me."

Miss Emily said, "That is true, but I would like you to be my executor in case I don't outlive you." They went into the judge's private office where he made a new codicil to Miss Emily's will making Millie her executor. Millie did not know the provisions of the will, and she preferred not to know the terms at this time. She assumed that Louis, the nephew, would be the main heir to her rather large estate.

When she had gone, Judge Campbell came into the outer office and said he was rather surprised at Miss Emily's decision today. He complimented Millie and said, "I am sure you will be a good and competent executor." Millie did not really know how to answer the judge because she had never had such an important request before. She thought much about the will, and she decided she would follow the terms of the will which any executor should and must do.

When she went to bed that evening, she lay awake hours thinking about Miss Emily and her will. She wondered why Miss Emily did not make her nephew, Louis, her executor. She also wondered what Miss Emily really thought about the engagement of Sarah and Louis. Before falling asleep, Millie felt that some day she might understand why Miss Emily made her the final executor of her will because she was second in charge of the law firm.

The next day Millie looked at the many wills in the large walk-in safe in the law office. She saw the will of Emily Blackburn, which had a seal on it that should only be opened in case of death. She decided that she would honor Miss Emily's wishes by keeping the provisions of the will secret. There were more than a hundred client's wills including that of Judge Campbell. She wondered how the judge would distribute his large estate.

Millie knew the contents of the wills because she had typed most of the wills for the clients of the judge. Each will required the signatures of two witnesses, and Millie was usually one of the witnesses. She was often amazed with the last wishes of many people. Some people used their wills as an instrument to get even with their heirs by only leaving them one dollar. One man who had only one son from an early marriage left the son a dollar. The man gave the residue of his estate to a lady friend he had only known three years. Millie had some definite private thoughts about this which she could not discuss with anyone. Surely there must have been friends or family who had been kind or helpful during his over eighty years of living.

One very elderly client, a woman of over ninety years of age, changed the heirs of her will every few months. When she met someone new to her (she usually liked them) she would include them in her will. Judge Campbell would always ask her about the present heirs. The client's usual reply was, "I don't want them in my will. Please take their names out of my will." Judge Campbell firmly had to put his foot down. In fact, he had to become emphatic about telling her that she must not constantly change her will.

He told her, "A will is meant to be your final wishes, and it is legally referred to as my last will and testament."

Millie felt that wills were interesting. If she became a lawyer, she would enjoy helping people write their last wills. Millie even liked the definition of a will which is a legal statement of a person's wishes about what shall be done with their property after they are dead. A will is really a document containing such a statement.

The last will and testament reveals many things about a person according to Judge Campbell. It reveals the inner character of the person. The judge said he could usually determine the attitude and personality of an individual after he read their will. The will gave him insight into the motives of the person who had the will drawn. Some people are kind and generous while others are selfish and resent leaving their property to anyone. Most people leave their estate to their next of kin which might be husband or wife or their children. Sometimes the heirs may be close friends or neighbors who have been kind to the person during their life time. There were a few unusual wills that Judge Campbell had made for clients. He did not always agree with the client on the terms, but he respected their wishes in almost every situation as long as it was within the laws of the state of Texas.

Millie Jean thought some of the wills were fascinating. She was astonished with that of one client who left her entire estate to her large house cat named Wilbur. The client was not very wealthy but she was not poor either. When she died, Wilbur inherited the house and his favorite furniture which he enjoyed resting upon. A caretaker was designated to maintain the house and yard for Wilbur. Wilbur lived several more years, and since he produced no heir or had any known heirs, the house was sold, and the proceeds of the property were given to local charities. Judge Campbell had faithfully administered the terms of the will for several years.

Laws were interesting to Millie, especially laws relating to estates. She decided that as a lawyer she would specialize in making wills and administering estates. She decided to study law until she could pass the Bar examination.

Millie told Judge Campbell of her decision. He said, "Wonderful, I could use a good lawyer in this office." Judge Campbell was extremely helpful to her in answering questions or explaining the legality of many given situations. He also suggested that Millie attend conferences and seminars for law students. Millie wrote to Clayton to find out if there would be any seminars or conferences which she could attend at the University of Texas.

Clayton replied immediately to Millie's letter, and he gladly arranged for Millie to attend a three-day conference at the university which would be opened for Texans who were planning to become lawyers. The conference took place during the spring break of 1941. Clayton suggested that Millie join him in Austin for his one week of the school vacation. She was thrilled because she was anxious to see her husband. Springtime was beginning with the elm trees turning green. She would enjoy the drive to Austin, and she hoped she would spot some fields of blue bonnets blooming on the way.

Judge Campbell and Millie arranged for Elizabeth Horton to cover for Millie while she was away in Austin. It pleased Millie that Elizabeth could substitute for her. Millie was fond of her and considered her to be a sincere employee of the firm.

The night before Millie was to leave for Austin, she spent most of the evening packing for her vacation with Clayton. Bessie was sending him some home made chocolate-chip cookies, and Bessie was not pleased that Clayton was not coming home for the Easter vacation. Millie explained to Bessie that she and Clayton were going to attend legal conferences during the week. She promised Bessie that Clayton would be home for the summer months.

When Millie had finished packing and was preparing for bed, the telephone rang. She answered the telephone, and a rather loud voice of a woman said, "Happy Easter to Clayton and Millie, and a very pink Easter to you both." Millie was not happy with the greeting; it was the voice of Sarah Bankstead. Sarah was calling to invite Millie to have lunch with her the next day at Bob's Cafe, and she emphasized it was the only decent place in Hillsboro to eat a hamburger. "The day after tomorrow," Sarah said, "I am leaving to spend the Easter vacation in New Orleans with dear Louis. Isn't that just peachy? Louis is just like peaches and cream."

Millie thanked Sarah for the kind invitation to have a hamburger with her, but she was glad to tell Sarah that she was leaving early the next morning for Austin to join Clayton for a week. Sarah said, "Give big Clayton a hundred hugs for me, and one very long kiss and also tell him that I miss him."

Sarah then mentioned the war in Europe. It was so horrible and devastating, and something must be done for them. She also mentioned that she and some of her girl friends were considering joining the U.S.O. to help do their share. Of course, she would have to obtain permission from darling Louis in New Orleans. "I know it will upset him, but we must do what we have to do is my philosophy," said Sarah. She continued, "Darling, you sound tired. Go to bed now and have lots of fun in Austin. Don't forget to hug Clayton for me."

Millie undressed and went to bed hoping that she would go to sleep immediately. She could not stop thinking about the telephone conversation with Sarah Bankstead, who always depressed her when she mentioned Clayton. She admitted privately to herself that she was jealous of Sarah and Clayton. She kept asking herself, "Why does Sarah continually ask me to hug and kiss Clayton for her?" She was most frustrated, and she decided sometime in the future she would tell Sarah in a most emphatic way to discontinue her remarks about giving hugs and kisses to Clayton. Millie resented Sarah using the words "big, handsome, and gorgeous" to describe Clayton. Some day she would have the courage to tell Sarah, "After all, he married me, not you, Sarah." She thought how wonderful it would be if Sarah joined the U.S.O. and was eventually assigned far from Texas.

Yet Millie was not totally pleased with these very personal thoughts. She remembered that her mother always said, "Be a nice person and be nice to every one."

She did not fall asleep for a long time even though she was leaving early the next morning. She was looking forward to seeing Clayton whom she missed very much. At this very moment she would love to run her fingers through his full head of blond hair. She would love to massage his big broad shoulders, and then place her arms around his strong masculine body. She gradually went to sleep while thinking about her beloved Clayton who was certainly not Sarah's "dear Clayton."

She slept peacefully most of the night until she awoke from a dream about Clayton. The dream was disturbing. She was in the city of Austin but she could not locate Clayton. His classmates said he had gone on a long trip. Millie was worried, and she could not understand why Clayton was not there to greet her. She could not believe that he had gone on a long trip; she felt he was somewhere in Austin. She was determined to find him. At this point in the dream, the alarm clock began ringing at 6:00 much to her relief.

She was so glad it was only a dream but it was a most frightening one to her. She decided not to tell anyone about it, and she remembered that her mother always advised never to tell a dream before breakfast because it might come true.

Millie arose from her bed, got dressed, and prepared for her journey to Austin.

III

Millie Attends a Seminar in Austin

Millie arrived in Austin at noon after the long drive from Hillsboro. While driving through the city to the university, she understood why Clayton enjoyed the University of Texas and the city of Austin. The setting was most delightful with large spacious parks, prestigious homes, and an abundance of many beautiful green trees. She drove to the campus of the university and to the men's dormitory where she would be permitted to reside with Clayton during the Easter break of 1941. Clayton was waiting in front of the red brick dormitory for Millie, dressed in a white short-sleeved shirt and navy-blue slacks. As she was parking the roadster, she thought she had never seen him look more handsome. He had wonderful posture and a marvelous physique. It was a great relief to see him waiting for her considering the dream she had during the past night. Clayton hugged and kissed her several times and said, "What a wonderful week we will have together here in Austin!"

He mentioned that there were many wonderful things to do and see in the capital city. She knew that Clayton would have the week planned and organized for them. Clayton was the most organized person she knew. Millie asked him, "What is first on the agenda?"

Clayton replied, "The first thing on the agenda will be going to bed together tonight."

Millie's face turned a pale pink, and she said, "Why, Clayton, you have no shame at all."

Clayton countered, "Millie, I love to shock you because you're so sweet and innocent."

Millie replied, "I don't think I am going to be innocent long while I am with you."

Clayton said, "Seriously, Millie, I think the first thing should be a tour of the Texas Capitol Building which is impressive, and it is important to the people of Texas. We will have a quick sandwich and a Coca-Cola before the tour."

After their lunch, Clayton and Millie went to Twelfth Street for the tour. Millie was most impressed with the large granite structure with a large dome in the center which resembled pictures she had seen of the Capitol in Washington, D.C. Clayton asked Millie, "Would you like a personal guided tour by me, or would you prefer an official tour guide?" Millie did not hesitate to say she would prefer a personal tour by Clayton.

He explained that the present Capitol Building was built between 1882 and 1888, and it was modeled on the Capitol in Washington, D.C. The original plan called for native limestone, but the limestone was unsuitable for the building. Finally, Texas granite was chosen as the primary building material. Clayton pointed out the cornerstone which was laid on March 2, 1885 on the forty-ninth anniversary of the date of Texas Independence. The pink granite stone which came from Burnet County weighed sixteen thousand pounds. It took sixteen yoke of oxen to pull a wagon to the nearest rail where it was shipped by train to the Capitol grounds. A great assemblage of people and important Texans from the government and civic officials were invited to witness the ceremony of the cornerstone. A forty-nine gun salute was fired in honor of the forty-ninth anniversary of Texas Independence. The state seal and the dates March 2, 1836<N>March 2, 1885 and the State of Texas were carved on the stone. Clayton mentioned that a zinc box was placed in the niche of the cornerstone containing various historical mementos. Among the items were currency from the Republic of Texas, a stone from the old Capitol, an 1862 meal ticket for twenty-five cents, and an Austin City directory. The stone was handsomely polished, and it weighed twelve thousand pounds when set.

Millie was amazed at the information that Clayton knew about the Capitol. He had always been a student of Texas history since his father introduced him to the Alamo and the struggle for independence

Before entering the Capitol Building, Millie observed the commanding view of the city of Austin. She commented to Clayton on the classical style of architecture and the immense size of the structure. The dimensions of the building at the extremes are five hundred sixty-six feet long by two hundred eighty-eight feet wide. The building is three stories in height above the basement with a fourth story running from the north to the south pediment. The dome of the Capitol rises to three hundred and eight feet to the star of the statue of the Goddess of Liberty. The building is only second in size to the National Capitol in Washington, D.C. for a similar structure. The Capitol building has nearly four hundred rooms, over nine hundred windows, and at least four hundred more doors. It took over fifteen thousand car loads of red granite for the exterior walls. Granite cutters from Aberdeen, Scotland were hired since there was a controversy with the International Association of Granite Cutters who voted to boycott the Capitol construction.

Clayton ended, "I think you have been told enough today about the exterior of the Capitol—let's go and tour the inside."

Millie was in awe of the enormous colorful terrazzo floors. Funds for the marble floors were appropriated by the forty-fourth legislature in 1935. The marble floors were quarried in Texas by a Texas architect. Several mosaic and tile companies were utilized who were not Texans. Their efforts created one of the largest and most beautiful floors in the world.

In the south foyer, twelve memorials of the battles fought by early Texans for independence are commemorated in marble. The floor of the Rotunda represents the seals of the six nations whose flags have flown over Texas. Millie was also impressed with the two marble statues in the south foyer which were created by Elisabet Ney, a German sculptress. The statues are Stephen F. Austin, who founded the first Anglo-American colony in Texas, and the other statue is Sam Houston, who was Commander-in-Chief of Texas forces during the Revolution. He was the first elected President of the Republic of Texas.

Millie enjoyed seeing the remainder of the tour, especially the Governor's Reception Room on the second floor, used also for signing bills and for many ceremonial functions. Many of the fine and beautiful Victorian furnishings are still in use from the time they were placed there in 1889.

Millie thoroughly enjoyed her tour of the Capitol, never dreaming that it would be so impressive. She was surprised at how much Texas history she had learned that day. She thanked Clayton, and she told him that she would never forget this wonderful afternoon tour. She was proud to be a native Texan.

Clayton and Millie had a pleasant dinner and evening at the famous Driskill Hotel, Austin's grande dame hotel. The Driskill was opened on December 20, 1886, by Colonel J. L. Driskill. Clayton and Millie were served an elaborate dinner in the main dining room. She enjoyed the elegance of the evening, but she told Clayton that she hoped they would not dine so elaborately every evening. Clayton replied, "Of course not, Millie, I am a student and my budget is limited. I thought we should have one high-class dinner and evening prior to your law seminar at the university." Millie realized Clayton always had the right reply, and he was usually in control of every situation. She continued to enjoy the evening. Clayton said, "Let's celebrate tonight, because we are together. We will have a bowl of Texas chili tomorrow night down on the river."

The next three days Millie attended and participated in the seminar for prospective lawyers who wanted to pass the Texas Bar Examination. She attended and heard outstanding lectures followed by discussion groups over two and one-half days, gaining much information on Texas law and the bar exam. On the last afternoon of the seminar, a sample test was given from 1:00 to 4:00 P.M. Millie felt competent about the written test, and she hoped that she would make a passing grade on the examination. She observed that several students were having problems with many questions. She could not have answered the questions if she had not been studying law at home each night.

There were forty students in the study group, and Millie was one of the five women participants. The thirty-five men were pleasant to her, but she wondered if they considered her serious about becoming a lawyer. "Well," she thought, "I will show them." She turned in her exam just before the deadline of 4:00, and observed that some students looked pleased while others seemed disappointed. All the students were invited back at 8:00 P.M. for a reception, and the results of the tests would be made known to each student. The law professors would make recommendations on areas of law and courses of study which might be helpful to each participant. Millie was nervous, but she felt good about the examination. She invited Clayton to attend the reception which was in the beautiful foyer of the law library. They enjoyed mingling with several participants and their guests who were from various areas of Texas.

At 8:30, the results of the tests were announced by the head of the law department, Dr. George Harris. The reception became very quiet as Professor Harris spoke to the group of future lawyers and their guests. He thanked everyone for their attendance and the wonderful effort by all the participants in the seminar for prospective lawyers of Texas. He emphasized that almost all participants showed good possibilities of becoming lawyers. In fact, over half of the group passed the sample examination, and five students scored ninety-five to one hundred per cent on the examination. Millie felt nervous, and Clayton squeezed her hand and gave her an encouraging pat on the shoulders.

The professor said, "It is now my pleasure to announce the five outstanding law students of this seminar. The anticipation was unbelievable in the reception area. Professor Harris continued, "The fifth outstanding student is Mr. Thomas Moreau. The fourth is Mr. John Clarke. The third is Mr. Stanley Jeffers. The second is Mr. Paul Nelson." The professor continued, "The most outstanding student, who made one hundred per cent in the examination, is Mrs. Millie Jean Campbell." Clayton hugged Millie, and Millie could not believe what she had heard. She asked Clayton, "Did I hear the professor correctly?"

He said, "You heard correctly, and you're a genius. But don't begin crying." Professor Harris asked the five students to stand for recognition and an applause from everyone. Everyone came around and congratulated them.

This recognition was a turning point in Millie's life. She knew that she would be a lawyer some day. She said to herself, "I will take the law exam in the near future, and I am confident I will pass." It pleased her to think she and Clayton would be a law team some time in the future.

Clayton was most proud of Millie's success at the law seminar. It was unusual for a woman to receive such an honor. The remainder of the week was enjoyable, but the highlight for the week was Millie's honor of being selected as the most outstanding student of the law seminar.

Sunday, the last day of spring break and the end of Millie's visit, arrived much too soon for them. They had a pleasant Sunday brunch at a good restaurant before Millie was to drive home to Hillsboro.

Millie mentioned to Clayton that he seemed very contemplative today. "Yes, I suppose I am contemplative today."

"Why?" asked Millie, even though she could surmise.

"Millie," Clayton said, "this is 1941 and a war is taking place in Europe, and I think America will become involved soon."

Millie said, "I hope not. We don't want a war."

"You're right," Millie, "but we have no choice. Unless someone stops the aggression, it will continue to spread. If America gets into the war, I will join the military service of our country."

Millie said, "Oh, no, I would not permit you to join the service."

But Clayton said, "I might not have a choice. But now you must return to Hillsboro and begin practicing law as soon as you can become a lawyer. Say hello to my father and dear old Bessie."

Millie kissed Clayton good-bye and told him that she loved and adored him. She thanked him for the most wonderful week of her life, and said she was looking forward to the time in the future when he would return to Hillsboro to practice law. Millie assured Clayton they would have a long and happy life together in Hillsboro. Clayton replied, "I hope you are right, Millie."

Millie was quiet and serious during the long drive home. She was pleased with her outstanding honor at the law seminar, but she was disturbed about Clayton's desire to join the military if America became involved in the war.

IV

The Law Examination

Judge Campbell had heard the good news from Austin about Millie receiving the top honor in the law seminar. The entire office staff of the firm congratulated her on her special honor. The law firm declared Monday as "Millie Jean Martin Campbell Day," and the judge and the staff took Millie to lunch to celebrate. They all realized that Millie would soon be a bona fide lawyer.

Millie continued to work during the day and study law each night. She studied volumes of case studies. She was blessed with an excellent memory for details which enhanced her progress in the study of legal matters. Within a few weeks, she received a registered letter from the Texas State Bar Examination in Austin. She could hardly wait to open the official letter from the Chief Examiner. To her amazement the letter read:

> Texas Bar Association
> Austin, Texas
> May 15, 1941

Millie Martin Campbell
Campbell Law Firm
Hillsboro, Texas

Dear Mrs. Campbell,

The Texas Bar Association was extremely pleased with the results of your examination at the Law Seminar at the University of Texas Law School and cosponsored by the Texas Bar Association. The committee has discussed and reviewed your examination, and we find it to be the most outstanding examination we have had the privilege of reviewing.

The Chief of the State Examiner's office and the Texas Bar Association cordially invites you to return to Austin as soon as possible.

We would like you to return to Austin for an additional written exam of three hours, and agree to be interviewed for an additional hour by the Office of the Chief of Examinations.

We would appreciate hearing from you as soon as possible. Please select any Thursday in the month of June for the final examination and interview.

Sincerely,

Benjamin Johnson
Chief Examiner

Millie Jean was overwhelmed and excited by the letter. The intention and tone of the letter was almost beyond her comprehension. She kept asking herself, "Am I qualified to become a lawyer? What would Clayton think? How would he react? After all, he has another year of law school at the university."

Millie decided to telephone Clayton in Austin and tell him the astounding news in the letter. His reaction was almost incredible. She said to him, "I truthfully feel I am too young and inexperienced to become a lawyer at this time; I think I should wait, Clayton, until you graduate from law school."

Clayton replied, "Don't be foolish, Millie, hundreds of law students would seize this marvelous opportunity!"

Millie asked, "Do you think Judge Campbell had an influence with the Texas Bar Examiners?"

Clayton countered, "Certainly my father has influence with the State Bar and the State Examiner, but he has no influence on who is going to pass or fail the examination to become a lawyer." He continued, "If my father had that kind of influence, his integrity would prevent him from using his position. Millie, you understand I must finish another year of law school and then I must pass the State Bar Examination before I become a lawyer. Millie, please take this opportunity; you deserve it."

Millie said, "I will think about it. I'll speak to Judge Campbell soon and maybe my mother." Millie thanked Clayton for his encouragement, and she ended the conversation by saying, "I wish I could give you this same opportunity."

Clayton chuckled and said, "Let's become one lawyer at a time in this family."

The next morning, Millie showed the important letter to Judge Campbell and he was very pleased. "I sure hate to lose a good secretary but I could use another good lawyer in the firm." Millie thanked him for his genuine support.

She then decided she would discuss the matter with her mother even though her mother would not have the knowledge or the experience to help her. The next evening she drove out to the farm surprising her parents, who were worried that something was wrong because of the unexpected visit. Supper was almost ready, but her mother tried to add a few things to the menu. J. D. said, "We would only have had fried potatoes if you had not come out to visit us tonight." Dora gave J. D. a warning look.

The family knew that Millie had something important to tell then. She explained about the law seminar she had attended in Austin and the honor she received which was followed by another letter asking her to return to Austin as soon as possible for more testing and an interview. Dora was thrilled and she expressed her pleasure. "Oh, my, my, my little girl is going to be a big lawyer." Jake said nothing, but he looked very pleased.

J. D. said, "That's real great Millie. If I ever get into trouble, you can defend me." Millie gave J. D. an unpleasant look.

After supper was over, Millie said, "I must return to Hillsboro before it gets dark, but I wanted to share this information with you."

The whole family congratulated her and wished her much success. Millie hugged all three before leaving. Her mother waved and watched the car raise dust as she drove away on the dirt road before reaching the pavement on the highway into Hillsboro.

She slept well that night, and awoke early the next morning. She made the decision to go to Austin for three more hours of testing and an interview. She typed her letter to the Bar Association and requested the third Thursday in June for the exam and the interview.

Clayton arrived home from the university during the first part of June. Millie was delighted to have him home again for the summer. He worked daily in the firm, and he and Millie usually stayed home in the evening so she could study and review complicated law matters which she might have to answer on the test. Clayton was most helpful and supportive. He constantly queried her on various legal matters.

The third Thursday of June arrived, and Millie decided to go alone to Austin for the test and the interview. Millie arose early since she had to be in Austin at 9:00 A.M., and she arrived a few minutes before 9:00. The secretary of the chief examiner welcomed her and explained they had the Bar Exam ready for her. Some of the minor questions had been eliminated, but she would be required to answer important questions. She began the test, and realized it was not going to be easy. Every question seemed difficult. She was permitted one fifteen minute break, but she only wanted a glass of water. Finally at 11:50, she was told she had only ten more minutes to complete the examination. Millie had finished the difficult examination but she decided to check her answers. She was uncertain about one part on corporate law in the state of Texas, but she decided to guess and speculate on the corporate law question.

Millie turned her test in at noon. The secretary smiled and thanked her, and she also told Millie to return at 1:30 for an oral interview by a panel from the Bar Association. When she returned at the designated time, she was ushered into the private office of the chief examiner. He greeted her cordially, and explained that he would moderate a panel of six attorneys who would have ten minutes each to ask her a question or questions. She must answer the questions to the best of her knowledge, and each panelist must agree that she answered the questions correctly or nearly correctly.

The questioning began, and each panelist promised they would not ask questions which were tricky nor would they try to confuse her. Millie felt more relaxed when she was told the manner of questioning. Each of the panelists took their allotted ten minutes. Millie was reasonably confident of her answers, and she felt good by the end of the interview.

She was naturally interested in the results of the written test and the interview which she had taken that day. The chief examiner told her she would receive a notice or letter within a few days stating the results. He thanked Millie for attending, and he hoped the results would be favorable for her.

Millie drove home in a somber mood. She hoped she passed the examination and the oral interview. She was disappointed that they did not give her the results today as she had expected them to have done. Millie thought how embarrassing it would be to her if she failed the exam and the interview. Clayton, Judge Campbell, and her family were anticipating her passing the examination.

Clayton welcomed her home, and he was anxious to hear the results of the exam and the interview. He was somewhat disappointed that she would have to wait a few days more before she learned of the results. Each day seemed like a month to Millie and Clayton. They were impatient for the results to be mailed to her, but Clayton constantly reassured her that she would pass the exam with honors and receive her license to practice law in the state of Texas.

V

Summertime, Again

The summers were always a most wonderful time in the town of Hillsboro. The streets were beautiful with the large green elm trees and the mimosa trees in bloom and the large green front lawns. The enormous old white houses looked beautiful among the tall green trees and various shrubs.

The summers were hot and humid. But the residents knew how to cope with the heat. They had electric fans and ceiling fans which kept the air moving inside the houses. If the fans did not work effectively, they sat on the front porch in white wicker chairs and hoped for a gentle cool breeze from the southeast.

Large blocks of ice were delivered to most homes every few days. Iced tea was the official summer drink for everyone. Not one family would consider having the noon and evening meals without a tall glass of iced tea which had been thoroughly sweetened with white sugar. Some hostesses took pride in having iced tea sets, a large glass pitcher and matching glasses. Round glass goblets on stems were popular with long narrow iced tea spoons which were made in nice silver plate. If it was a very hot day and most summer days were, iced tea would be served throughout the day. Life without iced tea in Hillsboro would have been boring.

Millie and Clayton tolerated the heat with numerous glasses of iced tea. They enjoyed picnics and backyard suppers. They enjoyed being together and doing simple things together. They enjoyed visiting friends and family. They often made impromptu calls on Judge Campbell, and Bessie insisted on serving food.

They enjoyed driving out to the country and having supper with Millie's parents. Dora expected them on each Wednesday evening for supper. Clayton enjoyed eating, and Dora tried to improve on each Wednesday with the fresh vegetables from her garden. Clayton enjoyed fried okra in corn meal, fried yellow squash in flour, fresh sliced red tomatoes, green onions, radishes, and leaf

176

lettuce followed by a large dessert. Jake would often tease Millie by saying, "Millie, you have a good husband, but you need to feed him more."

Dora was pleased that Clayton enjoyed eating, and she often said, "I have no patience with people who just pick at their food." Clayton and Millie returned home shortly after supper.

The summer was passing, and Millie had not heard from Austin regarding the results of her recent test and oral interview. She was becoming more anxious each day. Clayton reminded her, "No news is good news." Millie reminded Clayton that she was really curious to know the results, and he said, "Millie, curiosity killed the cat."

She became impatient with Clayton and said, "Please no more aphorisms for me."

Eventually, an official letter arrived from the Texas Bar Association. Millie was most excited. She opened the letter and read it while Clayton waited patiently for the results. Millie looked somewhat disappointed as she read the letter. After she had finished reading it, she passed the letter to Clayton who read it.

It was from the chief examiner in Austin, and he stated that one member of the panel had been very ill which had delayed the final decision by the committee. The committee of lawyers who interviewed her could not meet again until the sixth member was well enough, and then they would vote on a decision. He was most sorry for the delay, but he was pleased to announce that Millie had passed the written examination with high marks. The chief examiner said he would notify Millie whenever the committee would be able to meet.

Clayton said, "Millie, you have done it. You have it. This is a formality which they must go through in order to make you a bona fide lawyer for the state of Texas." Millie burst into tears. Clayton comforted her, and said, "I'm sorry you have had such a long wait, but I will guarantee that you will receive a positive and a unanimous vote by the committee."

Millie replied, "What if this lawyer who is ill does not recover from his illness?" Clayton replied, "Millie, you have to think and believe positively. You must have faith that good things will happen to you."

"You are right, dear Clayton. Somehow I misplaced my confidence and faith that my mother taught me a long time ago. I now believe I will pass the Bar Examination. Thank you for helping me to believe in myself."

The month of August in 1941 was very warm and dry. Millie kept hoping for rain showers to cool the Texas earth for a short time. Clayton preferred an east wind to blow to make it cooler in Hillsboro. They stayed indoors during the day to avoid the worst heat.

In the evenings, they listened to the news report on world conditions in Europe. They were concerned about the world situation in Europe and also in Asia. They agreed with the provisions of the Atlantic Charter issued by President Franklin Roosevelt and Prime Minister Winston Churchill on August 14, 1941. The Atlantic Charter issued a joint declaration of peace aims. The charter emphasized that sovereign rights and self-government be restored to people who had been forcibly deprived of them.

Millie hoped the war would end peaceably in Europe and other areas. She hoped her brother and Clayton would not have to serve in the military. She was most concerned when President Roosevelt signed a bill permitting the United States Army to keep men in the service eighteen months longer.

Millie knew how strongly Clayton felt about the war in Europe. Clayton's mother, Fiona, had been born in Scotland. She knew that some of his relatives might have to endure hostilities from the enemies of other countries. He felt badly about the aggression that many people had to endure.

They seldom mentioned or discussed the war with Judge Campbell because they knew it was painful to him since he served in World War I. When questioned, the judge said, "I pray everyday for the hostilities to cease."

Millie tried to prepare herself in case Clayton had to join the army in the very near future. She would be very lonely without him near her. She was proud of him, and she knew he would never be a draft dodger as many young men who tried to avoid the draft were called. Whenever the subject of his joining the service came up, Clayton reminded Millie that we have a great country which is certainly worth defending. "I'll fight for the United States of America, my country, anytime," said Clayton.

VI

Millie Becomes a Lawyer and the Death of a Friend

The long hot summer was almost over, and two things happened that would have a great influence on Millie's life. One of them was very good news. She received a letter from the Texas Bar Association stating that the chief examiner was enclosing a document which certified that Millie Martin Campbell was now a licensed and certified lawyer in the state of Texas effective on August 15, 1941.

Millie was deliriously happy as was Clayton, Judge Campbell, and her family. Judge Campbell insisted on a reception at Hillsboro House on the next Sunday afternoon from 3:00 to 6:00 to honor Millie. Invitations were sent to the local lawyers, close friends, and family members. Judge Campbell and Clayton planned the event including the food prepared by Bessie and the invitations. Clayton knew that his father would make an important announcement at the reception regarding Millie.

The Sunday for the reception arrived. Many guests came to the large white house with the Grecian columns on Craig Street. All of the local lawyers and their wives were present plus several important clients of Judge Campbell. Millie's parents, Jake and Dora Martin, came with their son J. D. who appeared uncomfortable in a white shirt and tie. Dora insisted that Jake and J. D. wear white shirts, neck ties, dress slacks, and their best slippers with matching socks. Millie was pleased that her family was present.

She was very happy to see her former teacher, Miss Emily Blackburn. Clayton whispered to Millie that Miss Emily looked pale and tired. Millie found her very cordial, and Miss Emily complimented Millie on her new status as an attorney. Miss Emily said, "I knew you would rise high in the world because you were a marvelous student with a brilliant mind." Millie thanked Miss Emily for her kind remarks. Miss Emily then took Millie aside, "I will make an appointment with you soon to discuss some very private matters which concern me."

"Of course," said Millie to Miss Emily, and smiled.

Before Millie could comment further, Judge Campbell asked for everyone's attention. He wanted to compliment and toast Millie on her new honor of becoming a lawyer. He also said he had an important announcement to make. "At this very moment," Judge Campbell said, "I am inviting Millie Martin Campbell, attorney-at-law, to become a junior partner in the Campbell Law Firm. If she wishes to think about it, she may do so. But if she wishes to accept now, I would be most happy."

Millie looked at Clayton, and Clayton whispered to Millie, "Do accept his offer to be a partner."

Millie glanced at her mother. Dora said, "It is a most wonderful opportunity, Millie."

Millie then said to Judge Campbell and everyone, "I want to thank Judge Campbell for this magnanimous offer to become a junior partner in the Campbell Law Firm. I accept with the greatest of pleasure. I pledge to do my very best as a lawyer for the Campbell Law Firm and the local community." Sustained applause and a toast were given to Millie. The reception continued for several hours because the guests wanted to talk and compliment Millie personally. When Millie had a quiet period, she looked for Miss Emily among the guests.

Bessie said, "Miss Emily Blackburn wasn't feeling too well and she left an half hour ago."

Before the reception was over, Millie thanked Judge Campbell and told him how much she appreciated his kindness and help to her in becoming a lawyer. She promised to be loyal and supportive of the Campbell Law Firm. She also mentioned that she would be glad when Clayton could join the firm.

Millie and Clayton said good night to the judge and thanked him again. Millie and Clayton had previously said thanks to all other guests when they left.

When Millie and Clayton arrived home to their house on Corsicana Street, they were still in a state of euphoria. Clayton had taken an extra bottle of champagne home with him. Millie protested that she did not need additional champagne. But it was not easy to say no to Clayton. They sipped the champagne slowly and discussed the interesting party that Judge Campbell had given in Millie's honor. The evening was getting late, and Clayton said, "I will carry you to bed tonight. You have had a big day, and we are going to have some pleasure before we fall asleep."

Millie said, "And you know how to do everything so well." Before Millie went to sleep, she experienced the most wonderful love-making of her life by Clayton. She could not believe the intensity of his lovemaking, but she would probably know nine months later.

They slept soundly the remainder of the night. She slept with her arms around Clayton all night, and her only thoughts were how lucky she was.

They were wakened early the next morning with the loud ring of the telephone. Millie was concerned about the early ringing of the telephone. No one ever called that early in the morning. She was worried since it was barely daylight.

She answered the telephone, and she could not understand who was talking. The voice was nearly hysterical, and it sounded like Bessie. She hoped nothing was wrong with Judge Campbell. The voice finally said, "No ma'am, I'se not Bessie; I am Beatrice."

Millie said, "Beatrice, what is the problem?"

"I ain't got no problem, Miss Millie—it it's Miss Emily."

"Oh, dear! What is the matter with Miss Emily?" asked Millie.

"She ain't here—she's gone, ma'am."

"What do you mean she's gone?" asked Millie.

"It's terrible, terrible, Miss Emily is dead and gone." Beatrice could not speak any longer.

Millie said, "I will be over immediately." She wakened Clayton again and told him the sad news. They left at once for Miss Emily's house on Craig Street.

Beatrice was crying with loud sobs when they arrived, and they did their best to calm her down so they could get the details of Miss Emily's death. Beatrice finally got herself under control, and she explained to Millie and Clayton the details as best as she could. She explained that she knocked on Miss Emily's door at 6:00

with a tray of hot coffee as she did every morning. Miss Emily did not answer. Beatrice waited another fifteen minutes and knocked on the door. Miss Emily did not answer. Then Beatrice was most worried, and she opened the door to check on Miss Emily who was still in bed. Her body was cold. Beatrice said, "I called the doctor, and he said she had been gone for hours."

The doctor said, "She probably died when she first went to bed."

Poor Beatrice began to cry with loud sobs and say intermittently, "My poor, dear Miss Emily."

Clayton said that he would walk down the street to his father's house and tell him about Miss Emily's sudden death. Beatrice continued to be emotional, saying, "What will happen to poor Louis down in New Orleans who does not have a mother now, and he never knew who his real daddy is?" Millie was glad Clayton did not hear what Beatrice had just said.

Millie said to Beatrice, "I always thought Louis was the nephew of Miss Emily."

"Oh yessum, you is right—a nephew he was."

Millie said, "Beatrice, you are lying to me."

"Oh, no, no, Miss Millie, I won't never tell a lie, I'se made a bad mistake."

Millie said, "I think I know the truth about Louis and Miss Emily." Millie admonished Beatrice never to discuss the relationship of Louis and Miss Emily ever again.

"Oh, Miss Millie, I'se promise never to say anything ever about dear Miss Emily and dear little Louis."

Millie told Beatrice that she was the executor of Miss Emily's will and final wishes. Beatrice said, "Oh, goodness, Miss Millie, what will I do now—I have no home?"

Millie said, "Don't worry, you will stay here for some time, and I'll find a place for you."

"Bless you. Bless you," said Beatrice.

Millie telephoned Louis in New Orleans and told him about the death of Miss Emily. Louis was most upset, and said, "I will leave for Hillsboro immediately, and you know I loved my aunt as much as I do my own mother." Millie expressed her sympathy to Louis. She explained that she was the executor of Miss Emily's estate. Louis was pleased that Millie was the executor of the estate. He said, "I know it will be in the best of hands."

Millie succeeded in calming Beatrice. She reasoned with her that Miss Emily would want her to remain calm and be helpful at this very time. Millie wanted to go home and bathe and change clothes before going to work. It was her first day as an attorney, and she was given a very pleasant office with her own secretary. However, this arrangement did not seem so important now because of Miss Emily's sudden death.

When Millie greeted Judge Campbell, she noticed that he was visibly shaken by Miss Emily's death. He could hardly speak, and she could tell that he had been crying. He had rescheduled most of his appointments since he had difficulty in maintaining a conversation. Millie expressed her sympathy to him and said, "I know you both have been very close friends for such a long time, and I am very sorry for you to lose such a good friend."

Judge Campbell gave Millie a strange look and said, "Emily and I were more than good friends." He returned to his office, closed the door, and Millie could hear a pounding on the judge's desk. Millie could also hear loud mournful sobs from the private office. She asked the staff not to contact the judge for several hours.

Millie began to think. Suddenly, she knew the big secret of Craig Street; the parents of Louis lived all these years on Craig Street. Judge Campbell and Miss Emily were the parents of Claude Louis Blackburn. Millie usually told or shared private matters with Clayton, but she decided not to tell him at this time that he had a half brother who was Louis Blackburn. Millie decided that she must learn to keep secrets. She was now an attorney.

Millie opened and read the last will of Emily Blackburn. The bulk of the estate was to go to Louis in New Orleans, some money to Beatrice, some scholarships for students at Hillsboro High School, and all of her fine jewelry to Millie.

Miss Emily had included instructions for her funeral—a very simple morning service at St. Mary's Episcopal Church near where she lived. She wanted only one hymn sung, "Amazing Grace", the twenty-third Psalm read from the Bible, and Clayton Campbell to read one of his favorite poems. She said he would know which one. When Millie asked Clayton about the favorite poem, he said, "It could only be `A Red, Red Rose' by Robert Burns."

The attendance at the funeral was large and it was conducted with great dignity. The flowers were most beautiful, with four red roses on the bronze casket. Millie was able to cipher the card when no one was looking. "I Love You" was scribbled on the donor's card.

Miss Emily was buried after the beautiful, simple service in the Blackburn plot of the Hillsboro Cemetery near the graves of her parents. The pallbearers were all her former students which included Clayton. Many former present students stood with tears in their eyes while the Hillsboro High School band played "Nearer My God to Thee."

After the burial, close friends were invited to Miss Emily's home for coffee and cake. Louis and Sarah were most gracious and thanked every one for their kindness. Louis hugged Millie and thanked her. Sarah Bankstead even hugged Millie and thanked her. Millie had never seen Sarah so sedate before. Sarah and Louis asked Millie to do a remembrance of Miss Emily for them and the other guests.

Millie had her own private thoughts of Miss Emily but she agreed to share them because Miss Emily had had a great influence on her. She began, "Miss Emily gave me encouragement, inspiration, and friendship. She taught me to enjoy life and to live life every day.

"She taught me that we live in a big world. Learn about the world by reading poetry and the works of authors. Believe in yourself and know yourself. Never be defeated by any one. Only you can let yourself be defeated. Don't be afraid to express your point of view, but also listen to the opinions of others. Sometimes they might be right, too."

She concluded by saying, "I think I am a better person by virtue of knowing Miss Emily Blackburn. Miss Emily will always have an impact on my life that will help me to be a stronger person, and I will always remember her and be grateful to her. Let us all treasure the memory of Emily Blackburn."

Everyone was pleased with this tribute to Miss Emily. Millie preferred not to show her private thoughts to everyone, but she was willing to make an exception for the sake of Miss Emily who had a direct influence on her and so many other students of Hillsboro High School.

Clayton was pleased with Millie's tribute to Miss Emily. He felt that Miss Emily had a positive and lasting influence on her many students.

VII

Millie Discovers a Secret

The transition from private secretary to Judge Campbell to an attorney was a large adjustment for Millie. She was fortunate to have her own private office but the law firm did not supply the office furniture. Clayton and Millie were busy the first week securing the basic furniture for her office. He found a good buy on a mahogany desk at Cheap Jim's Furniture Store in Hillsboro. He also bought two nice oak bookshelves. Lawyers always had bookshelves in their offices. Millie found two steel file cabinets which furnished the small but adequate office. Clayton was impatient to take a photograph of Millie Campbell, attorney-at-law.

The biggest problem for Millie and most new lawyers is the absence of ready clients. Millie had no clients to begin with except for the estate of Miss Emily Blackburn. Miss Emily had asked Millie to be her executor before she died, so the judge gladly passed the administration of the estate to Millie. Although it was very sad for Millie to administer Miss Emily's estate, it did give her some ready business.

Millie had already decided to specialize in wills and the administration of estates. Millie knew that a will must be filed as a legal document at certain times in a county or superior court. A copy of the will must be available to the public in case some one decided to protest its terms and to creditors who had claims against the estate.

Millie notified all the heirs who were listed as beneficiaries of the will. Louis Blackburn was the only heir who made an appointment with Millie to look over the will of his aunt. Louis greeted Millie warmly and thanked her for the nice tribute to his aunt on the day of her funeral. Millie shook hands with Louis and he held Millie's hand for a considerable time. She looked at Louis and studied his profile as he read Miss Emily's will. She was amazed at how much he resembled Miss Emily. Louis was astonished that he was the main benefactor, and said, "I did not realize my aunt was so fond of me."

Millie replied, "You will be very comfortable in the future as you are receiving a large sum of cash and several pieces of fine real estate which Judge Campbell has been managing for the estate of your aunt. What are your plans for Miss Emily's brick home on Craig Street?"

He replied, "I am uncertain at this time, but I think I would like to keep it for a while longer. I do enjoy coming to Hillsboro to visit friends like you and Clayton." Millie told him that Beatrice, the maid, was concerned about her future and what would happen to her. Louis replied, "That will be no problem; I want her to continue living in the house and take care of it when Sarah and I can not be here." Millie did not ask, but she was most curious about the wedding plans of Louis and Sarah.

Millie ventured to say, "I am sure you and Sarah will enjoy living in the house when you are married soon."

"I am afraid it will not be soon; Sarah and I will not be married until the war is over." Millie was surprised at this statement. "Have you not heard about Sarah?" asked Louis.

"Why, no, I have not," answered Millie. Louis continued, "Sarah has joined the U.S.O., and she will be leaving on the fifteenth of September which will delay our marriage for a few years. Sarah is very committed to helping obtain world peace. So our marriage must wait until the terrible conflicts of the world have ended."

Louis left her office, Millie was relieved that they would not be getting married soon. Millie told Clayton the news of Sarah joining the service when she went home that evening. Millie said, "Isn't that good news? Sarah Bankstead will not be living in the home of Miss Emily. I am so very pleased."

Clayton said, "Millie this is personal news of your clients, and I don't think you should care about the personal arrangements of Louis Blackburn and Sarah Bankstead. If you don't mind my giving advice, you should only be concerned about helping Louis receive his due inheritance from Miss Emily's estate and administering the legality of Miss Emily's will and its terms. The personal life of Louis and Sarah is no business of yours."

Millie was a little offended, and said, "Thank you, Judge Clayton Campbell; you have rendered an opinion. Well, Mr. Smarty-pants, you are right again. You should be the attorney, and I should still be studying law." Millie pretended she was upset.

Clayton gave her a friendly pat on the shoulder, and said, "Millie, it is all right being sensitive, but don't be too darn sensitive."

Clayton reminded Millie, "I must return within a few days to the university for my last year of law school. I am anxious to graduate from the university, but I am really more concerned about the future of the world. Millie, you may not understand, but if our country declares war in the next few months, I plan to join the service."

Millie said, "I love you, and I will respect you for doing what you feel you must do." Millie continued, "I hope and pray that the war in Europe will end soon."

Millie did not sleep too well that evening. She was thinking about her wonderful marriage to Clayton. She loved him very much, and she remembered that every girl at Hillsboro High School would have jumped at the chance of dating or even marrying Clayton. He was the most handsome and intelligent among the boys at Hillsboro High School.

Millie was going to miss Clayton when he returned to the university. During their few years of marriage she had to share him with the university while he was studying for a law degree. She had to conceal her disappointment when he spoke of joining the service in case America became involved. Hopefully, some day, Clayton would be finished with the university and that soon there would be peace in the world instead of wars which men had to fight. Millie did not feel as strongly about the war and joining the service. Of course, Millie was not a young man in 1941, and she could not fully understand a young man's situation regarding the war which seemed imminent.

In a few days, Millie said good-bye to Clayton at the Hillsboro train station as he was leaving for Austin to finish his last year of law school. She dreaded the thought of saying good-bye to Clayton if he should join the service. Millie did not enjoy saying good-bye; even the sound of the train leaving the station was unpleasant to her.

It was lonely the first few days after Clayton had left for school.

Millie preferred to be busy so that she would not have time to think about being lonely. In addition to being lonely, there was another void in her life since Miss Emily had died so suddenly. Millie knew she was going to miss visiting Miss Emily; she had enjoyed her conversations with Miss Emily.

She was most curious about the last brief conversation which she had had with Miss Emily. It was at the reception Judge Campbell gave for Millie when she became a lawyer. She remembered that Miss Emily had said she had some private matters to discuss with Millie. Millie wondered now about these private matters. She had not thought much about this conversation until Clayton had gone. Did these private matters of Miss Emily have something to do with the Campbells? Was Judge Campbell the father of Louis Blackburn? If so, Louis and Clayton are half brothers. Millie thought to herself, "Do I dare tell Clayton what I know?" But she was afraid to tell him because he was so forthright. Millie knew that Clayton would go directly to his father and ask him to tell the truth. She was uncertain how to approach Clayton, and she decided to delay telling this revelation to him.

As Millie thought about this family secret, she remembered that Bessie had once said she knew a very big secret. It was now time to approach and hear the big secret, and Bessie should know because Bessie and Beatrice were sisters. Their mother was Aunt Ettie, the first maid at Hillsboro House.

Millie waited for her opportunity to question dear old Bessie about the big secret. The opportunity came soon. Judge Campbell had to attend a lawyer's conference in Fort Worth a few days later, and Bessie became bored when she was not cooking for someone. Bessie called Millie at the office the next day to say that she had baked Millie a fresh green apple pie. Millie loved freshly baked apple pies, and she agreed to stop by in the late afternoon for one.

At the end of the day, Millie went directly to the big house on Craig Street. Bessie was in the rear of the house, but she came to the front door and opened it for Millie. Millie thanked Bessie for baking a special apple pie for her. Before leaving, Millie said, "Bessie, you and I have been good friends over the years, and I wish to ask you an important question. Would you be willing to answer the question for me because it relates to the Campbells?"

Bessie said, "I'll try, Miss Millie."

Millie said, "Bessie, you told me once there was a big secret you knew."

"Yessum, that is right."

"And your mother forbade you to tell it, and I think she said she would strike you dead if you ever told that secret."

"That is correct, Miss Millie."

Millie said, "I don't want Aunt Ettie to strike you dead, so please listen carefully to me." Millie continued, "Bessie, what do you know about Louis Blackburn and Miss Emily?"

Bessie said, "I know nothing about them."

"Did you know, Bessie, that Miss Emily was the mother of Louis?"

"No, no," said Bessie.

"And you know who the father is, Bessie."

"Of course not," said Bessie. "I know nothing, and I don't want to lose my job with the judge."

Millie said, "I know that you know who the parents are of Louis Blackburn."

"Oh, please, don't ask me no more questions about poor little Louis," said Bessie. "We all felt so sorry for him when he was first born."

"Where was he born, Bessie?"

"Oh, right here in Hillsboro, and me and my sister took care of him until he was six months old. He was such a good and pretty baby, and he never gave us any trouble. Then he was taken to New Orleans, and we never seen him again until he was a young man and plum grown. I'se went to sleep many nights crying about the poor little boy."

Millie said, "Thank you, Bessie; I believe I now know the big secret of Craig Street." Bessie looked worried. "Please don't worry, Bessie, the big secret of Craig Street will not be revealed by me." Millie thanked Bessie for the freshly baked apple pie, and then she left for her house on Corsicana Street.

When she arrived home, she picked up the receiver of the telephone to call Clayton. When the operator said number please, Millie replied, "Thank you, but I have decided not to make the call."

The operator said, "That is quite all right, madam."

Millie was most frustrated that there was no one she could

talk to regarding the big secret. Suddenly, she had an urge to see her mother and talk to her about the secret. Millie put the apple pie in the car and drove the eight miles into the country where her parents lived. Her parents were surprised to see her. They were not expecting her, but Millie said, "Bessie had baked me an apple pie which I wanted to share with you."

Dora said, "We love apple pie. Jake and me was only going to have a glass of milk and cornbread since J. D. has gone to see a girlfriend."

Millie said, "I'll have cornbread and milk too, and we will save J. D. a slice of apple pie."

Jake said, "You had better make that two pieces—that boy can sure eat."

Millie was quieter than usual, and Dora was aware that something was troubling her daughter. After supper, Dora suggested to Jake to check on the livestock because J. D. had been in a big hurry when he left for the visit with that girl.

Dora said, "Millie Martin, what is bothering you?"

"Oh, nothing, Mama."

"Yes, there is something bothering my child."

"Well, you are right, Mama, something is bothering me very, very much," said Millie.

"Well, you can tell your mother, I hope," said Dora.

Millie said, "I have learned a disturbing secret about Judge Campbell and Miss Emily. I would like to tell Clayton, but I am afraid it will hurt someone. I also promised the person I heard the secret from that I would not tell it."

Dora said, "Then Millie, you don't tell secrets which will hurt people. Millie, we all have things in our life which it is best to keep secret. Just ask God to help you keep this secret from hurting anyone."

Millie agreed with her mother and said, "Thank you, Mama, I know you are right. I don't want to hurt anyone." Millie hugged her mother, and said, "I must leave for home as it is almost 9:00." Dora reminded her daughter to drive carefully on the way home.

Millie felt better after talking with her mother about the secret. She could depend on her mother to give her good advice. Millie was amazed that her mother had not asked her to tell the secret.

She admired the strength and character of her mother. She hoped that someday she could develop the strength and character of her mother.

Even though Millie felt better after the visit, there were some unresolved questions that she could not solve by herself. She could understand why Miss Emily had maintained the long secret about her son, Louis. Miss Emily had a reputation to be protective while living in a small town. She was a most popular teacher in the Hillsboro school system.

But Millie could not understand Judge Campbell who had always been so kind and helpful to her. Judge Campbell was very fond of Clayton because his wife had died such a long time ago. He had been so generous to her and to Clayton by giving them a nice frame bungalow house for a wedding present. Millie could only believe that Judge Campbell would enjoy being a father to Louis.

After analyzing the complicated situation, Millie could not be critical of either one. Miss Emily had been a wonderful teacher and a good friend whom Millie was going to miss for a long time. The judge had been a wonderful friend and father-in-law to Millie. He had selected her as his private secretary, and had helped Millie in the self-study of law which was a major influence in her becoming a lawyer. She did not forget that the judge accepted her as a partner in his law firm.

Millie decided that she was not going to let the discovery of the secret tarnish her feelings toward Judge Campbell or mar the memory of her favorite teacher. She was pleased that she had made that decision.

When she was preparing to go to bed the telephone rang which was a call from Clayton in Austin. Millie could detect a slight annoyance in his voice. He said, "I have tried to call you several times this evening, but I did not receive any answers from you." Clayton continued, "Did you have an important business appointment or did you and Louis go to a party tonight?"

Millie replied, "Goodness gracious, no, my dear charming husband. I don't have evening business appointments, and I only date my husband when he is in town. I drove out to the farm to visit my parents and take them an apple pie Bessie baked for me.

I just had a feeling that I must see and talk to my mother about a problem I could not resolve."

Clayton said, "I hope it was not a serious problem."

Millie replied, "No, it was not a major problem. I was only lonesome."

Clayton continued, "The reason I am calling you is that I had a telephone call from Louis Blackburn this evening. He asked me for permission to invite you to a social event he wishes to attend in a few days." Clayton continued, "I told him he did not have to ask my permission, but he must secure your permission."

Millie said, "Why can't Sarah attend the function with Louis?"

Clayton told Millie that Sarah had left Hillsboro to join the service.

Millie thanked Clayton for the telephone call, and said, "I only want to go to social events with you."

Clayton said, "Millie, I am not a jealous husband. I would be most happy for you and Louis to attend the social event which is really important to him."

Millie said, "I love you very much, Clayton, and I wish I could see you very soon." Clayton said, "I love, you very much, Millie, but it is past bedtime and we must say good night to each other."

VIII

Miss Emily's Jewelry

Judge Campbell returned from the Texas Lawyer's Convention in Fort Worth, and gave Millie a summary of the conference. He heard some outstanding lectures by lawyers who were from various parts of the United States. There were many new laws which had been passed by the Texas legislature, and more new laws pending within the new legislature.

Millie thanked Judge Campbell for giving her a written summary of the conference. He also gave her a list of the new laws which were recently adopted by the Texas legislature.

Before leaving her office, the judge inquired about Emily Blackburn's estate. Millie explained that Louis Blackburn was the principal heir. Judge Campbell said, "He is a fortunate young man because Emily left a sizable estate."

Millie told the judge, "I understand that she was very fond of her nephew."

"So I have heard," said Judge Campbell.

Millie asked, "How did Miss Emily acquire so much property and leave such large bank accounts?"

The judge said, "Emily was an excellent manager, and she received a large inheritance from her father, Dr. Benjamin Blackburn. Emily was a good investor, and she knew how to double and triple her investments. Emily was most generous with people whom she admired, but she was frugal for herself. She did buy expensive clothing and jewelry, but only if they were on sale or she received a good buy. And now I must get busy this morning and earn some money or I will not have any estate to leave for my heirs."

Millie thanked the judge for sharing his opinions on Miss Emily. She remembered that according to the bequests of the will, she was to inherit Miss Emily's fine jewelry. She decided that she should collect the jewelry soon. She knew from experience in the law office that good jewelry often disappears when someone dies.

194

Millie telephoned Louis and told him she would like to collect Miss Emily's jewelry as soon as possible. Louis was pleasant to Millie, and said, "You may come at anytime for it." Millie agreed to come by at 5:00 that day for the jewelry.

She arrived shortly after 5:00, and Louis greeted her warmly. "I am so glad you came for the jewelry because Sarah really wanted to have two or three pieces of my aunt's jewels before she left for the service." A sudden thought struck Millie; why had Miss Emily not left her best jewelry to Sarah? She knew Louis and Sarah were to be married. Wouldn't she want her good jewelry to stay within the family? Louis noticed that Millie was thinking about something. Millie said, "Well, Louis, I will tell you what I am thinking, but it is somewhat embarrassing. I was just thinking why did Miss Emily not leave her jewelry to Sarah who is going to be your wife?"

Louis said, "I have thought about this, and I am uncertain if my aunt really liked Sarah. On the other hand," said Louis, "jewelry is so personal with a woman, and my aunt might have thought Sarah would have preferred selecting her own jewelry."

Millie was pleased with the last explanation about the jewelry. She said, "Louis, I must tell you something that Miss Emily said to me before she died. In fact, it was the last time I saw her alive, and the last day of her life." Louis seemed most interested, and Millie continued, "Your aunt's last words to me were, `Millie, I want to make an appointment with you to discuss some private matters which concern me!' " Millie asked Louis, "Do you know what those private matters were?"

"No," said Louis, looking very concerned. Louis then said, "I will check with our family in New Orleans and ask them."

Louis said, "Now, I think we should go upstairs and look at the jewelry." Louis took Millie upstairs to Miss Emily's bedroom, saying, "Nothing has been touched in the bedroom since she died. Beatrice can not stand to go into the bedroom, and Sarah and I have not changed anything." Millie glanced sadly at the dark mahogany bed where Miss Emily died with the pink satin cover and pink silk sheets. There were framed photographs of her parents and a few photographs of Louis. An open book of poetry was next to her bed. There was a nice dresser with a silver dresser-set on it with the initials E. B. A large matching chest of drawers was near, and Louis opened the third drawer where Miss Emily kept her best jewelry. There were three beautiful boxes full of the most wonderful jewelry Millie had ever seen. There were gorgeous diamond rings, earrings, brooches, necklaces, gold bracelets, emeralds, and pearls. Millie could not even count the number of pieces. Some of the jewelry was very old because many pieces had belonged to Miss Emily's mother and grandmother.

Emily told Louis that she would take the jewelry and compile a list of it for the estate. Louis indicated three pieces of jewelry Sarah was willing to purchase from the estate. Millie told Louis that it would not be necessary for Sarah to purchase them as she would share them with Sarah. Millie said, "I will see that Sarah receives this set of three pieces: a ring, a necklace, and a pair of earrings." Louis spontaneously put his arms around Millie's waist and hugged her closely to him and thanked her for the jewels for Sarah. Without realizing what was happening, Millie put her arms around Louis and his arm strong body felt good. They stood embraced for a few minutes.

Millie then pulled away from Louis, and looked at her watch. "It is time for me to leave. I must take the jewelry to the office and put the jewels in the safe." Louis invited Millie to have a glass of claret before leaving, but Millie declined in order to get to the office before it closed. Millie was relieved that she had this good excuse to leave quickly.

She was nervous when she left Miss Emily's house, but she thanked Louis for the visit and for his help with the jewelry. Louis stood at the front door and waved to Millie as she drove down Craig Street. Millie was glad Louis did not mention the social event he wanted to attend and invite her to be his guest. Millie was certain that she must never again be alone with Louis Blackburn.

When she arrived at the office, she placed the three boxes of jewelry in the big office safe. Millie opened each box to make sure that all the jewelry was there before taping each box twice. She admired all the jewels, but she did not see any wristwatches. She remembered that Miss Emily often wore a small gold wristwatch, and on special occasions, she wore an interesting platinum and diamond wristwatch. Everyone use to admire that beautiful watch.

Millie could not understand how Miss Emily had acquired

such fabulous jewelry. Even though Miss Emily was affluent from her family inheritance, she could not afford such expensive jewelry. Millie sat at her desk for a few minutes contemplating the jewelry and its history. Millie was the only one left in the law building; it was time to go home. She was startled by the sudden ringing of her telephone. The caller was Judge Campbell.

He had telephoned to inquire about Miss Emily's jewelry. He was pleased that Millie had inherited the jewelry. He told Millie if she did not want it and if she was considering selling various pieces, he would be very interested in buying them. He emphasized to Millie to give him the opportunity to purchase any of the jewelry she did not wish to keep. Millie assured the judge she would give him first choice of any jewelry which she might sell in the future. She told him she was inclined to keep most of the jewelry for a possible future daughter. The judge seemed pleased, and he agreed with her thinking.

After she had finished speaking with the judge, Millie was most confused. Why would Judge Campbell desire any of the jewelry? He had no daughter to inherit it, and he had no wife nor any prospect of a wife. There had to be a reason why the judge wanted to purchase some of Miss Emily's jewelry.

Even though it was getting very late, Millie decided to examine Miss Emily's jewelry again. She went into the large office safe which was down the hall from her office, taking a letter opener with her in order to open the boxes. Millie opened one box at a time, and when she had opened all three boxes, she was beginning to see a likeness in the design of the jewelry. There were a few brooches which looked Celtic in design. A few other pieces had thistles in various sizes. Could they be Scottish thistles? Millie did not feel the jewelry had been made in America. From the thistle design, Millie believed that some of the jewelry came from Scotland.

Millie decided to take a few pieces home with her to study. She would stop by Judge Campbell's house and borrow a book on jewelry design. She recalled one particular book in his library which might be helpful. She remembered Clayton telling her about the book on Celtic jewelry which had belonged to his mother, Fiona Campbell. Clayton had shown the book to Millie on one occasion. He proudly told her that his mother had pieces of her Celtic jewelry illustrated in the book. Millie was anxious to read the book.

When she arrived at Judge Campbell's home, the judge was on his way out to have dinner with some clients. Millie did not want to delay him, but she showed him three pieces of jewelry. "Oh, my God," he said. "I have not seen those pieces for over twenty years." Millie thought the judge's strong reaction to the jewelry was most strange. He seemed to have a familiarity with and knowledge of the jewelry.

The judge left for his dinner engagement and Millie went into the library to read about jewelry design. She located the book which she was seeking and found the information she desired. The book which had been published in the early part of the century gave the history of Celtic-design jewelry. She found some astonishing information regarding the three brooches. They were illustrated in the book with a history of each piece. The three brooches were authentic Celtic brooches. Millie was curious now. These brooches belonged to Clayton's mother, Fiona McGill. Did she bring them from Scotland when she came to Texas to live with Judge Campbell? How did Miss Emily get possession of these valuable pieces of jewelry?

Millie was preparing to leave, and she called Bessie to tell her she had finished and she was leaving for home. Bessie came into the library. "Mercy me," said Bessie. "What is you reading about now?"

"Just about some jewelry," said Millie.

Bessie looked at the brooches on the library table, and she almost screamed aloud. But she put her hand over her mouth. "Oh, my goodness, where did you get that jewelry? I ain't seen it for many years."

Millie said, "The jewelry belongs to an estate, and I am trying to determine the value of it."

"Oh, I'se understands," said Bessie.

"I must be going soon, but Bessie, tell me who owned this jewelry. Did it belong to Clayton's mother, Fiona?"

Bessie became very quiet, and she did not want to reveal any information she knew about the jewelry. "I'se knows nothing about this here jewelry," said Bessie. "Now I must go and turn down the judge's bed before he comes home."

Millie said, "Bessie, I think you have another secret tucked into your sleeve."

Bessie said, "And I'se never tells secrets to nobody."

PART FIVE

I

Wonderful News

The fall of 1941 was most disturbing to Millie. The daily news from the radio report each evening regarding the European war seemed to intensify. The Nazis intensified their anti-Semitic campaign by forcing all Jewish people to wear a yellow star on their clothing.

During the past summer, the American State Department ordered German and Italian consulates in the United States to close, and the State Department ordered German and Italian monetary funds and property frozen. American borders were closed to German and Italian travelers.

President Roosevelt was greatly troubled about the problem of keeping the sea-lanes open. The "Robin Moor" had been sunk by a submarine in the South Atlantic in May. Many other sinkings of American ships followed these events. On September 11, President Roosevelt in a broadcast to the world warned that American warships and planes would fire at sight on Axis warships which entered waters vital to America's defense. The President called for the arming of American ships, and to authorize their entry into combat areas and also safe entry into belligerent ports. A government bill was passed by the United States Senate and the House of Representatives to guarantee the safety of ships and planes.

Millie Jean continued to listen every night to war reports which were broadcast on the radio. Millie's neighbors and friends did not discuss the war openly but their quietness did not keep them from thinking about the seriousness of it.

Millie went to her office at the law firm each day. She was beginning to acquire several new clients which kept her busy. Early one morning Millie saw Mrs. R. V. Metcalfe enter Judge Campbell's office. Mrs. Metcalfe usually took a few minutes to say hello to Millie after she had finished her business with him. Mrs. Metcalfe always came early for her meetings with him because she wakened at 4:00 A.M. each day. Mrs. Metcalfe had her breakfast at 4:30 each morning, ready to begin her day at 5:00. She usually did her correspondence and bookkeeping between 5:00 and 7:00 A.M.

When Mrs. R. V. Metcalfe had finished her conference with Judge Campbell, she came by Millie's office to greet her. She would never stay more than five minutes because she did not wish to interrupt Millie's schedule. Millie's door was open, and she looked at Mrs. Metcalfe as she came into her office. She noticed that Mrs. Metcalfe was large in size, and was wearing a large flowing skirt. In fact, all of Mrs. Metcalfe's skirts were usually large and flowing and made by herself. Her hair was short and thin; she was in a jovial mood. In fact, she was always laughing. Millie was envious of people who were constantly jolly and full of laughter. She had always been serious in her outlook on life. Mrs. Metcalfe greeted Millie with a quick hug and several chuckles of laughter. Millie reciprocated by saying "Hello, how nice to see you, Mrs. Metcalfe." After a few more pleasantries, Millie invited her to have a seat and a quick chat. Millie became more serious and said, "I would like to ask you about the terrible situation in the world today. What do you think about the war in Europe?"

Mrs. Metcalfe said, "I don't think about it at all. I don't think we should be concerned about the war; I think the people of the world should all love one another, and we would not have wars. Now, I must be going. Just remember, Millie, people of the world must learn to love and respect one another."

Millie said, "I agree with you, but it is a very complex situation."

Mrs. R. V. Metcalfe replied, "I don't bother with the problems of the world. I prefer looking after the robins and squirrels on Craig Street."

Millie said, "Well, it is always nice to see you. We must get together soon and have a cup of coffee or a glass of ice tea."

Mrs. Metcalfe replied, "I never drink coffee or tea, but we could have a glass of fruit juice."

Millie was glad when Mrs. Metcalfe left. She had always been fascinated by her, but Millie was experiencing another side of Mrs. Metcalfe. She was inclined to agree with Mrs. Metcalfe on her personal views, but realized that the greater part of the world did not. Nevertheless, Millie had a different view of the world's problems, and she was glad that other people had the total freedom to express their viewpoint.

Millie thought that Clayton would have answered her differently. He felt that people must be willing to fight for their freedom, or they would eventually lose it.

When she had finished her morning work, she decided to walk to the park and have her lunch, a cheese sandwich and an apple. There was a wonderful feel about autumn in Hillsboro. A slightly cool wind was blowing from the north, and that meant that bitter cold "northers" would be bringing colder air to Hillsboro soon. The leaves of the large elm trees were beginning to turn gold and brown. A few leaves were falling and blowing with the wind.

Millie enjoyed the serenity of the park and she had a very special feeling about life. She was glad to be alive and suddenly felt wonderful in spite of the world situation. She enjoyed watching a family of squirrels running up trees and jumping from tree to tree. One squirrel came close to the park bench, and she tossed her apple core to it. The squirrel ran away with it, and Millie watched it take the core to a nest. He only wanted the apple seed for his young.

Millie thought it was wonderful for the family of squirrels to look after their young. Some day she would enjoy having children and taking care of them. Millie's spirits were high; she felt elated. Suddenly, Millie had a revelation. There was something about her physical condition that made her feel different. She had to admit to herself that a change was taking place inside her body. Millie then realized that she was pregnant; she was carrying a child.

She returned to her office in a state of ecstasy. She telephoned Dr. Wainright, the family physician, and made an appointment with him to conduct an examination.

Judge Campbell noticed a difference in Millie when it was time to close the office in the late afternoon. "Millie, why are you so happy today?" asked the judge. "Did you acquire a new client that I don't know about?"

Millie laughingly told the judge, "I can't tell you just now, but it is possible."

When she arrived home on Corsicana Street, some of her happiness diminished as she looked around the house. She wondered what Clayton's reaction would be if she was pregnant. They had not planned a family so soon. They were going to wait until Clayton had finished law school. Millie decided not to call him until she had a consultation with Dr. Wainright. She went to bed that evening, and read a book until she was sleepy. She was anxious for the next day to arrive so she could visit the doctor and receive his opinion.

The next morning arrived, and Millie had no appetite for food. She decided to have only a cup of coffee before seeing the doctor. Millie arrived at Doctor Wainright's clinic promptly at 9:00. The doctor greeted her warmly and asked about the judge and Clayton. The examination only took a few minutes, but Millie's wait in the examining room seemed a long time to her. Dr. Wainright returned and told Millie that she had been pregnant for three months. He congratulated her, and Millie asked him for any additional advice for her. He recommended that she eat a balanced diet, take a short walk each day, and have plenty of bed rest. The doctor asked her to return each month for his observations.

Millie thanked him, and then returned to the office. She was glad that she had only three appointments that day because her mind was on her pregnancy. She was anxious to telephone Clayton about her new status. She hoped he would be pleased even though they had no plans for a family at this time. Millie looked at her calendar, and the month was mid-November. The doctor estimated that she was three months pregnant. She was thinking that she had become pregnant in the month of August.

Millie remembered the night in mid-August. It was the night after the reception Judge Campbell had given for her when she became a lawyer. Clayton had taken an extra bottle of champagne home with him after the reception. Millie thought to herself, "I will never forget that night with Clayton. It will be our secret for the rest of our lives."

When she went home in the late afternoon, she telephoned Clayton at the university to tell him the news, saying, "I have some very important information to share with you. You are going to be a father in six months, and I am going to be a mother in six months."

Clayton said, "Oh, my God, Millie, are you adopting a new child?"

Millie said, "I think you had better sit down on the side of your bed while I continue. I went to see Dr. Wainright today, and he confirmed that I am three months pregnant. I probably became pregnant in mid-August when you were here."

Clayton continued, "Why, Millie, that is just amazing, just fantastic, and just wonderful. Just think, darling, I will be one proud father of a new son."

Millie said, "You might be the proud father of a new daughter."

"I would love her too," said Clayton. "Millie, what can I do for you? You must take care of yourself. You can't go to the office each day."

She said, "Don't be silly—I can go to the office every day. Clayton, you be careful and very cautious because you have never been a father before."

Clayton said, "Next week is Thanksgiving, and I'll be home to look after you for a few days. We have a lot to be thankful for this Thanksgiving. I am thrilled, and I love you. Please take good care of yourself."

Before ending the telephone conversation, Millie promised to look after herself, and told Clayton how much she loved him. Clayton promised to be home soon from the university.

Millie Jean had never felt or experienced the marvelous feeling she felt now. She could not define it but it was most wonderful. Of course, she had never been pregnant before. She could now understand the miracle of motherhood. The maternal instinct was important and a powerful force. She wondered if most women had this feeling when they were pregnant.

She was anxious to tell her mother that she was pregnant. She would not tell her father at this time but she would like to talk privately with her mother. Millie drove out to the farm the next day. Her parents were always happy to see her. She told her mother that she wanted to speak with her privately. Dora sent the men, Jake and J. D., on an errand to the nearest neighbor to borrow some kerosene for the oil lamps. When Millie told her mother about her pregnancy, Dora Martin could not believe it. Dora tried hard to conceal her surprise that she would be a grandmother in the near future, but she hugged and kissed Millie and congratulated her. Dora said, "It will be a great pleasure for us to have grandchildren." Dora offered to come and stay with Millie if she was needed, but Millie did not think it was necessary.

Millie said, "I must leave soon because the doctor wants me to rest regularly."

Dora had tears in her eyes when her daughter drove away. She knew the day would come when it was time for her to be a grandmother, but this announcement by Millie had caught her off guard.

When Jake and J. D. returned from the neighbors, Dora told them the big family news. Jake said, "I suspected this since you sent us to borrow kerosene when we have five gallons in the shed near the smokehouse." Dora began to cry, and Jake said, "Your Mammy had tears in her eyes when we told her the big news that you were expecting; your tears will dry up when you see your first grandchild. You'll be so proud. You won't be crying; you will be laughing."

J. D. had been listening to the conversation between his parents from another room. In a loud voice, J. D. asked, "Does that mean I am going to be a real uncle in a few months?"

"Of course," said his mother.

Jake said, "That's what happens when young people get married."

J. D. said, "Well, it won't happen to me because I don't plan ever to get married."

Dora said, "The Lord Almighty would not want to hear that you don't plan to get married and raise a family." J. D. gave his parents a very strange look.

His father ended the conversation by saying, "J. D. will change his mind when a pretty young girl takes a fancy to him."

II

The Announcement

Clayton Campbell arrived home two days before Thanksgiving. He said to Millie, "I have come home to take care of you. Do you feel all right? Do you hurt?"

Millie replied, "Goodness, no, Clayton. I feel fine. Women have been having babies for many thousands of years!" She gave him a large kiss and said, "I suppose father's-to-be need tender-loving-care."

But Clayton could not do enough for Millie. He wanted to clean the house and cook the meals.

Millie said, "I suppose you wish to prepare Thanksgiving dinner for our families."

Clayton said, "I had not thought about it, but it is a wonderful idea. I will invite your parents and your brother J. D. I will also invite my father."

Thanksgiving Day was an important day in Hillsboro. It was a wonderful day for families who joined together and prepared a feast. However, it was not a great day for turkeys unless they wanted the honor of being the national dish for the day. Most families never considered the wishes of the turkeys.

Clayton prepared a most superb feast. He roasted a large turkey, and Millie and he made the stuffing and gravy. Dora insisted on making pies—two pecan pies and two pumpkin pies. Bessie was not happy because she felt it was her duty to prepare the Thanksgiving dinner at Hillsboro House as she had done for many years, but Clayton had a way with Bessie to keep her happy. He permitted her to make her famous potato salad and the cranberry relish which she made every holiday. When Clayton went to see Bessie, he said, "You know none of us could top your potato salad and cranberry relish."

Bessie said, "Little Clayton, that ain't true—you just want to pamper poor old Bessie."

Clayton hugged Bessie and said, "I will always pamper you, Bessie. You and your mammy took good care of me when I was born and my mother died a few hours after I was born." Bessie had tears in her eyes, and so did Clayton. He said, "Bessie, what was my mother like?"

Bessie said, "Why, Clayton, she was a beautiful blond woman. There was no other woman like her here in Hillsboro. I was only a young girl, but I'se remember her. She was full of fun and laughter, and she spoke her mind, just like you do sometimes. Every one liked her even if she was different."

Clayton asked, "Bessie, why was she different?"

"Well, her ways were not our ways," said Bessie.

"For example?" said Clayton.

"Well, she stayed up late at nights, and she did not get up early. We had to serve her breakfast in bed. She read books during the day, and wrote many letters to her family and friends across the waters. At night, she wanted a five-course dinner, and we had to serve it very properly for her. She always wore a long dress with her best jewelry in the evenings. She had something about her that caused us all to like her. We always tried to please Miss Fiona because we liked her so very much."

"Bessie, did my mother have nice jewelry?"

"Your mama had de most beautiful jewelry I ever saw," declared Bessie.

Clayton continued, "But Bessie, do you know what happened to her beautiful jewelry?"

Bessie replied, "That is a secret, and I ain't telling no secrets, no sirree."

Clayton said, "Bessie, you're wonderful and you're terrible. I think you know a lot of secrets on Craig Street."

Bessie became quiet and serious. She did not want to talk any more about the past. Clayton said, "Will you help me serve Thanksgiving dinner because I have an important announcement to make?"

"Yes, I will, as long as you're not going to say you is joining the army to fight," said Bessie.

Clayton said, "I am not joining the army for a while."

"Then I'll be there," said Bessie.

The Thanksgiving feast was wonderful. Before it began, Dora

said the blessing. It was simple and sincere.

"Thank you, dear God, for this most wonderful day to celebrate and thank you for our many blessings—good health, food, good family, good friends, good neighbors, and a good country where we enjoy freedom. We are most grateful and thankful for our blessings. Amen."

Clayton thanked his mother-in-law for her appropriate words, but before eating, he offered a toast to everyone and wished them much health and happiness. He continued, "I wish to make a most important announcement which pertains to Millie and me." Clayton was not aware that the Martin family knew about Millie expecting a child.

The judge said, "I suppose you and Millie are leaving Hillsboro for a larger town." "Oh, no, Daddy; it is more important than that. In fact, we are going to increase the population of Hillsboro. Millie and I would like you to know that we are going to be parents within a few months."

Judge Campbell was very surprised, and the Martins pretended to be surprised including J. D. The judge said, "That means another lawyer for the Campbell family."

And Clayton said, "He might want to be a farmer like his other grandfather."

The announcement was a happy occasion for the Martins and the Campbells. Everyone enjoyed the bountiful food, and second helpings were encouraged. Dora was amazed at the amount of food Clayton and J. D. consumed at the dinner table. But the judge reminded Dora that it was the one day of the year which had no limits on the amount of food they ate.

The guests stayed an hour after eating their big meal. Their conversation was only about things that were good and wonderful which had happened in the past year. The Martins told about having bountiful crops and a good harvest. J. D. had saved enough money to purchase a pick-up truck. Millie and Clayton were happy about the blessed event which would occur in a few months. Judge Campbell said that he was happy about everything. Bessie came from the kitchen, and said, "God already knows what I am thankful for cause I'se thanks Him every day of my life."

When the guests had left for their homes, Clayton and Millie sat on the sofa and held hands. They discussed the new baby and how much they were looking forward to its birth. "What will we name it, Clayton?" asked Millie.

"I have been thinking about a name and names for it. If he is a boy, let's name him Robert Martin McGill Campbell."

"What a very long name," said Millie.

"But it includes all of our family names."

Millie said, "If it is a girl, let's name her Roberta Martin McGill Campbell."

"That's great; it's a deal," said Clayton.

Clayton returned to Austin on Sunday for the university. Millie would miss him, and as usual was sad for a few days when he left. However, she was happy this time because she was thinking about the new baby.

She returned to work on Monday morning because of numerous appointments that day. There was a message from Louis Blackburn that he would like to make an appointment to see Millie as soon as possible. Millie telephoned Louis who wished her a belated Happy Thanksgiving. She courteously asked about his holiday. Louis had spent the day with the Banksteads who had many visitors and a large feast, but they all missed Sarah who could not be excused from her service in Washington.

Louis indicated that he would like to speak to Millie privately about Miss Emily's estate. Millie invited him to see her at 2:00 P.M. in her office. When the conversation had ended, Millie was not too happy about seeing Louis Blackburn again, but it was her duty since she was the executor of Miss Emily's estate.

Louis arrived promptly. He was wearing expensive slacks, shirt, and shoes. He smelled very good from his Old Spice aftershave. In spite of her dread of seeing him, she found him rather handsome. He shook hands rather firmly and kissed her right hand.

Louis said, "I must tell you my big news. I have joined the United States Navy, and I'll be leaving in a few days for San Diego." Millie was surprised. She did not realize Louis would enter the military. "Yes, Millie," he said, "it will only be a short time before America enters the war. I feel my opportunities will be better now instead of being drafted later."

Louis said, "Millie, would you do two things for me while I am away?"

"Of course," said Millie.

Louis continued, "Please manage my aunt's estate carefully for me and withhold your usual commission. Secondly, please write to me and keep me informed of the news here." Millie assured Louis that she would honor both requests. Louis said, "I must leave now as I have many things to do. Also, permit Beatrice to remain in my aunt's home to maintain it."

Louis stood up to leave, and Millie extended her hand to him. He hugged her ever so gently and whispered in her ear, "I love you." He left quickly, and Millie did not feel upset with him. She regretted that she did not tell him her own and Clayton's big news.

III

The War and Decisions

Sunday, December 7, 1941, began as a normal day for Millie. She attended church on most Sundays, and on Sunday afternoon, she wrote Clayton a long letter relating events which had happened with her, the law office, or news of Hillsboro for the past week. She was in her second page of writing, telling him about Louis Blackburn joining the Navy, when the telephone rang. Millie was surprised because she did not usually receive telephone calls on Sunday afternoons.

She answered the telephone, and it was Clayton who sounded very excited. He told Millie, "Turn your radio on at once. The news is coming in from Hawaii where the Japanese have attacked Pearl Harbor. I'll speak to you later."

Millie was in shock, but she managed to say, "Thanks, Clayton, I will listen to the radio report."

The news reporter was giving a summary of the tragic devastation which resulted from the attack on the Pearl Harbor naval base at 7:55 that Sunday morning. Within two hours, the Japanese had destroyed six American battleships, many small vessels, and three hundred planes. Hundreds of casualties had been caused.

The reporter continued, "Hangars and air fields were bombed. Fuel tanks and military installations were destroyed. The Japanese planes were able to return to their carriers and make repeated attacks on the American base." The reporter continued to tell of the widespread and horrible destruction of the military base on Oahu in Hawaii.

Millie Jean remained in a state of shock, like many people of the United States. The people of Hillsboro were disturbed. The news of the attack traveled swiftly. Millie received numerous telephone calls from relatives and friends who confided their fears about the disastrous attack on Pearl Harbor. They were all afraid this meant that America would declare war on its enemies who were responsible for this destruction.

Millie looked out of her front window, and saw neighbors on Corsicana Street who were sharing their fears with each other by grouping together and discussing the fate of the country. Others remained still and silent with concerned looks on their faces. Many residents had opinions on the grave condition of the world. Some people feared there would be immediate attacks on other American military bases or even on our largest cities which were in danger of being destroyed by bombs.

After the initial shock of the attack and destruction on Pearl Harbor, Millie maintained her self-control, knowing the future would require it from everyone. The radio reported that the President of the United States would probably declare a state of war the next day on Japan and possibly later on Germany and Italy.

When Millie retired to bed, she prayed to God for courage and strength for the future. She did not feel sleepy. She would have preferred staying awake to think about the events of the world, but she knew she must cope with the war which would most certainly begin soon. As an attorney, she felt it was necessary for her to show strength and courage. She thought America would need strong leaders and strong citizens.

She felt inclined to telephone Clayton, because she was sure he had definite thoughts on the Pearl Harbor attack and what America must do. She did not wish to discuss the matter with Clayton at this time considering his strong views on defending his country. She believed in defending her great country with force if necessary, but she also strongly believed in negotiations among nations to avoid war whenever possible.

The following day, after the attack on Pearl Harbor, President Roosevelt asked Congress to declare war on Japan. He told the Congress of the United States, "December 7 will be a date which will live in infamy." Congress declared war on the Japanese within a few hours. There was only one dissenting vote.

Millie heard the Declaration of War from the lobby of the law firm. The judge, Millie and the staff listened to the President's address. He sounded tense, but he never faltered. Judge Campbell looked tense. When the President had finished speaking, Judge Campbell said, "I dread to experience another world war, but as head of this firm, I encourage the entire staff to expend every effort to help win this war." He encouraged everyone to become involved and do their utmost to help our country win the war efforts.

In the evening, Millie received a telephone call from Clayton who had heard the Declaration of War earlier in the day. He told Millie that he and two friends would like to join the service within three days. Clayton asked Millie for her permission to enlist. He said, "I would like to join the service at the beginning of the war instead of being drafted at a later time. If you totally oppose my joining now, I will not do so. You are my wife and pregnant with my child, and if you say no, I will not join. I'll wait until I am drafted."

Millie replied, "Clayton, please give me an entire day to think about this. At this moment, I cannot say no, and I cannot say, yes. Please let me think about it. I will telephone you tomorrow."

The decision was most difficult for Millie. If Clayton should be drafted later, he might be unhappy with his military assignment. She continued to think about the birth of their child. She would like Clayton to be with her when it was time for the new baby. Millie always prayed to God when big decisions had to be made. She knew that her mother could not help her with this decision even though she would tell her about it. As always, Millie prayed to God before going to sleep to help her make the right decision. The next day came. Millie had made her decision to tell Clayton if it was important to him and he felt it was in his best interest for a better military position, he had her approval to enlist now.

She telephoned and gave her approval. Clayton said, "I love you, Millie, and I appreciate your giving me the approval to enlist. I will be home in a few days before I join the army and hopefully I can enter an Officers' Candidate School."

Millie said, "I love you, Clayton, and I'll be proud of you, but I will miss you when you are away. I hope it will not be for a long time."

Clayton said, "Thanks, Millie I will be home for a short visit soon before I join. Don't be unhappy about my joining the service now. It is what I wish to do."

Millie felt better after talking to Clayton. So many thoughts came to her and she became philosophical. She was always re-

lieved when she had made a decision. There were so many decisions to make in life. There were so many decisions to make daily,
and there were big decisions which required time to contemplate.
It seemed to her as soon as one major decision was made, another condition would evolve which required further decisions. Millie thought to herself, "Life is a series of decisions."

IV

Clayton Joins the Army

The World War continued to worsen. Germany and Italy declared war against the United States on December 11, 1941. The Japanese continued their assault on American installations throughout the Pacific. Japanese planes destroyed American air power in the Philippines.

Within a week after the attack on Pearl Harbor in Hawaii, Americans learned of an estimated loss of lives numbering 2400. Frank Knox, the Secretary of the Navy, went to Pearl Harbor to assess the losses. His account revealed the wide destruction of ships and planes as well as the great loss of lives.

When Americans learned of the extent of the tragedy in Pearl Harbor, they became united in helping in the war effort. All must do their part. Many young men joined the army before they were drafted.

Clayton arrived home shortly from the university. He had been granted permission to leave school for the duration of the war. Millie was glad to have him home with her for these few days, but she knew she would be counting the ten days before he departed for training at the Officers' Candidate School at Fort Hood. Millie assumed that Judge Campbell had some influence which allowed Clayton to enter the Army's Officers' Training School.

Millie attempted to make each day seem normal but it was not easy. Tears came into her eyes often, and she often sought some place to cry in private.

Judge Campbell did not seem at ease during this time. Millie knew what he must be thinking. She surmised that he would be thinking that Clayton is my only son and I will miss him while he is away. Millie could sympathize with these thoughts.

Christmas came and the big Christmas dinner was given by Judge Campbell at Hillsboro House. Millie's parents, Jake and Dora, were invited as well as her brother, J. D. There were three or four other friends of the judge including his former secretary, Agnes Clarke. Only small gifts were exchanged this Christmas due to the war efforts by everyone. Gifts were not a priority because of the war.

Bessie served the big traditional dinner. Everyone tried to act normal, but no one could forget that the lives of Americans were being lost somewhere every hour. Judge Campbell asked Dora to say the blessing, but it was more a prayer for our boys than the traditional blessing. She prayed to God to watch over and protect Clayton as he began his duty in the army. She prayed for other young men in the army.

The guests ate their dinner quietly. When they had finished, Clayton said, "You're all too quiet. Don't worry about me. I am going to go and help get this war over with quickly. Now, let's all cheer up and walk along Craig Street and sing some Christmas Carols." No one, not even the judge, could say no to Clayton.

They all walked along Craig Street and sang "Silent Night, Holy Night." It helped them forget the war for a short time. The cold winter air felt good on their faces after the big warm dinner they had consumed.

When the guests returned from the Christmas caroling, Bessie served eggnog in the large parlor. After a few minutes of conversation, the guests thanked the judge and said good-bye to Clayton, who would be leaving in two days for his enlistment in the army. Some guests said their good-byes well, but others were awkward. Everyone gave Clayton an embrace and wished him well and a safe return to Hillsboro when the war was over.

When everyone had gone except Clayton and Millie, the judge asked Clayton to come to his office for a private talk. Millie helped Bessie put the food away and clear the dining table. Bessie dropped a large silver stuffing spoon on the wood floor making a loud noise. She said, "Oh, dear me, I'se been dropping things all day. I just can't believe that little Clayton is going to be a soldier boy."

"Yes," said Millie, "he is going to the army to help protect us and our country."

Bessie said, "If I'se was younger, I'd go with him. There ain't no one going to take my freedom from me."

Father and son returned from their private conference, and overheard what Bessie had said. The judge smiled, and Clayton said, "Bessie, pack your clothes, and a few cooking pots, and come along and cook for me."

Bessie said, "Just give me about an hour and I'll be ready to go with you." Clayton hugged Bessie and told her he would always love her and never forget her. He shook hands with his father and said he would telephone before he left for the army. Millie thanked the judge and Bessie for the Christmas dinner.

The day after Christmas, Millie canceled her appointments so that she would be free to visit with Clayton. She decided to let Clayton decide what he wanted to do for the last days before leaving for the service. Clayton slept late, and then indicated he would like to go for a drive in the country. He would like to look at the farms his father owned and perhaps buy one from his dad someday. He reminded Millie that he wanted to live on a farm. Millie did not relish farm life but she would be happy to live with him on a farm.

Clayton and Millie enjoyed the drive in the country even though the trees were no longer green as they had lost their leaves for the winter, but they enjoyed looking at the black land of Texas with its valleys, small hills, lakes, and streams. They came upon a hill with a wonderful view of the valley in the distance. Clayton said, "This would be a good site for building a home." Millie agreed with him. Clayton said, "I will tell my father to reserve this site for us because he owns this land."

They both liked the view of the valley which could be seen for miles. Clayton said, "We will build our house here or just up the hill." They parked the car and climbed the incline to where they thought the house should be. A very large old oak tree was at the top of the hill. Clayton said, "The oak tree will be in our yard when we build the house." They stood holding hands and looked at the valley below them. Clayton said, "Our children will grow up here on the hill." Millie embraced him, and he held her closely to him as the wind blew around their bodies.

When they drove away, Millie looked at the hill and the landscape. She wished the house was there now. They drove slowly back into town. They kept their private thoughts to themselves. Before arriving home to Corsicana Street, Clayton said, "May I cook dinner; you know, I enjoy cooking. Millie said yes, even though she had dinner planned. She wanted him to be happy on his last day before joining the army.

Bessie had sent them a large portion of turkey which was left over from Christmas dinner. Clayton made a wonderful turkey casserole for the main course. He served a green salad, green beans, and hot dinner rolls with butter. For dessert, he made a rum sauce for two slices of pecan pie which Bessie had sent with the turkey.

Millie said, "What is in this wonderful turkey casserole? Where did you learn to cook so wonderfully?"

Clayton said, "You asked me two questions. I'll only answer one of them. Bessie and I used to make this casserole together with leftovers from holidays. The ingredients except for the turkey are a secret."

Millie said softly, "Another secret of Craig Street."

"What do you mean another secret of Craig Street?" asked Clayton.

Millie said, "I only meant that good cooks must have some secrets which they keep to themselves. Bessie is a good cook and she must keep some of her recipes a secret."

"I suppose you are correct," said Clayton.

When Millie and Clayton went to bed, he told her how much he loved her and that he would think of her everyday that he was gone. He said, "I will also be thinking about the new boy or girl who will arrive in a few months. The only thing I regret is that I won't be here when Robert or Roberta is born." Clayton continued, "I'll be away helping our country to become a safer place for our children. We must go to sleep, but before we do, and please don't get upset, I have written a short letter to our child. Just in case I should never make it back from the war, please save it for my child until he or she is old enough to understand it. The letter is in our large Bible in the entry hall." Clayton said, "I wish my mother had written me something before she died because I never knew her." He then fell into a peaceful sleep.

The next morning came too soon for Millie. They only took toast and coffee for breakfast because they had had two days of large meals. Millie knew why she did not have an appetite.

Clayton telephoned his father for a brief chat before leaving.

Among the things he discussed with his father was the land that he and Millie looked over yesterday. The judge assured him that it would be his land as soon as he could arrange it.

While Clayton was speaking to his father, the postman delivered the mail. There was a Christmas card from Ensign Louis Blackburn with a postmark from San Diego. The card was addressed to Clayton and Millie. Louis wrote a brief note to them. He said, "I am ever so busy learning about the navy, and undergoing basic training as a seaman. I miss you both very much, and I hope you are both fine."

Clayton was pleased to hear from Louis. Clayton wrote Louis's name and address in his address book. He said, "I will write to Louis because he always seemed like a brother to me instead of a friend." Millie's heart beat faster when she heard this comment about Louis. She was tempted to tell him about the secret she had discovered when Miss Emily died. She now knew that Clayton would be pleased to know that Louis was his half brother, but Millie refrained from telling him. She said to herself, "I will tell him sometime in the future but today is not the day because he has so much to think about."

It was time to drive Clayton to the small Hillsboro train station. Clayton made a brief inventory of the things he was taking with him: photographs of Millie and close relatives, an address book and fountain pen, a small New Testament from his mother-in-law, a diary, and shaving kit.

The drive to the station was hard for Millie. It meant saying good-bye to Clayton perhaps for a long time, and facing the immediate future alone when a child would be born without his father present. The train was pulling into the station when they arrived. Millie had never heard the wheels make so much noise. There were more people at the station than Millie had ever seen before. Many other young men were leaving to join the army and the train cars were crowded with young men. Millie thought, "This is war time."

She only had a few seconds to hug Clayton and kiss him. She told him she would always love him. "Write soon," she said. He walked into the train car nearest them, and the train began moving. She waved until the train was out of her sight, and tears came into her eyes when she heard the last whistle of it. She drove home slowly in a mental daze, and she went to their bedroom where she lay on their bed and cried for an hour.

The long cry had been good for her. It had relieved some of the tension she felt because of his enlisting in the service. She realized their lives would be different now. Clayton was devoted to a cause that was important to him. Millie realized that she must overcome her tears, and she must begin preparing for a new child which was due in about four months.

V

The Problems of Sarah Bankstead

Although Millie had much work to do at the office which kept her mind occupied, she felt the loneliness in the evenings and at night since Clayton had left for the army. She had a strong belief in God which she had inherited from her mother. She prayed to God every night to help her overcome her loneliness and to protect Clayton from danger.

She found the days easier for her. She walked to work whenever the Texas weather was favorable. Dr. Wainright had recommended walking daily. Most days she walked up Corsicana Street to Pleasant to Elm Street. On one sunny morning, she walked along Craig Street to Pleasant, and she came to the large white house where Clayton grew up.

Bessie was in the backyard hanging the laundry on the clothes line as it was such a nice day. Millie waved to Bessie, and Bessie said, "My goodness, Miss Millie, you is really getting into the motherly-way. I believe you is going to have twin babies."

Millie said, "Oh, Bessie, don't talk like that. I know I am not going to have twins."

Bessie continued, "Me and the judge thinks you should come here when it is time to have the baby. Me and my girl, Delila, could take care of you."

Millie said, "Thanks, Bessie, for your concern, but I think I will stay in my own home. Now, I must get to the office and do some work before the new baby arrives."

When she arrived at the office, she told the judge about her encounter with Bessie. She told him she preferred staying in her own home when the child was born. He said, "I understand your reasons. It is only natural that a mother would want her child to be born in its own home. But if you need us, please let us know." The judge continued, "Don't be upset with Bessie because I give her credit for rearing Clayton. My wife died a few hours after he was born. Bessie took over like a nurse and a mother. Clayton and I are most grateful to Bessie." Millie told the judge she understood his feelings toward Bessie.

Millie had a considerable number of estates to close that week. She was also due in court at 11:00 A.M. for the final closing of the Emily Blackburn Estate. She arrived a few minutes before eleven o'clock in an excited state because it was the largest estate she had administered, and she was representing Louis Blackburn who was the principal heir. Judge Blaine called the court to order, and asked Millie, "Are you ready for the final closing of Estate Case 0303944400?"

"Yes, Your Honor," said Millie.

The judge then announced the final allocation to each heir. All real property was awarded to Louis Blackburn. Various sums of money were given to scholarships and local charities. All fine jewelry was given to Millie N. Campbell except for three gold wristwatches which were given to Sarah Bankstead. Judge Blaine then asked, "Are there any objections?"

"Yes, your Honor," replied Millie. Millie stated, "The will did not make provisions for Miss Bankstead to receive three gold watches."

The judge asked Millie to approach the bench for a conference, and he told her to look at the bottom of the last page of the will where she would see a codicil stating her gift of three gold watches to Sarah Bankstead. Millie looked at the will, and she had overlooked the codicil. "Your Honor," Millie said, "my apologies to the court; I neglected to observe the codicil of the will."

The judge then asked her if she would like to continue the estate longer, or would she like to close it now. Millie said, "Your Honor, may I study the will another five minutes?" He granted a fifteen-minute intermission for her to reexamine the will. Millie reread it and studied carefully the codicil near the end of the last page. It read, 'I, Emily Blackburn, being of sound mind, do hereby bequeath my three gold wristwatches to Sarah Bankstead, a former student and friend who is now engaged to my nephew, Louis Blackburn.' It was dated April 10, 1941.

Millie studied the signature, and it looked like Miss Emily's. Millie was cautious. She telephoned the law office and asked the secretary to check the list of clients who had examined their wills on April 10, 1941. The secretary read the names of clients who saw their wills that day. To her amazement, Emily Blackburn had seen her will on April 10, 1941. Millie wondered where she was on April 10, and then she remembered that she was in Austin with Clayton for the law seminar.

After the time granted for studying the will, Millie told the judge she was satisfied with the codicil. She had been awarded twenty-nine pieces of fine jewelry.

When Millie returned to the office, she looked at Miss Emily's jewels. There were no gold watches. She was upset with herself because she had not noticed the codicil, and she had forgotten to ask Louis about Miss Emily's gold watches. She would write to Louis, immediately, to inquire about the watches. She sent an air mail letter that afternoon to him at his naval training base in San Diego.

In a few days, she received a reply from Louis admitting that Sarah had taken three watches just before she joined the U.S.O. because she knew that Miss Emily had willed them to her. Louis mentioned that he would soon complete his basic training and then he would be given a permanent assignment. He sent his best wishes to everyone in Hillsboro.

Millie was pleased to hear from Louis, but she was disappointed with Sarah Bankstead. She was required by law to have Sarah sign an affidavit stating that she received three gold watches from the estate. She did not have Sarah's address in Washington, and she would lose time writing to Louis again. How would she get Sarah's address?

She decided to ask Sarah's mother for it. Mrs. Bankstead answered her telephone call cordially and inquired about Millie's well-being. Millie thanked her, and said she needed Sarah's address in order to contact her regarding Miss Emily's will. Mrs. Bankstead said, "Oh, my darling girl, Sarah came home today on a furlough! Would you like to speak to her?"

"Oh, please," said Millie.

Sarah's voice came on the telephone, saying, "Hello, dear Millie. It is so wonderful to receive my first call from you. I just arrived home for a week of rest and relaxation."

Millie said, "I am calling you regarding Miss Emily's will. You were bequeathed three gold watches by Miss Emily, and Louis told me that you had taken them."

Sarah said, "Yes, that is correct. I did not think anyone would mind because they were willed to me by Miss Emily."

Millie said, "You must sign an affidavit for my files that you have received the watches."

Sarah promised to come by the next day to sign a receipt for the watches. Sarah said, "Millie, I must talk to you about something very personal tomorrow."

Millie replied that she would be pleased to listen. Millie asked, "May I ask what it is that you wish to discuss?"

Sarah said, "It is most personal but it pertains to Louis and me."

Millie said, "I will see you tomorrow afternoon." She knew that Sarah slept late which was the reason she said for her to come in the afternoon. Millie was anxious for the next day to come because she was curious about this visit from Sarah.

Millie walked to work again on Craig Street the next day. Halfway down the street, she met Mrs. R. V. Metcalfe who began laughing as soon as she saw Millie. "Oh, Millie, Millie! How wonderful to see you!" said Mrs. Metcalfe. "How are you, Millie?"

Millie said, "I am fine but so very lonely."

Mrs. Metcalfe asked, "Why are you lonely? You should never be lonely."

Millie replied, "My husband joined the service last month and I miss him. I am lonely."

Mrs. Metcalfe said, "I missed my husband when he died but I was never lonely for Mr. Metcalfe. I just love being alone because I can do as I please. I just have more fun doing the things I have always wanted to do."

"That's very interesting," said Millie. "I am on my way to work, and I must be going, Mrs. Metcalfe."

Mrs. Metcalfe said, "Now don't be lonely, just have fun doing what you want to do."

Millie was glad to continue her walk, and thought, "It is difficult to agree or disagree with Mrs. Metcalfe." Millie never felt she had an adequate or immediate answer for Mrs. Metcalfe.

The morning went quickly, and the time came for Sarah's appointment. She arrived wearing her U.S.O. uniform, looking attractive in the neat trim skirt and jacket. Sarah hugged Millie, and said, "I am surprised to see you in the family way. Of course, I should not be surprised considering you are married to the most gorgeous man in the world. But I am here to sign the paper for the watches which, I will do, although you may ask for the watches to be returned after our conversation."

Sarah signed the affidavit acknowledging the three gold watches.

Millie then asked, "What personal matter do you want to discuss?"

Sarah said, "Oh, Millie, I am so upset; I don't know if I can really tell you." Millie listened patiently and waited while Sarah wiped tears from her eyes.

She asked, "Sarah, have you done something wrong or unlawful?"

"No," said Sarah. "It is even worse!"

"Well, do tell me," said Millie. Sarah said, "It is so very embarrassing for me. You know I have been gone for several months, and I was assigned to the head office of the U.S.O. in Washington, D.C. I am with the very top people and I meet so many wonderful people. I met this wonderful man who is handsome and charming. We have marvelous times together. He is in love with me, and I am in love with him." Then Sarah burst into sobs of crying. Millie gave her tissues for her eyes and closed an outer door to her office so that others could not hear Sarah crying. Between sobs of crying, Sarah said, "What am I going to do because I love Albert?"

Millie said, "Tell me about Albert."

"Albert is most kind and gentle and so patient with me," answered Sarah.

Millie asked, "Does he know about your engagement to Louis?"

"Yes," said Sarah, "and he wanted to stop seeing me."

Millie asked, "Why didn't you stop seeing him?"

Sarah began to cry loudly and said, "I tried to stop loving him, but I can't. What am I going to do, Millie?"

Millie asked, "Does he have money from his family?"

"Yes, his family are well off," said Sarah. "He doesn't need my money. Money does not matter because I love him."

Millie continued, "Have you told Louis about this affair?"

"Oh, no," said Sarah.

Millie said, "You must tell him. It is the decent thing to do."

Sarah said, "I want to hire you to write a letter to Louis explaining what happened. I no longer love Louis Blackburn. I love Albert Worcester, and I want to marry him."

Millie said, "I cannot write the letter to Louis because he is a good friend.

"Oh, please do," pleaded Sarah.

"No," said Millie. "It is your duty to write to Louis and tell him what has happened between you and Albert."

"But what do I say?" said Sarah.

"Just tell him the truth," said Millie. "Of course, it will hurt him very much."

Sarah said, "I will write Louis a letter tonight."

"Millie responded, "Good luck, Sarah."

Sarah said, "I will return the watches to you because I don't deserve them. Millie said, "I would appreciate if you would return the small white, round, gold watch that Miss Emily wore to school each day. You may keep one of the other watches as a gift from me."

Sarah hugged Millie before leaving, and thanked her for listening to her problems. Millie said, "I wish you well."

VI

World War II

Millie happily received letters from Clayton every week. In each letter, he told her how much he missed her. His officer training at Fort Hood was most comprehensive. Most days began at 6:00 A.M., and he was not finished with training until 7:00 P.M. Some letters were brief because he was so tired in the evening. Each letter told of his progress in the various segments of his training, and he usually scored among the top in his class.

Millie answered each letter shortly after she received it, and related the happenings on Corsicana and Craig Street. She saved every letter and photograph she received from Clayton during his training. She also kept Clayton informed of the news at the law firm and any news of interest about his father and Bessie. They exchanged photographs of each other. His photographs were mostly taken of him during training exercises, but Millie was pleased with every photograph which she kept in the cedar chest.

She reluctantly sent Clayton photographs of herself, reluctant because she was pregnant. Clayton was pleased with each picture, and he was impatient to become a father. He thought Millie was beautiful in her pregnancy.

Millie wrote to him about the war efforts at home. Everyone was encouraged to buy United States Defense Bonds. There were posters every where with pictures of Uncle Sam asking you to purchase United States Saving Bonds to help finance the war. Even school children were given stamp books in school, and students were encouraged to buy a ten, twenty-five or even a fifty-cent stamp each week.

Many items were rationed, and each household was given rationing books in order to make purchases of many food items. Coffee, sugar, butter, and meat were rationed as well as many other things. Automobile tires and gasoline were rationed. Millie was glad she had purchased four new tires for her car just before the

Declaration of War. Passenger car introduction was discontinued until after the war. Many citizens complained because it was nearly impossible to purchase a new or used automobile.

The American government had declared price controls on many things such as houses, where rents were frozen for the duration. There was a shortage of housing in America since there were few building materials and almost no workers available. Most young men were serving in the military.

Defense plants, which made supplies, equipment, and machinery for the military, opened in the large cities of Texas as well as many other cities in the various states. Workers flocked to defense plants to seek jobs, and many families migrated to California where those jobs were plentiful.

Small businesses had difficulty in finding employees. Many women and teenagers worked in stores and shops because of the shortage.

Most people wore a V button which stood for Victory. The V emblem could be seen everywhere. There was a positive psychology to the sign V for Victory. It had been introduced to convince all citizens that they must believe our country would be victorious in winning the war.

All citizens were encouraged to plant Victory gardens in their back yards. The vegetable gardens would help relieve food workers from producing food and give them more time to work on other projects helpful to the war effort. Millie planted a large area of tomatoes in her yard while the other neighbors planted a vegetable which they would share with everyone.

There were shortages of service people. There were shortages of doctors and school teachers. Most young doctors and young men teachers had gone to the war. Many former and retired teachers were asked to return to teaching until the war ended.

Every bus and train station in the state of Texas was filled with soldiers in their military uniforms. Motorists were encouraged to give the service men a ride when they saw one who might need a lift.

The service men were often times given a free meal by a restaurant. Some families would invite them to their homes for a home-cooked meal and a visit. Some women formed groups to knit socks for the men who were serving overseas.

There were shortages in all aspects of civilian life in Texas during 1942 but most citizens did not complain about it. They gladly accepted these conditions if it would help win the war. Most people were willing to make personal sacrifices for the war efforts.

VII

The Secret Room

The time was rapidly approaching for Millie to give birth. She felt ill almost every morning, and one morning she felt so ill that she knew she must have help. She called Dr. Wainright who told her to come to his office when he opened at 9:00. He advised her that the baby was not due for at least another month, but Millie told him she would attempt to be there even though she was feeling very ill.

At 9:30 Millie had not arrived at the doctor's office, and he called the judge to say that Millie had called earlier reporting that she was not feeling well. Judge Campbell was concerned and he called Bessie. He told Bessie to go to Corsicana Street and check on Millie's condition.

Bessie went immediately to Millie's house, and was shocked when she saw her. Bessie called the doctor to come soon. Dr. Wainright rushed to Millie's house. After examining her for several minutes, he said, "It is not labor pains; it is a complication with the pregnancy which will require bed rest until the birth of the child." Millie agreed to bed rest, but someone would have to care for her.

The doctor and Bessie persuaded Millie to go to Hillsboro House where Bessie and her daughter, Delila, would look after her until the new baby was born. The doctor told Millie, "If you stay in bed for the next few weeks, I think you will have a healthy new baby."

Millie was driven to Hillsboro House, and was given a pleasant bedroom upstairs facing Craig Street. She enjoyed looking at the beautiful large green trees along the street. She could see them if she used two pillows. She had never really studied an elm tree before and now saw parts that she had never observed before. The tree had a natural balance. It was not just a green tree with brown bark. There were thousands of leaves but no two leaves were identical even though they were all similar and related.

Millie had wonderful care while she rested in bed. Bessie who was patiently teaching her daughter to become a housekeeper introduced her daughter Delila to Millie. Delila was very shy, but she had a kind nature which Millie appreciated. Bessie or Delila came frequently to see if Millie needed anything.

Judge Campbell stopped in every evening for a brief visit with Millie. He gladly took over her law business and clients until she could return to work. He kept Millie informed of each client and each law case because he did not want her to lose contact with them, and Millie herself was most anxious to be kept in touch.

She looked forward to the daily visits from Judge Campbell. One evening the judge told Millie there had been a communication from Louis Blackburn. Louis had been severely injured in a naval training accident, and he was in the hospital in San Diego. However, he was improving and he expected to receive a medical discharge from the service in a few weeks. Millie was concerned but relieved that Louis was improving.

The only other visitor Millie was permitted was her mother. Dora was disappointed that her daughter could not come home to the farm because she wanted to take care of her, but the doctor felt Millie should remain near him in case of further complications. Millie told her mother she would like her to be with her for a while when the baby was born.

The days passed slowly for Millie, but she felt content just resting and waiting for the baby. She stayed in bed all the time except (as permitted by the doctor) for five minutes every morning. Millie hardly left her room.

She had never really been upstairs before at Hillsboro House. The house had sounds and smells that were characteristic of a large old house. One morning Millie looked down the central hallway and all the doors to each room were open except one bedroom near her room which always had the door closed. She was curious about this room with the closed door and she asked Bessie about it. Bessie said, "Oh, Miss Millie, don't bother about that room. It is just a room that the judge keeps closed."

Millie said, "I was only curious, Bessie, because the door is always closed."

Bessie changed the subject of the room, and began talking about the good spring weather. The abrupt change of subject was

Bessie's method of avoiding the answer to a question.

The next day, when it was time for Millie's five minutes to be up and about, she looked out of her door and could determine that Bessie and Delila were occupied with chores and neither was upstairs. Millie walked out of her room, into the hall, and over to the room where the door was always closed. She tried to turn the knob of the large wooden door, but it was locked tightly.

She returned to her room, and back to bed, where she lay thinking about the room with the locked door for several minutes when Bessie came into her room and said, "Miss Millie, I heard footsteps in the hall. Did you need something?"

"Oh, no, Bessie," said Millie. She explained that she felt like walking a few steps. Bessie gave Millie a strange look and said, "Let me know when you need me."

Millie tried to forget about the room with the locked door until Tuesday morning when she discovered a pattern. Someone went into the room at 9:00 every Tuesday morning. She could hear a key inserted into the lock and the dead bolt turned for opening the door. She waited a few minutes and decided to investigate. She looked into the hall, and could see cleaning items just outside the door. So Bessie cleaned the room every Tuesday morning but no one ever used the room.

Millie knew a secret must exist in this room, and she named it the "secret room" of the house. She wondered how she could ever discover the secret but she was determined to do so.

When Dora came for her daily visit the next day, Millie told her mother she must do something of utmost importance for her.

"Why, of course, my dear," said Dora.

Millie said, "Mother, I want you to telephone Bessie next Tuesday morning at exactly 9:10. Give Bessie enough time to go downstairs to answer the telephone. Please keep her talking for at least five minutes."

Dora said, "I will do so, but I don't understand why you want all this done. But if it is important to you, I will do so."

Millie waited impatiently until the Tuesday morning. At exactly 9:00 she heard the key inserted into the lock of the door. She heard the squeak or the door when it opened, and shortly the cleaning activity began in the "secret room." Millie looked at her watch, and prayed for the telephone to ring downstairs. Soon the telephone rang, and she listened for Bessie to go downstairs to answer it. When she heard Bessie's footsteps going down the stairs and heard her speaking on the telephone, she quietly tip-toed into the hall and saw that the door to the "secret room" was slightly open. She tried to push it further, but it made a squeaking noise. She could only open it a few inches without Bessie hearing the noise.

Millie looked into the "secret room." It was an elegant lady's bedroom. There was a large photograph of a beautiful woman in a pretty silver picture frame. A silver bud vase with a fresh red rose was near the picture. Everything else looked very old. There were wonderful objects of art which decorated the bedroom. She admired an expensive silver dresser set on a dressing table.

Millie looked at another framed photograph of a man and a blond woman. It was Judge Campbell and a woman, but it was not Miss Emily. Millie studied the photograph carefully and she noticed the jewelry looked familiar.

She had been in the room for about five minutes. As she looked at her wristwatch which she had inherited from Miss Emily, she noticed that the woman in the photograph was wearing an identical watch. Millie was most confused. Who was this woman?

She started to leave the room when she met Bessie at the door. Bessie screamed, "Miss Millie, you are not supposed to be in this here room. No, no one is ever supposed to be in this room." Bessie was terribly upset and she was shaking. Then it occurred to Millie; this was Fiona Campbell's room. She said to Bessie, "So this is Fiona Campbell's room."

"Yes," said Bessie. "No one except me and the judge has seen this room for over twenty years."

Millie said, "So this is the room where Fiona died."

"Yessum," said Bessie.

"And she died in that bed," said Millie."

"Yessum," said Bessie.

Millie said, "This is a very strange house." Bessie was still upset, and Millie said, "Stop shaking because I will never tell anyone I ever saw this room." She continued, "Now, Bessie, you're going to let me go home because I wish to have my child in my own house."

Oh, no!" said Bessie. "I have been told to keep you here."

Millie said, "If you don't take me home this moment, I will tell every secret I know about you.

"Now go call my mother, and tell her to come with my father who will drive me to my own home."

"Yessum, yessum, I'll call your mama, right now," said Bessie.

VIII

Millie Becomes a Mother

Millie was glad to be back in her very own home. She believed correctly the new baby would be born soon, and she had only been home a few hours when she began to feel labor pains. It was a new experience for her but she knew the labor pains were genuine this time. Dora was spending the day with her. In the early afternoon, she told her mother to call Dr. Wainright to come immediately.

The doctor arrived shortly, and indicated that it was time for the new baby. Within ten minutes, Millie gave birth to a new son. Her first thoughts were how happy Clayton would be. Millie asked, "Is the baby fine and healthy?"

Dr. Wainright said, "The healthiest boy I have ever seen."

Millie said, "I am so pleased."

The doctor said, "You're not through; here comes a second new baby, a beautiful girl."

Millie replied, "Doctor, please stop teasing me."

Dora said, "Millie, the doctor is not teasing. You have given birth to twins, a nice boy and a pretty girl."

Dr. Wainright said, "They are both fine and healthy. I suggest you have a good rest now, and we will care for the new babies."

Millie said, "I am very tired, but please contact Clayton and tell him about the twins. I so wish he was here." A telegram was sent to Clayton by Judge Campbell who had just arrived to see his new grandchildren. The telegram read, CONGRATULATIONS, CLAYTON. YOU ARE THE FATHER OF TWINS, A BOY AND A GIRL.

In a few hours, Clayton reciprocated with two telegrams from Fort Hood. The first was to his father, and it read, "I am overwhelmed—I do things by the numbers." The second telegram was to Millie, and it read, "I love you—thanks for making me the father of twins."

The grandparents were thrilled with the new twins. There had never been twins in the family before. J. D. was most pleased, and he said, "I am twice an uncle." Judge Campbell told every one he met about the new twins. He passed out cigars to his male clients, and kept an enormous box of chocolate candy on his desk for women clients to sample.

When Millie woke, she had to pinch herself in order to believe she was the mother of twins. They brought the new boy and girl for her to view. She said, "They favor Clayton."

Dora said, "It's possible because he is the father of the twins."

Bessie came to see the new twins, and she was amazed. She kept saying over and over again, "I just don't believe it, Miss Millie."

Millie said, "It is true. Don't you think they favor Clayton?"

Bessie said, "Yes, they look like Clayton. They is the prettiest babies I'se ever saw in my whole life," Bessie continued, "I think you need my Delila to help you."

Millie said, "You are absolutely right; I do need Delila to help me with the twins."

Delila moved into the back bedroom near the kitchen. She was very gentle with the new babies, and Millie felt she was fortunate even though Delila could not cook as well as Bessie could.

When Millie received her first letter from Clayton, it revealed that he was ecstatic over the birth of the twins. He reminded Millie of the preselected names: Robert Martin McGill Campbell for the boy and Roberta Martin McGill Campbell for the girl. He continued, "I can hardly wait until we win this war, and I can return home to you and my babies. I am afraid I will be sent overseas immediately after I graduate from Officers' Candidate School." Clayton also wrote, "I think we should have a godparent for our children, and I suggest Louis Blackburn to be the godfather of the twins unless you have an objection. I will write to Louis, and ask him if he would consider doing the honor for our children. My love to you and our twins."

Millie answered Clayton's letter agreeing with him that Louis should be the designated godfather of their children. She reported that each day the twins became stronger and more alert. She also mentioned that little Roberta had some very strong lungs and vocal chords when she was hungry or needed attention. "The little boy is more gentle, and I suppose he takes after me," wrote Millie in the letter, "I do wish you could see them because they are beautiful babies."

Millie and Delila were constantly busy with the new babies. Everything had to be done twice. Millie did not return to the office until she was sure that Delila could manage the babies alone. Bessie was kind enough to come every day and help for a couple of hours.

Millie received another letter from Clayton. It was brief and serious. It read:

June 1, 1942

My dear Wife,

I am now an officer in the United States Army, and I have received orders to go overseas to the European command in three days which means I will not see you and the twins before I leave.

Please take care of them until I can return from this dreadful war. I love you and the twins, and I miss you so much.

I'll write again soon with my new address which will be an A.P.O. number from New York.

Stay well, and give the twins a big hug and kiss for me.

Love,

Clayton

Millie was disappointed that Clayton did not get a leave to come home and see the twins before being sent overseas. Somehow Millie did not believe the war was fair.

One day Millie received a telephone call from a man whose voice sounded familiar. After he said a few more words, Millie realized it was the voice of Louis Blackburn. "Where are you, Louis?" asked Millie.

"I am at my Aunt Emily's house on Craig Street. The navy gave me a medical discharge due to the injury of my right leg and my right arm."

"Oh, I am so sorry, Louis," said Millie. "What really happened?"

Louis replied, "There was an explosion on the training ship, and I was very near when it happened. I lost the use of my right arm, and I have little use of my right leg."

Millie said, "Louis, you are fortunate to be alive."

He replied, "I am not sure that I agree with you, but I suppose God wanted me to live so I will try to live as normally as I can. May I come to see you and the twins? I understand I am to be their godfather."

"Of course," said Millie, "please come soon."

When Louis came for the visit, Millie was shocked to see him. He had to walk with crutches and his right arm and hand were limp. He had lost a lot of his sparkle and enjoyment of life. He seldom smiled or laughed, yet he greeted Millie warmly and with tears in his eyes. Millie knew at that moment she would always hate war, and she would do every thing possible to keep her baby son Robert from ever joining the army.

Louis seemed more natural when he saw the twins, Robert and Roberta, in their cribs. He gave each one a gentle pat, and said, "I am happy to be your godfather." Millie observed a sudden change in him. The babies made him more restful and contented. He asked, "May I come to see the babies often?" She was pleased that Louis liked Robert and Roberta.

Millie returned to her normal routine at the law office and was glad to be back meeting clients and helping them with their problems. The entire office staff had a small party to welcome her back.

Delila was a great help to Millie at home. She was competent, and the babies loved her. The twins responded to her especially when she sang old minstrel songs to them. Delila knew how to keep them happy and smiling.

Louis came every day to see the children, and he helped with the evening meal. Delila had not learned to cook very well, and Louis volunteered to prepare evening meals whenever possible. He was beginning to feel stronger, and he seemed happier. He was a great help to Millie because she had two babies to rear and a law career to develop. Any help was appreciated.

Judge Campbell often came to see the grandchildren after work and he sometimes stayed for dinner. He enjoyed some of the

New Orleans cuisine which Louis enjoyed preparing. When Louis made a special dish, he would invite the judge for dinner.

One evening, after a special delicious dinner which had been eaten by the judge, Louis, and Millie, Judge Campbell said good night to the babies, who were almost asleep. He thanked Millie for the nice evening. Before leaving, he went over to Louis and put his arm around his shoulders, and said, "Thank you, my son, for such a great dinner." Millie could not believe what she had heard.

When the judge and Louis left together, Millie believed a miracle had happened. The judge offered to drive Louis to his home. Something told Millie a father and son had discovered each other.

IX

Missing in Action

Several weeks passed and Millie was very concerned that she had not heard from Clayton who had recently been sent overseas. She hoped he was safe and that she would hear from him soon. She told Louis about her concern over Clayton, and he did not think it was unusual because he had only recently been sent overseas.

She was reluctant to tell Judge Campbell about her concern. The judge asked her one day if she had heard from Clayton, and she told him that she had not and she was worried about his welfare. The judge looked serious and nervous, and said, "I am sure we will hear from Clayton soon. War circumstances might have prevented him from writing."

Millie continued to be uneasy about him. One morning just before she was ready to leave for the law office, she heard a knock at the door. Millie told Delila she would answer the door. She looked through the small glass window of the door where she saw men in uniform. Her heart almost stopped beating; she could hardly open the door. One of the soldiers was a captain and the other a sergeant from the War Department. The captain and the sergeant introduced themselves, and asked if Millie was the wife of Lieutenant Clayton Campbell. The captain asked if they might come in for a short time. Millie realized by their behavior that they had unpleasant news for her.

She invited them into the living room. She noticed that the sergeant stopped briefly and looked at a photograph of Clayton in the hall. Millie said, "Are you here to tell me news of my husband?"

"Yes, Mrs. Campbell," said the sergeant.

"Is my husband dead?" asked Millie.

The captain said, "We hope not Mrs. Campbell, but the War Department has sent us here to tell you that Lieutenant Clayton Campbell is missing in action some where in Italy". Millie could not speak but the captain continued. He said, "The only thing the

War Department knows is that your husband arrived safely in Italy a few weeks ago. He was assigned to a combat group near the front. On his way to the front, Lieutenant Campbell, his driver, and their jeep never arrived for his assignment."

Millie began to ask a question, but the captain said, "I am sorry, Mrs. Campbell, but we have no more details on where Lieutenant Campbell might be. No one knows what happened."

The sergeant asked, "Mrs. Campbell, would you like us to remain with you until relatives or friends can come to be with you?"

Millie said, "No, thank you." Millie wanted them to leave because she wished to be alone. They left quietly.

Millie went to her own and Clayton's bedroom where she cried and cried until her eyes were red. After several hours, she realized she must tell Judge Campbell that his son was missing in action. She called Louis Blackburn to come quickly to Corsicana Street.

When Louis arrived, he knew it was news about Clayton. Louis listened sympathetically to the awful news. Millie asked Louis if he would go to the office and tell Judge Campbell. He said, "I will go now, but how sad for him that his only son is missing in action."

Without thinking, Millie said, "No, Louis, there is another son."

On the way to the office, Louis thought about what Millie had said to him, "No, Louis, there is another son." He began to ponder more about Millie's statement, and questions began to form in his mind. He asked himself, "Who is this other son? Where does this son live? Who was the mother of the other son?"

A sudden revelation came to Louis. He knew his mother in New Orleans was not his natural mother. She was a cousin to Miss Emily, who had always told him he was her nephew. He had believed all these years that Miss Emily was his aunt. He continued to think about his relationship to Miss Emily. Another thought came into his mind, "Why was I the only, or almost only, heir to Miss Emily's estate?" Louis then asked the ultimate question, "Was Miss Emily my actual mother, and is Judge Campbell my real father?" He was in a state of confusion. For some moments, he believed they were his parents, but in the next few minutes, he could not believe that they were his actual parents.

When he arrived at the office and informed Judge Campbell that Clayton was missing in action, the judge was shocked and visibly shaken by the bad news of his son. The judge finally said, "Who else do I have to lose? I have lost my wife, my sons, and a woman whom I loved." Louis remained quiet for a period so that the sad news might be accepted by the judge.

After a lengthy silence, Louis said to him, "You do have a son here today. " The judge gave him a strange look. Louis had tears in his eyes.

The judge stood up from his massive desk and said, "I have always suspected that I might have another child." The judge began to cry. He walked over to Louis and put his arms around him, and said, "Welcome home, my son."

Louis asked the judge, "Was Emily Blackburn the woman you really loved?"

The judge nodded affirmatively, and said, "But I also loved my wife, Fiona."

Louis persisted, "Was Emily Blackburn my natural mother?"

"Yes, I believe so," said the judge. "I was overseas at the time you were born, and Emily never told me or any one that she was carrying my child. I would never have married Fiona if I had known Emily was pregnant with you."

The judge continued, "I was a lonely soldier when I was overseas, and I was in the prime of my life. Fiona McGill offered me companionship and passion which I could not resist when I was a young man. I fell deeply in love with Fiona, and I could not live without her. I had to marry her. I know it hurt Emily when I wrote the letter to her breaking our engagement. She never forgave me for that letter."

The judge was inclined to talk more about this situation, and Louis encouraged him to continue. "I finally discovered that Emily had given birth to a child," said the judge.

"How did you discover this?" asked Louis.

"It was gradual like a crossword puzzle. After my wife died and I recovered from the loss of her, my maid Bessie kept telling me about Miss Emily's new nephew who was almost an orphan. There were other clues from family and friends which I don't recall now. I do remember that Bessie suggested I should contribute to helping to rear this child. Well, I offered Emily Blackburn money, and she flatly refused it. She told me what I could do with my money!"

I told Bessie how Emily had rejected my offer of money. Bessie said, "Mr. Campbell, you don't know how to handle women. I tell you what you got to do. There is a lot of fine jewelry upstairs in this here house which belonged to your own mammy and some fine jewelry from Miss Fiona. I'se knows that Miss Emily would love that jewelry. Give it to her and say, 'You can keep it or you can sell it to support your nephew.' "

The judge paused and looked plaintively. Louis said, "Did you give her the jewelry?"

"Yes," said Judge Campbell, "and she accepted it graciously."

Louis said, "So the jewelry Miss Emily bequeathed to Millie was really your jewelry."

"Yes, that is correct," said the judge.

The judge realized that the news was upsetting to Louis. He said, "Louis, my son, will you forgive me for keeping this secret from you for over twenty-five years?"

Louis asked, "Did you actually keep the secret for twenty-five years?"

"Yes," said the judge, "and I am asking you to forgive me for withholding this knowledge from you for such a long time."

Louis said, "I think I would like to leave now. I don't wish to know any further details about my early life." Louis left abruptly without saying good-bye to the judge.

The judge watched him leave, and said to himself, "He certainly has the attitude and behavior similar to Emily Blackburn."

Louis returned to Miss Emily's pale yellow brick home on Craig Street. He could not readily accept the news about the identity of his parents. Miss Emily had been wonderful to him all of his life. She always told him that she was his godmother, and she would always care for her godson.

Louis was experiencing much anguish and had tears in his eyes when he returned home. Beatrice said, "Lord a mercy, what is wrong with you, Mr. Louis?" He told Beatrice about the sad news of Clayton Campbell who was missing in action. "Oh, no," said Beatrice, "poor Miss Millie and those poor twins. What will happen to them now? And poor Judge Campbell! Young Clayton was his only son."

Louis became very agitated, and said to Beatrice, "That is not true. He has another son, and you know who he is, Beatrice."

"Oh, dear me!" said Beatrice. "I don't know nothing about another son."

Louis said, "Beatrice, you helped raise me the first six months of my life before I was sent to New Orleans to live with Miss Emily's cousin. You do know that Miss Emily was my mother, and Judge Campbell is my real father."

"I never heard such ridiculous thing in my whole life."

Louis said, "I am going upstairs to Miss Emily's bedroom to study her personal effects for clues to my origin."

"No, no, no," said Beatrice, as Louis started for the stairs. Beatrice ran ahead of him and stood in front of the door to Miss Emily's bedroom to block it. Beatrice was a large woman whose frame easily blocked the door.

Louis said, "Beatrice, go down stairs immediately. If you don't do what I say, you are fired as of this minute."

Beatrice slowly removed herself, and she cried and moaned as she made her way down the stairs mumbling and crying, "My poor, poor Emily. She ain't here to keep her secret."

Louis entered Miss Emily's bedroom and looked around at the beautiful old mahogany furniture. He began looking through the drawers of her dressing table but found nothing of any importance to him. He looked through the tall highboy which was on legs, but he only found neatly arranged clothing of Miss Emily's. The two bedside commodes revealed only small interesting items which belonged to her. He looked into the clothes closet where he saw only lovely dresses and coats hanging with many shoes neatly arranged on the floor of the closet.

Louis was ready to give up and leave the room when he saw a small cedar chest that was covered with a tapestry and books. He removed all the books and carefully removed the antique tapestry. He tried to open the chest but it was firmly locked.

He felt that a key must be in the room. He looked inside the bedside commodes, but, there was no key. He decided to give up and maybe apologize to Beatrice. He admired the silver dresser set, and he observed that with the mirror, comb, and brush, there was a silver box with the initials E. B. Louis opened the top lid to find that it was filled with buttons, pins, coins, and similar items.

He saw in one corner of the box a small gold key. He tried the key and the cedar chest unlocked.

When he opened the lid and gazed at the contents, he had a twinge of guilt. Here was Miss Emily's most private things that she did not want to share with the rest of the world. There were photographs of family and friends. Louis found pictures of Robert Campbell and Miss Emily. There were photos of him as a baby with writing on the reverse which said, "My darling baby."

There were stacks of letters. Louis observed many were from New Orleans. They were mostly from his foster mother who gave reports on his growth and development. Miss Emily was assured that her baby was receiving the best loving care.

He picked up another stack of letters which were from overseas. They were from Robert Campbell before he married Fiona McGill. The letters were very personal; and he skipped to the last letter which he read sadly. This was the letter which Lieutenant Robert Campbell had sent breaking their engagement.

Louis also discovered a small file of very important documents. There were several birth and death certificates of people he really didn't know. He noticed a birth certificate with the date of his birth 1917. He had found his own birth certificate. It was from the state of Texas, and it listed Emily Rose Blackburn as his mother. The father was listed as unknown.

Louis had discovered enough evidence to support the theory about his natural parents. He was about to close the lid of the trunk when he noticed a small diary, on whose first page was written, "The Personal Diary of Emily Rose Blackburn." He read several interesting entries and continued to read until he found the entries of 1917. The new baby was mentioned several times. One entry stated, "I hope Robert Campbell will some day discover his marvelous son. He would enjoy knowing his dear little son."

Louis cried as he continued to read the diary. He could not understand why Miss Emily had kept the big secret for so long. Did she not know that he might discover it? He loved Miss Emily dearly, but it would take sometime before he could accept the fact that she was his mother. He had very mixed feelings about the judge. Why did he wait so long to tell the truth?

X

The Death of Bessie

When Louis Blackburn had first learned the news about his real parents, he was bitter and frustrated. It was not an easy adjustment for him. In time, he accepted the truth about his real parents. He had a personal conference with the rector of the Episcopal Church. The rector explained that it was a delicate situation. He further explained that Hillsboro was a small town, and a child born out of wedlock would have been disastrous for Miss Emily who was an educator and Judge Campbell who was an important attorney.

After much personal deliberation, Louis wrote Judge Campbell a letter stating that it was an honor to be his son. However, he agreed with Miss Emily that it should be kept a secret instead of being general knowledge in the small town of Hillsboro. He pledged to Judge Campbell that he did not seek or need financial help, or even public recognition that he was a son of the judge.

When Judge Campbell received the correspondence from Louis, he was amazed. Many children would have been demanding their position and financial support from a newly discovered father. He changed his will to include Louis Blackburn as one of his heirs. He hoped Louis would some day feel close to him. The judge was beginning to feel the strain and stress of life, and he missed Clayton who he had hoped would take charge of the law firm in the near future.

Life would never be the same for the judge due to the probable loss of Clayton in the war. The judge did not take life too seriously and nothing was vitally important to him anymore.

Bessie who was beginning to slow down and was showing her increasing years reminded the judge that he still had two wonderful grandchildren. She suggested that he must learn to enjoy them. He told Bessie he would consider what she had suggested. He was really slowing down and so was Bessie. It took Bessie twice as long now to prepare a meal as in the past, but the judge would never reprimand her or even think about a replacement for her.

One morning the judge wakened early, and he was feeling very chipper. He had decided life must go own even though he had probably lost a son in the war. He was looking forward to breakfast, and he already had a joke for Bessie. He went into the breakfast room to have his usual breakfast but there was no evidence of Bessie. Where was she? In forty years he had never known her to oversleep. He went to her room and opened the door slowly. The judge called her. "Bessie, Bessie, have you overslept? Where is my coffee, toast, and orange juice?"

Bessie did not answer him. She would never speak to him again. She had died in her sleep. The judge returned to his breakfast table and bowed his head in his hands and cried aloud, "What will I do without Bessie? She was the only person who could tell me what I should do or not do."

Everyone was sad about Bessie's death. Her sister Beatrice was distraught, and Delila, her daughter, was overwhelmed with grief.

Judge Campbell paid for the entire funeral expenses. He purchased a plain bronze casket and had an enormous spray of yellow roses placed on the lid. Yellow roses were Bessie's favorite flower. A yellow ribbon banner was placed on the casket with the inscription **Love to our Bessie**.

The funeral service was held at the Black Baptist Church in the southern part of the town. Judge Campbell attended the funeral, although he had never been inside the simple, plain wood church before. The minister gave a long and glorious talk about Bessie, and the elders of the church gave eulogies. The choir sang many spiritual hymns. At the end of the service, every one stood, held hands, and sang, "When the Saints Go Marching In." All the mourners had tears in their eyes when they filed out of the church.

Bessie was buried in a small country cemetery a few miles out of town. Judge Campbell went to the burial, and her family asked the judge to speak about Bessie.

The judge marched up to the grave which was under a large oak tree, and rested his hand on the bronze casket. In a strong voice, the judge said, "My family and I loved Bessie. We appreciated her many years of loyal service to the Campbell household. She helped me raise my son, Clayton. We will always remember her sincerity, her loyalty, and her wonderful sense of humor. We express our sympathy to her family and friends today. We loved her. May God bless you, and may God bless, dear Bessie." The mourners all said in unison "Amen, brother" several times.

Judge Campbell drove his big Cadillac slowly back into town. He wondered what life would be like in the big house on Craig Street. Everyone was gone except himself; he knew that his life would be lonely there.

XI

Conclusion

Millie Jean had a dreadful time dealing with the loss of Clayton. She experienced times when she thought he was surely dead or badly injured. There were other times when she had hope that he was alive and well. After many weeks of worrying and grieving about him, she knew she must find some way to control her grief.

The twins grew quickly and required much of her time for their care. Delila was most helpful, but she could not manage both of them alone; Millie had to help her. This was good for Millie. It helped her to be busy yet she kept hoping to hear from Clayton. She kept hoping he would be home from the war soon to see his children.

The months passed and Millie was amazed at how much young Robert resembled his father. His personality was going to be similar to his father. He was developing a sense of humor similar to Clayton's. Roberta was more serious. She was going to take after Millie.

Millie continued her law practice in spite of her grief over Clayton. She found it difficult to listen and concentrate with clients but she knew that Clayton would wish her to pursue her profession.

Her children were a consolation to her. She often had tears in her eyes when she looked at them. The children were growing bigger and they would soon need a father to do things for them. She had the strong support of her family during this difficult time. Her parents and brother came almost daily to see her. Judge Campbell tried to be helpful but Millie knew he had his own private grief about Clayton.

Louis Blackburn was a steadfast friend who always was helpful and available when Millie needed encouragement. He came almost every day to visit Millie and the twins, who became fond of him as they grew. Louis brought them books and read them stories. He often took them to the Double Dip for ice cream. They wanted to go every day during the summer months. Louis had promised to take Robert to his first softball game when he was old enough to understand the game. Louis was a fine godfather.

Louis cooked dinner on special occasions. He cooked an ornate and delicious dinner for Millie's birthday. He and the twins organized a birthday party with decorations, balloons, and hats. Millie was surprised when she came home from work. It was a Monday night, and Louis had made red beans and rice, New Orleans style. The food was mild enough for the children. He had also baked a delicious birthday cake for Millie.

They all had a great time. The children had been taught to sing "Happy Birthday" to mother. Millie had tears in her eyes. Louis knew what she was thinking. The children became sleepy, and were put to bed. Louis and Millie listened to *Lux Theatre* on the radio in the living room. It was a most romantic drama. When the program ended, Louis and Millie stood up ready for him to leave for the evening. He spontaneously hugged her. He said to Millie, "I hope Clayton will return soon. If he should not return from the war, would you marry me?"

Millie did not know what to say, but replied, "I cannot answer your question at this time."

Louis said, "I understand your feelings and I will wait patiently for your answer." Louis continued, "Millie, I think you need to go away for a weekend to get away from the memories you have here, and it would be good for you to be away from the children for a couple of days."

"Oh, no," said Millie, "I could not leave the children."

Another thought occurred to Louis. He would try this approach. Louis said, "All right, Millie, but we are going to a new movie this Saturday night in Waco. It is called *The Best Years of Our Lives*. I hear it is very good, so be ready at 6:00 for me to pick you up."

Millie was about to say no when Louis said, "Judge Campbell is going to look after the children. I have spoken to him, and he has agreed. Good night, I will see you at 6:00 on Saturday."

Judge Campbell came for the children at 5:00 on Saturday to take them for ice cream at the Double Dip, and then on to Hillsboro House for the evening and the night. He had several games for them to play; and then they could go to bed and spend the night with their grandfather.

Louis and Millie left for the movie at 6:00 and arrived at the Palace where they got good seats. She enjoyed the movie even though it was about three soldiers returning from the war to their families. They all had difficulty adjusting to civilian life. Millie enjoyed the acting and she thought Clayton looked like Dana Andrews.

When the movie was over, Louis took Millie to the Elite Cafe where they each had a toasted cheese sandwich, coffee, and apple pie. Millie sat closely to Louis on the drive home and they held hands.

When they arrived in Hillsboro, they drove by Judge Campbell's home. His lights were still on. They checked on the children. The judge gave a good report on their behavior. He insisted on them remaining the night. The judge told Millie, "I would like you and the children to join me in living here. It is a large and lonely house for me alone." Millie thanked him and said she would consider it for the future.

Louis took Millie home, and he asked if he could come in for a late visit. Millie said, "Only a visit, Louis." Louis always respected Millie's wishes. He said good night after a visit and a hug. She whispered something into his right ear which had been injured in the navy. Louis thought he heard Millie say, "Please wait for me and be patient."

The next morning Judge Campbell returned the children to their home. They were very happy and so was the grandfather. He told Millie, "I will be glad when you and the twins decide to live with me at Hillsboro House." She thanked him, and he said goodbye. As he walked to his car, Millie noticed the judge was frailer than he used to be. He was walking with a slight limp that she had never noticed before. His hair was becoming thinner and was changing to gray. She felt sorry for him because life had given him many things, but it had not given him a long time with his family.

She asked her children if they had enjoyed the visit with their grandfather. "Oh, yes," they said. "He wants us to come and live with him."

Millie asked, "Do you want to live with grandfather in the big house?"

"Oh, yes, yes! Can we all move there?"

"I will think about it," said Millie.

Millie was at her office early the next morning to work on numerous wills for her clients. At 8:00, Judge Campbell had not arrived for work. He was always in his office by 8:00. When 9:00 came, Millie was worried. She telephoned his house, but there was no answer. She then telephoned Louis who lived nearby on Craig Street. Louis rang the doorbell of Hillsboro House. There was no answer. He looked through the window of the parlor and saw the judge slumped over in his arm chair with a book. He knew where a passkey was hidden and he entered the house. The judge was still breathing, and Louis called an ambulance.

The judge was rushed to the hospital where Dr. Wainright came and examined him. The doctor said the judge had suffered a severe stroke. He predicted that he would recover but it would take a long time.

Millie was concerned about the judge because he was Clayton's father. He was also Louis's father. His recovery was slow, and he had to have help when it was possible for him to return home. Louis volunteered to take care of him.

Louis did an excellent job of helping the judge regain his strength, but he never fully recovered. One evening Louis helped him from his wheelchair to his bed, where he died quietly and peacefully with Louis holding his hand.

The judge requested a very simple service similar to the one for his wife Fiona so many years ago. He was buried beside her at the city cemetery. It was another sad time for Millie and her children but Louis said, "He was ready to go."

Millie delayed opening the judge's will for a week. It was too painful for her. When she read the will, she learned the main heirs were herself and her children, but she found a recent codicil attached to the will stating that he had left Hillsboro House to Louis Blackburn. The judge had written an explanation for this. It said, "Knowing human nature as well as I do, I think Louis Blackburn may need a large house in the future."

When Millie told Louis about the codicil and his inheritance of the large house, Louis said, "My father expected us to be married soon. May I have your answer?"

Millie hesitated for a short time. She thought about Clayton, who had not been heard from for a long time; the War Department presumed him to be dead. Millie realized if she did not say yes to Louis, he would never ask her again.

Epilogue

The years passed, but Millie Jean never forgot Clayton Campbell. She often went alone to the big hill in the country which overlooked a green valley and a river where Clayton had selected the place for building a home when he returned from the army. Everytime Millie went to the hill and stood for a few minutes, she felt Clayton's presence was near her. When the wind blew upon the hill, Millie could hear Clayton say, "I love you, Millie."